The Stone Collie

We all chose scoops of ice cream in different flavors. When Brent came back, carrying a tray with ice cream and iced water, he said, "Now Lucy. Explain why you lost your cool in there."

She picked up a plastic fork and swirled it around a scoop of coconut ice cream.

"Everything was going well until... I looked up and saw Cassandra and Madeline in the audience."

"Who are they?" Annica asked.

Lucy took a deep breath. "You're not going to believe this."

"Try us," Brent said.

"They're characters from my book. Come to life."

"From *Devilwish*?"

"No, from *The Stone Collie*. That's the book I'm working on now."

I stared at her. This might happen in a Stephen King novel, but not in one of Lucy's stories. Not to Lucy.

Annica said, "How is that possible? Unless you used real models."

"I didn't. I never do. They're my own creations. Cassandra and Madeline both have blonde hair. Madeline's hair is lighter and longer. Cassandra envies her. Cassandra wears her hair in one braid. She has freckles across her nose. She tries to cover them with powder. Madeline wears make-up. She likes bright pink lipstick.

"The girls are sisters. They resemble each other slightly, but Cassandra is convinced that Madeline is the pretty one. I named them. I had a doll named Cassandra when I was a little girl, and Madeline was my cousin."

"You've just described 'Anygirl,'" I said.

"Yeah." Brent finished his ice cream. "All teenaged girls look alike."

Annica cast him an indignant glance. "No they don't."

"So," I said, "you saw two blonde girls, one with long hair wearing bright pink lipstick, one with a braid and freckles."

What They Are Saying About

The Stone Collie

Eerie goings-on are happening in *The Stone Collie*, Dorothy Bodoin's twentieth installment in *The Foxglove Corners Mysteries*.

The story begins with the heroine, Jennet Ferguson, school teacher/amateur sleuth, finding a collie puppy tied behind a vacant house. Immediately, the reader is engaged with questions about the welfare of the wee dog, why she was left there and if she will be okay.

However, the biggest question that looms over Foxglove Corners is—What is going on with Lucy Hazen?

A dear friend of Jennet's, Lucy, who writes popular horror stories for teenagers, is hard at work on her newest novel. Shocked over what is beginning to happen in her life, she summons Jennet to her home, where she confides that something she wrote in her fictional world came true in real life. She had written about a stone statue in the woods, then found one in her own woods. Shortly after that, Lucy gives a reading at the local library and two girls arrive to listen, looking identical to Hazen's made-up characters. The plot heats up when copies of Hazen's recent release *Devilwish* keep on disappearing from the library, and then dozens of them appear on Lucy's porch, with black X's defacing their covers.

In the meantime, Jennet discovers yet another puppy tied behind the vacant house; a young girl named Jennifer disappears, and who in the world is Zachary Drummond and what is he up to?

Once again Foxglove Corners is in jeopardy, held hostage to the evil surrounding it.

With the help of Jennet's colorful compatriots, notably Annica and Brent and, of course, her loving husband Crane, she plugs away at the strange occurrences, gets to the bottom of it all, and restores peace to Foxglove Corners. But not for long, I am sure.

Bodoin's tales of Jennet Ferguson are delightful and always leave you wanting more. There is a cast of characters that quickly wins over your heart, making them feel like your best friends, and an aura of spookiness hovers over each story. This one doesn't disappoint, for I found myself riffling through the pages to get to the end. I heartily recommend it and will be looking forward to the next installment.

Suzanne Hurley
Author of *The Teddy Bear Eye Club* and *Love?*

Other Works From The Pen Of
Dorothy Bodoin

The Silver Sleigh, August, 2015—As Jennet attempts to solve the mystery of a ghostly blue merle collie, who haunts the woods of an abandoned kennel, an antique silver sleigh leads her into danger.

A Ghost of Gunfire, January, 2015—Months after gunfire erupted in her classroom at Marston High School, leaving one student dead and one seriously wounded, Jennet begins to hear a sound of gunfire inaudible to everyone else.

Dreams and Bones, May, 2014—A renovation at Brent Fowler's newly-purchased Spirit Lamp Inn turns up human bones buried in the inn's backyard, rekindling interest in the case of a young woman who disappeared from the inn several decades earlier.

The Door in the Fog, November, 2013—A wounded dog disappears in the fog. A blue door on the side of a barn vanishes. Strange flowers and a sound of weeping haunt a meadow. And a curse refuses to die. It's another typical summer in Foxglove Corners.

The Stone Collie

Dorothy Bodoin

A Wings ePress, Inc.

A Cozy Mystery

Wings ePress, Inc.

Edited by: Jeanne Smith
Copy Edited by: Joan Powell
Executive Editor: Jeanne Smith
Cover Artist: Trisha FitzGerald

All rights reserved

Wings ePress Books
http://www.wings-press.com

Copyright © 2016 by Dorothy Bodoin
ISBN 978-1-61309-753-3

Published In the United States Of America

February 2016

Wings ePress Inc.
3000 N. Rock Rd.
Newton, KS 67144

Dedication

In memory of my brother, Dr. Nicholas J. Bodoin.

One

The sun burned down on my bare head as I trudged along Jonquil Lane. The gravel beneath my feet felt like hot coals, and the 'Raze the Construction' petition, so fresh and crisp when I'd left the house, was wilting like my sleeveless cotton blouse and the wildflowers that bloomed at the lane's borders.

Get ready for a scorcher, the morning *Banner* had warned. *Heat, humidity, wind, afternoon storms.*

It wasn't the best weather to go door-to-door collecting signatures, but my friend, Sue Appleton, the president of the Lakeville Collie Rescue League, had volunteered to help me, and this was the only day she had free.

As an English teacher at Marston High School in Oakpoint, Michigan, I had several weeks of vacation, but procrastination thrives in summer heat. Life slips into slow motion. The lightest task requires the greatest effort. Finally, Sue and I chose a date, mapped out our routes, and here I was, broiling in the late June sunshine.

My dark brown shoulder-length hair felt like a stringy mop, and my skin was damp and prickly. I should have worn a sun hat, should have taken the car, stopping at every house on its ten-acre parcel. The next time I'd be better prepared.

I was glad I'd left five of my collies at home drowsing in air-conditioned comfort. Only Raven, the bi-black who lived happily outside in a Victorian dog house built especially for her by my husband, Crane, had chosen to accompany me.

Apparently she was having second thoughts, lagging behind to sniff at every enticing new scent along the way.

"Heel, Raven," I said.

Having a mind of her own, like most of my collies, she dashed ahead of me.

The idea of circulating a petition to demolish the long abandoned construction on Jonquil Lane had been mine. The builder's original vision involved elegant French chateau-style houses on a heavily wooded section of the lane, but his project had fallen apart when he went bankrupt. Subsequently he fled Michigan for parts unknown, leaving skeletal structures to deteriorate into an unsightly ruin.

Before long, wildlife staked their claim to the crumbling half-houses. The site became a haven for vagrants and various unsavory individuals with evil intentions of which I had first-hand experience. The entire area was dark and dangerous, well on its way to being reclaimed by nature.

Today I planned to canvass every household on the lane with my petition, enlightening my neighbors about the construction's violent past and collecting signatures. The sooner the doomed development was erased from the Foxglove Corners landscape the better.

But it was so hot. I twisted off the cap of my ever-present bottled water, took a long drink, and rounded one of the many curves on the lane. Ahead, about a dozen yards away, one of the newly-built houses beckoned. Its soft blue siding glowed in the afternoon light, and white gingerbread trim gave it a frosted fairy tale look.

Pale blue was my favorite color for a house, and on a day like this, no shade was cooler or more inviting.

2

Raven took off toward the house like a land-bound comet, her black and white fur blowing. I followed much more slowly, and as I approached the house, realized that it was vacant. It sat in a vast unlandscaped space, its roof shaded by a lone weeping willow tree in the back. Windows without curtains stared out at emptiness. There were no cars in sight. No sign of human habitation. A scent of sawdust still lingered on the air.

The people haven't moved in yet, I thought. *Go on to the next house and come back later. You have all summer.*

While I'd been admiring the house, Raven had disappeared, probably into the woods across the lane that would provide the new homeowners with a lovely rustic view.

"Raven!" I called. "Come!"

She didn't come, but she *did* respond with a single imperious "woof." The sound came from behind the house rather than the woods.

"Raven!"

Another bark. Translated into dog language: '*You* come!'

Leaving the lane, I stepped on sunbaked ground, thinking how raw the surroundings were, how grass and flowers and perhaps a small pond would transform the blue house into a showplace.

In the shade of the wraparound porch, I walked to the back where I came upon Raven's discovery—a collie puppy chained to the trunk of the tree. She was standing, wagging her little rope tail madly. A rusty lock secured the chain to the tree.

She was a little beauty, a baby perhaps four months old. Her coat was the color of butterscotch with a full white collar and white markings. She reminded me of a plush Lassie toy all fluffy and pretty and fresh from the store.

Raven nudged her gently, licked her as a collie mother would. The puppy watched us with sparkling dark eyes.

Near her but out of reach lay an empty bowl. Nothing else.

3

You never, never chain a dog to a tree, especially in hot weather. Especially without water.

Or food?

The puppy was a little thinner than she should be. How long had she been here? And was her owner inside the house?

My rescue instincts flared to angry life. Here was a collie who might be in distress in my own neighborhood. When I was driving, I had dog treats in my car and a spare leash. Today I had only water, but there was plenty of dog food at home in my pantry. I had only to retrace my steps. But first, I'd knock on the door. Someone must be inside. Who would chain a little puppy outside in this relentless heat and leave?

She *did* have shade, though.

I poured the last of the bottled water into my palm and held it to the puppy's mouth. She lapped it eagerly while at my side Raven whimpered.

That's not enough, she might have said.

There must be an outdoor faucet. I looked and found it. Now if the water was turned on…

It was. I filled the bowl and placed it close to her. Tentatively I stroked her little head. It was like touching warmed velvet.

"Stay with her Raven," I said. "Stay."

Knowing that Raven wouldn't leave the puppy's side, I went back around to the front and climbed the six stairs to the porch. I knocked loudly on the door, rang the bell and waited.

It was as I had feared. No one was inside.

Lucky for him. Or her.

Disheartened, I headed back into the sunshine, back up the lane to my green Victorian farmhouse where I had bags of kibble and every kind of dog treat imaginable. Not puppy food, but it would have to do.

~ * ~

Every rescue is different. When you come across a collie in peril, you follow the Rescue League procedure. Remove the dog from the dangerous situation, if possible, taking care not to get bitten. Offer water and food. Take the dog to our vet, Doctor Foster, for an initial health examination, then to Sue Appleton, who would find a foster parent for her and eventually a forever home.

Remove the puppy from the dangerous situation? My husband, Deputy Sheriff Crane Ferguson, would consider that theft. But if the puppy were abandoned, how could I possibly be accused of stealing her? Sometimes, for the sake of the rescue, you have to take chances.

You don't know that she's abandoned, an inner voice whispered. *Her owner may be at work.*

Then he should have made other arrangements for his puppy. The day was only going to grow warmer. A predator might decide she would make a tasty lunch. I shuddered at the thought.

Another consideration reared its head. I couldn't cut through the chain or open the lock without a key.

That left me with providing food and doing everything in my power to find out who had left a puppy chained to a tree behind an unoccupied house.

Even before I turned onto the walkway, I heard my dogs barking. Two collie faces appeared in the picture window, one black and one white. Candy, my mischievous tricolor, and Misty, the white puppy who had appeared on our porch one snowy Christmas Eve, were always the first to greet me.

I let myself in through the side door that opened to a spacious country kitchen. Candy and Misty had already raced through the house. They pranced around my feet, wild with excitement. Sky, the timid blue merle, emerged from her safe haven beneath the kitchen table and stretched. Halley, my first tricolor collie, and Gemmy, a sable, padded in from the dining room.

Was that everyone?

They crowded around me as I reached into the cupboard where I kept the kibble. Candy tried to shove past me, and Halley licked her chops.

"You poor starved babies," I said. "It isn't dinnertime yet."

Thinking of the lonely puppy at the blue house, I scooped a generous portion of chicken and lamb mix into a bag, then remembered I needed a small bowl.

A plaintive whine reminded me that charity begins at home, and I set out biscuits for the entire crew.

"I'll be right back," I said, with a glance at the petition I'd tossed on the table. Signature gathering was over for today.

~ * ~

To save time, I drove back to the blue house, stepping into the scene I'd recently left. Nothing had changed. There was no car. No sign of the person who had left a collie puppy chained alone in the heat of the day.

Raven lay close to the puppy who hadn't moved. They were both quiet, and the water bowl was empty.

I spilled the kibble into the bowl I'd brought from home and poured the puppy fresh water. She pounced on it.

"It's good," I said. "Yummy. My dogs' favorite."

Leaving her to her dinner, I walked around to the front and pounded on the door again, although I knew it was hopeless. No one travels in Foxglove Corners without a car. But maybe someone had taken the car, and someone else stayed behind?

No one responded.

When I returned to the puppy, I saw that the dish was empty. I'd done what I could. When Crane's shift was over, he would help me. Together we'd figure out how to free the puppy. He could cut through the chain or force the lock.

I believed Crane could do anything, and certainly he wouldn't enforce the letter of the law if it meant keeping a helpless animal from danger.

"I'll be back, baby," I said. "Take a nap. Coming, Raven?"

She looked at me but didn't get up. I understood. The butterscotch puppy was her charge, and she wasn't out of the woods yet. Dogs always know.

In the meantime, I was supposed to meet Sue back at the house, and I had a few chores that wouldn't wait. Like preparing dinner.

I hated to leave the puppy, but I did.

Two

Ice cubes sparkled in their tumblers as I poured the lemonade I'd made this morning and set the pitcher, still half full, on the white wicker side table.

Ice turning to water necessary to sustain life.

I hoped the puppy wouldn't spill her water. As a pup, Halley had like to play in her water pail. Maybe her owner was a novice and didn't realize that sometimes puppies spilled their water in play.

I handed one glass to Sue Appleton and settled in my favorite wicker chair with the other one.

The temperature had soared into the high eighties. A fragile haze bathed the yellow Victorian across the lane where Camille, my friend and aunt by marriage, lived with her husband, Gilbert, who was Crane's uncle.

The woods on the lane looked dark and cool, but no one in his right mind would seek relief from the heat with a robust woodland hike. Here on the porch of my green Victorian farmhouse, we had a pleasant oasis of shade.

The collies had already discovered this. They were grouped around us, panting and watching for deer or other interlopers in their territory. Occasionally they took turns lapping at the pail of water I'd set out for them.

Sue removed her pink sun hat and fanned herself, letting her strawberry blonde hair fly around her face. "I can't stop thinking about that collie puppy, Jennet," she said. "Whoever left her on a chain to bake in this ungodly heat deserves a long jail sentence in a small, hot cell. And I hope, wherever he is, he's thirsty."

I'd made a second trip to the house to refill the puppy's water bowl, debated about calling nine-one-one, and decided to wait for Crane to come home. He'd be through with his shift shortly.

I had my own image of the puppy's owner—guzzling beer by a shady lake, his hat pulled down low to conceal his villain's features. Fairly or unfairly—it didn't matter to us— we both assumed the guilty party was a male.

I took a sip of lemonade. This batch was just right, neither too sweet nor too tart. "He'll change his ways if I have anything to say about it," I said.

"You'll have to find him first."

"I will."

Sue set her hat on the glass-topped round table and stirred her drink with a straw, setting the ice cubes tinkling. "I have nine signatures," she said. "Not bad for a day's work. The people on Sagramore Lake Road were all cooperative—those who were home, that is. I showed them the pictures on my cell phone."

"I only collected two."

Camille had been the first to sign the petition. She also had first-hand knowledge of the evil that flourished at the abandoned development. Then, I'd found my other nearest neighbor, Doctor Linton, hard at work pulling weeds in his large vegetable garden. He, too, thought the area was a hazard as well as a blight on our picturesque landscape.

After securing his signature, I'd come to the blue house, and Raven had found the puppy.

"As Scarlett O'Hara said, tomorrow is another day." Sue liked to quote from her favorite novel, *Gone with the Wind*. In our case, with Sue's schedule, giving riding lessons and breeding horses, it would be more likely a week from tomorrow.

"If the pup were on a rope instead of a chain, we could just take her," Sue said. "After all we're the Collie Rescue League. Who has more right?"

In my opinion, anyone was justified in doing whatever was necessary to rescue a dog in peril from the heat. Usually, though, summer rescue involved dogs trapped in locked cars.

"Until we find the man responsible for her plight, we'll have to be satisfied with giving her food and water," I said.

"Did Raven come home yet?" Sue asked.

"Not yet."

She wouldn't leave the puppy unless someone drove her away from the house. In any event, I didn't worry about her. Of all my collies, Raven could take care of herself. She had once lived in the wild and only on rare occasions joined us in the house. As for water, Foxglove Corners abounded in streams and ponds. She wouldn't be thirsty.

"I know the place," Sue said. "I've been watching it go up since the spring. When I leave, I'll check on the puppy and make sure she has fresh water. And your Raven too."

"I'll give you more kibble for her, and when Crane comes home, I'll ask him to walk over to the house with me."

"I'll see if I can line up a foster home for a puppy. Just in case." Sue glanced at her watch and rose. "Lord, it's hot. I'm melting."

I nodded, draining my glass.

Hot for people, worse for long-haired dogs. Misty had gotten up with Sue, anticipating imminent change. The cool house, possibly treats, fresher water with ice cubes in it. It was time for Sue to go home to her horses, and I had a stew to make.

As we parted, I thought of the puppy who couldn't look forward to change. I hoped she would be all right.

~ * ~

Now that summer had freed me from the drudgery of lesson plans and homework, I resisted the temptation to bring home take-out from Clovers, my favorite little restaurant on Crispian Road. Crane deserved home-cooked meals, and I made sure his dinners were always substantial and savory, served by the light of tapers in the heirloom candlesticks that had belonged to his Civil War ancestress, Rebecca Ferguson.

Born in Tennessee, but a long-time resident of Michigan, Crane still retained a trace of his accent and his fondness for southern food. He was unfailingly appreciative of my modest culinary efforts, and I was eager to please him.

Anyone would think I was a newlywed. Most of the time I felt as if I were, thanks to my handsome, gray-eyed husband who was the only man I'd ever wanted. Whenever he came home after a long day patrolling the roads and by-roads of Foxglove Corners, our house burst into vibrant life.

He was home now. Outside. Parking his Jeep behind my Taurus. I knew it by the rush of collie feet to the side door. Candy as usual was in the lead, and Misty had her favorite toy, a plush goat, in her mouth. They waited for him at the door in a confusion of wagging tails, leaping bodies, and barking voices.

I gave the stew a final stir. Done. Rice, asparagus, rolls, an apple pie cooling on the counter safe from inquisitive collie noses. "Ready and plenty and piping-hot," in accordance with the creed of Stephen Vincent Benet's Southern Lady.

The door opened, and there he stood in the middle of his welcome committee resplendent in his uniform with the shiny badge he wore with pride. A bit more sunburned since this morning. A bit wearier. Streaks of gray in his fair hair and crinkles about his frosty gray eyes that held all the warmth in the world.

He greeted the dogs one by one. Finally it was my turn.

"Hot out there today," he said.

"Well, it's June."

"Something smells good."

"Beef stew. Or it could be apple pie."

We could do better than that.

"I missed you," I said, and a few kisses later, he unbuckled his gun belt. On his way to the cabinet where he kept his guns, his gaze dropped to the petition on the table.

"Only two signatures, honey?" he asked. "That isn't good."

"Sue has nine, but I got distracted."

I told him about the puppy chained at the blue house and my efforts to help her.

"No one lives there yet," he said. "Who would leave a dog at a vacant house?"

"That's what we have to find out."

"The Rescue League is on the job, I take it."

"With a vengeance," I said. "Some people should be banned from owning a dog."

"True enough. Unfortunately if people have the money, they can buy one most anywhere or pick one up at a shelter."

"It goes back to the breeder. Responsible breeders know their clients. They don't sell a puppy to just anyone with the price."

"No argument there," he said. "Let's check it out before dinner."

That was what I hoped he'd say. I turned off the stew and moved the rice and asparagus to the oven. I was ready.

As a rule, the Lakeville Collie Rescue League was a formidable force, but it never hurt to have the law in its corner.

~ * ~

We set off down the lane, Crane holding the leashes of Misty and our wild child, Candy, while I led my gentle Halley. For some time, Crane had insisted on handling Candy himself. In the past she had proved too difficult for me to control when she spied something or someone she wanted to pursue.

We passed the woods, so silent and secretive, casting long shadows on the lane. They were beautiful but rife with mosquitoes and other undesirables. At the Linton house, the lure of barbecue drew the dogs' attention. Around one curve, then another, and there was the blue house. Exquisite but lonely on its raw expanse—and quiet.

Too quiet.

Crane led Candy and Misty onto the property. I followed with Halley.

"There's no puppy back here," he called.

My heart began to race. "Where's Raven?"

"I don't see her."

I came to a stop beside him. The chain, lock and bowl were gone, along with the butterscotch puppy. If it hadn't been for the weeping willow tree, I'd think we had come to the wrong house. Three other houses on the lane were newly built, and one was blue.

But this was the right place. There was no doubt about it.

"I don't understand," I said.

Had her owner taken her away and removed the evidence of neglect from the scene? Including my bowl? He'd taken my bowl. Stolen it.

And where was Raven?

"Don't jump to conclusions," Crane said. "Could be that her owner picked her up."

In which case there would be nothing to save her from. Except the person who didn't have enough sense or humanity to protect a dog from killing weather. How could I find that person and where was the puppy now?

While I was glad we hadn't found her still tethered on that cruel chain, I was far from cheered by the outcome of our investigation.

There were too many unknowns and a young dog's health and well-being at stake.

Candy pawed the ground and pulled mightily on her leash, but Crane pulled back with a gruff command to heel.

"We might as well go home, honey," he said. "Maybe Raven's there."

"We didn't pass her on the lane."

"You know our girl. She took a shortcut through the woods."

"I hope so," I said.

If not, we had another collie to worry about.

Three

The air was muggy, the day stifling, as I walked up the lane. The magnificent flower beds that graced Camille's yellow Victorian had an ethereal shimmer in the haze. Beauty aside, the high humidity made me feel damp and crumpled. And I'd only stepped out of the shower an hour ago.

It felt strange to walk this way without dogs, but I needed both hands free today. First I planned to follow Sue's example and take pictures of the new construction on my iPhone. Pictures were more persuasive than words. Soon I would be moving on to houses whose owners I didn't know well. It was possible that not everyone knew about the ruin on Jonquil Lane. Or cared.

Afterward, I intended to head in the opposite direction and visit the blue house again in case the puppy was there.

Raven caught up to me, barking and wagging her tail. She had come home before dark last night, her fur covered with burrs and bits of leaves, attesting to a long romp in the woods. Crane had brushed her in spite of her reluctance, and I fed her, wishing for the hundredth time that dogs could talk, knowing they communicated in other ways.

"What happened to the puppy?" I had asked her.

She tilted her head and looked at me. Not even a woof or a whimper.

Lassie would have led me to her. I smiled at my fantasy. Raven was no Lassie, and my life wasn't a movie script.

Take one problem at a time, I told myself. First pictures of the unfinished construction.

I could see the first of the houses already, a structure without a façade and a fallen wall. They would have been an impressive addition to Jonquil Lane, those elegant French chateau-style mansions, if the builder had finished them. Each house would have been unique, all imaginatively landscaped. A few almost completed structures still stood, after a fashion, mute testament to grandeur unrealized.

The rest was a jumble of collapsed walls, broken glass, and orphaned lumber, not to mention trees brought down by the wild winds of Foxglove Corners. Darkness and danger and booby-traps lying in wait for the unwary.

Not to mention the ghosts.

I half expected one to materialize beneath a free-standing arch and warn me away from its haunt. It needn't worry. I had no intention of going any farther.

At the edge of the lane, I aimed my phone at the mess while Raven explored the underside of a thick crawling vine.

"I want to see woods here again," I said aloud, "and the last of the skeletal wood burned or carted away or whatever happens when an area is razed."

Satisfied with the views that appeared on the camera roll, I called Raven and turned around, heading down the lane. I passed the yellow Victorian and my own house where the dogs, sensing my presence, set up a clamor from inside. Next the Linton house and the curves, baking in the increasing heat.

Now for the puppy.

~ * ~

She was there again, behind the blue house, chained to the willow, her water bowl overturned. The ground was still wet where the water had spilled. I didn't see my bowl, but I had her breakfast wrapped in plastic tucked in the pocket of my denim skirt.

She seemed even livelier this morning, standing and wagging her tail. Of course it was early, hot enough, but by afternoon it would be hotter still.

"Hello, Butterscotch," I said. "Didn't they remember to feed you?"

She yipped her answer. That high pitched puppy bark. No? Yes? A puppy could always eat more.

As I had anticipated, there was no sign of habitation in the blue house, no one to storm through the back door and demand that I leave the premises. I didn't bother to knock on the front door.

Why couldn't Crane have been with me this morning? Not that he had doubted me, but he could have done something.

I found the same obstacle to the puppy's freedom: a chain secured by a lock.

Wait! I could cut through leather! Why hadn't I thought of that? All right. When I came back, I'd bring sharp scissors and a collar if I had one that would fit her. If not, I could carry her home.

And be accused of dognapping?

You'd better rethink that, I told myself. *Just keep checking on her, filling her water bowl, bringing her food.*

I spilled kibble into the bowl and watched while the puppy ate daintily, devouring every crumb. While she ate, I snapped pictures: a close-up of the lock, one of the empty water bowl, one of the house, so obviously untenanted. One of her sweet face licking her chops.

"I'll come back, baby," I promised her.

With more kibble and some chunks of beef from our stew.

Before I left, I filled her water bowl and made a fuss over her. She lapped it up as if it were the tastiest kibble. Had anyone ever held her or showed her affection?

I reminded myself that puppies were attention hogs.

I didn't want to leave her. On the other hand, I couldn't stay here. I had the evidence of the chain and the empty water bowl on my phone. My next step was unclear, but I knew I would return to the blue house as often as I had to until one day, the butterscotch puppy's owner would be home.

~ * ~

As always I was glad to be home with the air conditioning and a refrigerator filled with snacks and cold drinks. Refreshed and energized, I took Gemmy, Sky, and Halley for a short walk and returned to the harsh ringing of the landline which we used less and less as I became accustomed to the intricacies of the iPhone.

The caller was Lucy Hazen, Foxglove Corners' celebrated writer of horror stories for young people. She sounded a little out of breath and more than a little nervous. In other words, not like herself.

"Good morning, Jennet," she said. "I was wondering if you'd be able to come to lunch today."

"Sure. That sounds nice. We haven't had a visit in ages."

"We'll make up for it today. We'll have tea," she added. "Say around twelve-thirty?"

That meant after lunch she would read my tea leaves. Lucy had many talents, among them an uncanny ability to foresee future events. While I tended to think of tea leaf reading as an amusing parlor game, I had to admit that many of Lucy's past predictions had come true, often making me aware of dire happenings before they became reality.

Whenever something out of the ordinary happened, my first thought was to consult Lucy.

"What shall I bring?" I asked.

"There's no need..."

"I'm driving right by the Hometown Bakery," I said. "What sounds good? Cupcakes? Fruit tarts?"

"You choose," she said. "Thank you, Jennet. I knew I could count on you."

We said our goodbyes, and I glanced at the clock. It was almost noon. I had to hurry. Out of denim and into my orange sundress. A three-strand necklace of coral and gold beads. My new Peach Frost lipstick. For a summertime tea party with my friend, I wanted to look my best.

But why had Lucy thanked me? She'd sounded as if I were doing her a favor, as if the favor were of the utmost importance.

I found my keys and the multi-colored straw bag I used in the summer and dodged Misty's airborne toy goat. Whenever I prepared to leave the house, at least one of the dogs tried to prevent my departure with a ball or Frisbee or toy, whichever was closest.

I left them with an admonition to be good and a promise of glorious future rewards to be dispensed on my return.

Through the hustle and bustle of leave-taking, I'd had time to wonder what lay behind Lucy's invitation to Dark Gables, her atmospheric home on Spruce Road. By the time I was in the car and driving out to the lane, I had come to a troubling conclusion.

Something was wrong.

Four

No one could see Dark Gables from the road, which suited its slightly reclusive owner, Lucy Hazen. Once she had told me that her house, surrounded by dark evergreens and hardwood forest, provided her with the solitude and atmosphere needed for a writer who consorted with fictitious werewolves, vampires, and other assorted horrors.

The long driveway with tall conifers on either side, shadows, and curves like those on Jonquil Lane, concealed the view ahead. Already feelings of claustrophobia and forebodings were creeping up on me.

At the end of the driveway, the house appeared in all its Gothic glory with clean, classic lines, heavily curtained windows, and dark gables rising to the sky.

Carrying the box from the Hometown Bakery, I walked up to the porch where Lucy was waiting for me with her collie Sky, the little blue merle who shared a name with my shy rescue. Lucy had glossy black hair and usually wore black. Today's ensemble was a long gauzy dress complemented by gold chains and bracelets.

She loved to dress like her vision of a horror story writer whether at home or in public.

I detected a fleeting glint of surprise in her eyes which puzzled me. Surely I was expected.

"You look so nice, Jennet," she murmured. "All dressed up. Come in."

"Well, yes," I said. "A tea party at Dark Gables calls for something pretty."

Sky padded after us through rooms filled with heavy dark furniture to the sunroom at the back of the house. Here summer bloomed in perpetuity with white wicker furniture, green and blossoming plants, and French doors that offered a soothing view of Lucy's back yard fountain and the woods beyond.

A round table, covered with a floral cloth, was set up on the shaded patio.

"We're having chicken salad," Lucy said, eyeing the box. "What did you bring from the bakery?"

"Cream puffs. They just came out of the kitchen."

"Perfect."

And it was a perfect lunch with a soft breeze to add atmosphere and a subtle splash of water in the background. Sandwiches cut in quarters, potato chips, and two kinds of pickles. To drink we had iced tea. Cups of hot tea would follow for the tea leaf reading. As I rarely ate outside, usually grabbing lunch on the run, this was a special treat.

Something was missing, though. I couldn't find a name for it, but it was there, hovering over the table.

Finally I said, "What's troubling you, Lucy?"

She looked up from her sandwich. "You're astute, Jennet, but then I knew that. Does it show?"

"Not to just anybody, but I know you."

"All right." She picked up a potato chip and examined its shape. Her bracelets clanged together, a curiously ominous sound. "There's something very wrong, and you're probably the only person who can help me. Yesterday I found something in the woods. An object. It disturbs me."

She broke the chip in half. I waited.

"What did you find?"

"A stone statue. I have no idea how it got there. It's the the kind you find in any garden or on a front porch. It looks like Sky."

"It's painted then?"

"No, but the dog's expression reminded me of Sky."

Hearing her name, Sky tilted her head and moved closer to the table. Unlike my Candy, Sky was no food bandit. She was willing to wait for a handout—but not too long.

We were both avoiding the main point. What was a garden statue doing in Lucy's woods?

"Where did it come from?" I asked.

"I have no idea," she said. "Ordinarily I don't go strolling through the woods. They're my view. My inspiration. But yesterday Sky, my docile little Sky..."

She broke off and caressed the collie's head. "She's usually so good, but with food, all bets are off. I had a rotisserie chicken on the counter. I'd sliced most of the meat off and was going to wrap the carcass in old newspaper paper and put it in the garbage. I reached for the paper, and Sky..."

I laughed, visualizing the scene. Similar ones had been enacted in my own house dozens of times. "Say no more."

"Sky grabbed the carcass and ran with it, right out the French doors I'd left open. I chased her, picking up chunks of meat that fell, but she wouldn't surrender it."

"They never do."

"The little demon took off into the woods. I had to follow her. You know how dangerous chicken bones can be for a dog?"

I nodded. My chases usually involved pork chop bones, the dogs' favorite.

"Well, there we were, tearing through the woods. Sky is a whole lot faster than I am. I never did catch her until the carcass was gone. All those bones."

Lucy shuddered, paused to catch her breath. It seemed she had just relived every minute of that chase through the woods with their endless roots and vines and depressions hidden by last fall's leaves. She appeared to have experienced again the fear that those bones would choke Sky or pierce one of her organs.

"It's a wonder I didn't break my neck," she said.

"That's a worrisome story, but it's not unusual. Dogs will be dogs. Sky seems to be fine."

"So far."

The stone statue had gotten lost in Lucy's tale. I steered the conversation back to it.

"So you don't know how the statue came to be in your woods?"

"None."

"Or how long it's been there?"

"It could have been days—or years. People don't usually trespass on my property. Not even hunters."

"Well," I said. "It's mysterious, but..."

I didn't see how discovering a statue could cause the haunted look in Lucy's eyes or the barely discernible trembling of her hands.

"I thought we could go back into the woods together so you could see the statue," she said, "but in your pretty dress and those shoes..."

She glanced at my strappy orange sandals. "It won't do. We can go another day."

"We can go today," I said. "I can throw my dress in the washer if it gets dirty, and I'll walk carefully. The heels are low."

She brightened. "If you think you can manage it..."

"I can, but I have a feeling there's more to your story, Lucy," I said. "What did you leave out? What's really wrong?"

"It's my book," she said.

"*Devilwish?*"

I knew Lucy's latest release was a gruesome little novel about three teens who make a pact with the devil and then try desperately to renege on their bargain. As in *Doctor Faustus* or *The Devil and Daniel Webster*. It was an old story. Using her magic with words and her knowledge of young people, *Devilwish* would be new and relevant.

"No," she said. "My work-in-progress. It's about two sisters who move to a spooky old house in the country and find a stone collie statue in their woods. My title is *The Stone Collie*."

"That's quite a coincidence."

"I think it's more, and here's the problem. I'm only half way through the first draft of my book. No one else has read it, and I haven't discussed the plot with anyone. Nobody could possibly know about a stone statue in the woods unless they *had* read my book. Besides, collie statues aren't exactly common."

"It has to be a coincidence then," I said.

"I wish it were."

"Back up," I said. "In your book, how did the statue find its way to the woods?"

She smiled for the first time this afternoon. "Aliens from the planet Voltar left it," she said. "Fiction is easier than life."

Five

The stone statue sat in a clearing in Lucy's woods under a gnarled old tree around which a glossy green vine had twisted its way up to the first branch. It was impossible to tell how old the statue was or long it had been there. It was intact without a single crumbling ear or paw, and it had an eerie luminous gleam.

Eerie? I'd prepared myself to encounter a supernatural entity. In truth, the color was grayish-green. Its expertly carved face was reminiscent of Sky or of any regal collie.

"There are no vines growing around it," I said. "No moss anywhere near. I don't think it's been out here that long. But I can't say for sure."

"That was what I thought."

Sky sniffed around the base, pawed at the ground. Lucy grabbed her collar and pulled her away.

I couldn't resist touching the stone head lightly, as if the statue were a real dog. It was, as I'd anticipated, rough—and warm, whereas I'd expected it to be cold.

Well, it was a hot day, even in the dense shade of the trees.

"Drat!" Lucy slapped at her arm. "Mosquitoes. Now you see why I don't go walking in the woods."

I had a few bites, too. I should have brought a shirt or sweater. But how could I have known that our tea party would move beyond the patio? No matter. Bugs were all around us, thick in the humid air. There was no escaping them.

"What do you think, Jennet?" Lucy asked.

"I've seen sculptures like this, usually spaniels holding baskets in their mouths. I wonder why they chose this particular breed? It's as if they knew a collie lives at Dark Gables."

Whoever they were. He, she, or—because these were the woods of Dark Gables in Foxglove Corners where ghosts were welcome—it.

Lucy pulled on Sky's collar. The collie responded with a little squeak of protest. "I was afraid of that."

"Maybe it doesn't have anything to do with your book."

"But if it's because I have a collie... What then?"

I stepped back, and a vine that looked like ivy grabbed my heel. Not poison ivy, thank heavens. I yanked it free, then felt a pin prick on my ankle. The insect had bitten and run.

"Is there a planet named Voltar?" I asked.

"I made it up."

"The statue isn't hurting anything, and it's pretty," I said. "Why don't we move it to your porch or maybe the back yard?"

Lucy's quick answer startled me. Clearly she'd had the same idea and rejected it. "I don't think we should do that. Besides, it must weigh fifty pounds or more."

"And the aliens would be upset."

Lucy paled, clearly not amused. I knew she was superstitious. She didn't believe in her own Voltarians. Of course she didn't. But she had faith in her power to glimpse occasionally into the future. Perhaps she had seen something that unnerved her.

Still, I wasn't used to seeing her so unsure of herself. So apprehensive. Even fearful.

I didn't ask her to explain. I doubted she'd be able to.

"I feel we might be tempting fate," Lucy said. "Interfering with some plan."

"Then we'll leave it here."

"I wonder if it's a grave marker," Lucy said.

"Way out here in the woods? Was this ever a cemetery?"

"Not to my knowledge."

Last winter I'd dealt with a secret grave in another wood. I wasn't eager for a repeat performance.

"Let's not think about bodies just yet. I can't imagine where it came from, but let me think about it. If we're through, I'd like to sample those cream puffs."

"And we'll have our tea."

"Maybe the answer will be in the leaves."

"I never could read my own fortune successfully," Lucy said. "Yours, yes."

"Well…" We turned around and started retracing our steps. More vines underfoot, more mosquitoes.

"The collie statue didn't just wander into the woods and decide to sit down in the clearing," I said. "There has to be an answer to this puzzle. We just have to find it."

"Then you'll help me?" Lucy asked. "We'll work together?"

"Definitely. What would summer in Foxglove Corners be without a mystery?"

~ * ~

We moved inside for our tea and dessert. Lucy seemed calmer, no doubt because she no longer felt alone with her strange mystery. Later, after we had eaten all the cream puffs—as light as air and therefore not an extravagant indulgence—we drank our tea, which Lucy poured in plain white cups. Patterns would interfere with the formation of the leaves.

And the leaves held the answers. Some of them, anyway. I was well acquainted with the ritual. Drain the cup in the saucer, turn it toward you three times while making a wish. This allowed the leaves to arrange themselves into symbols.

Peace. The charm's wound up. Or something like that.

Lucy peered into my cup. "I see your wish," she said. "Everything in your home is clear."

That was always a good beginning.

"And Jennet, look at this." Lucy pointed to a light leaf that had settled close to the top. Her gold bracelets jingled softly. "What does this look like to you?"

"A blob?" I said.

"Look again. Notice the shape of the head."

"It looks a little like a dog."

"A collie," Lucy said. "My statue."

Now that Lucy had planted the idea in my mind, I saw the hint of a collie head tilted in the whimsical collie fashion.

"If the statue is in my cup, then it's going to play a part in our lives," I said. "But I've recently come across another collie."

I told her about the chained puppy in the blue house on Jonquil Lane. "Sue and I are going to try to find out who owns her."

"That's terrible," Lucy said, reaching out again to Sky. "Dogs need the company of their people. Puppies especially shouldn't be left alone for hours at a time. On a chain, no less."

She sighed. "There's so much inhumanity in the world. So much stupidity."

"We have our work cut out for us," I said, adding on an impulse. "What happens next in your book, Lucy? After the sisters discover the statue?"

I knew she didn't like to discuss her work in progress but this time thought she'd make an exception.

"Chaos and a hearty dose of mayhem. According to my plan, when the girls find the statue, it's only the beginning of their adventure. Eventually they're going to make contact with the aliens."

"Let's hope life doesn't imitate art," I said.

~ * ~

Crane came home with information that evening. "The owners of the blue house are Jonathan and Rebecca Brooks. They're both lawyers. They have two children, a boy and a girl. No pets yet, but they want to buy a dog for the kids. They plan to move in next month."

"How did you find out all that?" I asked.

He gave me his most infuriating grin. "Sheriff's secret."

Misty trailed after him with her toy goat in her mouth as he locked his gun in the cabinet. He tossed the toy into the dining room and she scampered after it.

"Where does the puppy fit in?"

"It doesn't. Someone else must be using their property to keep her during the day."

"The question is, did the Brooks family authorize it?" I asked.

"I doubt it."

"I'm going to talk to the neighbors tomorrow," I said. "Someone must hear whining or barking. Don't tell me a little puppy is going to be quiet all day."

"Go ahead. But hearing animal sounds isn't unusual in the country."

"I need more signatures for the petition, too. Most people aren't home during the day, but I'll try."

Sue couldn't join me tomorrow, but I wanted to catch up to her nine.

"Good luck," he said.

When he went upstairs to shower, I turned my attention to dinner. Roasted chicken tonight, brussels sprouts and white rice. Dessert was strawberry shortcake which I'd assemble later.

I hadn't told Crane about the statue in Lucy's woods. It wasn't a distressing subject, not yet, so I'd do so while we ate.

As I tossed the salad, I couldn't help wondering about coincidences. To be sure, they existed, but this one was extraordinary.

Lucy writes a book titled *The Stone Collie* and shortly thereafter finds a stone collie statue on her property. Not in front of the house, which would be mysterious enough, but in the woods where, normally, she would never have seen it were it not for Sky and the stolen carcass.

The significance eluded me.

What troubled me most was its effect on Lucy, who had always seemed so unflappable. She was truly worried about the artifact, about a possible connection to Sky, and about the power of her written word to make something happen. Which, in my opinion, wasn't possible.

On the other hand, this was Foxglove Corners, the quiet, the picturesque, the strange, with many an inexplicable occurrence taking place within its borders. People disappeared into thin air, ghosts walked, mysteries took form while Lucy sat at her computer and wrote horror stories.

Now, it seemed, it was her turn to experience horror.

Six

As soon as Crane left the next morning, I set out down Jonquil Lane with my petition and the pictures of the abandoned development on my phone. Because I thought an icebreaker would help my cause, I took Halley with me, and in case the puppy was at the blue house, I had a packet of kibble in my pocket. I was prepared for any eventuality.

It was one of those rare June days, warm but not oppressive, with a breeze rather than a robust wind. Sweet scents rode the air, and the wildflowers on the lane glistened with dew. Raven dashed out of her house to join us, and I suddenly felt optimistic about my missions.

"If the puppy—what's her name? Butterscotch?—is still being chained without water, don't hesitate to call nine-one-one," Crane had said last night. "I'll see if anyone noticed a collie puppy in the area or a person who doesn't belong here. We'll catch up with her owner."

Optimism was invigorating. If only Lucy's mystery could receive such attention.

Raven ran ahead of us as if she were on a mission of her own. As she was, for I was sure she remembered the puppy. Halley and I followed at a more sedate pace. On a morning such as this, it would be folly to hurry.

I heard the puppy yipping from a distance, a high pitched sound that sliced through the heavy country silence. A sound that could get on a human's nerves if it continued.

The yipping grew louder as the blue house came into view, a pale blue jewel shining against an azure sky. It needed landscaping. Shrubs and flowers planted around the foundation. Perhaps a pond and a miniature tree.

Were the nearby houses too far away for the puppy to be heard? I doubted it. In the country, sound carries.

She was there, behind the blue house, frantically communicating her desire for company to the world. Her cries changed to joyful yelps as Raven added her own barks to the melee. I glanced at the windows, still uncurtained, with no one peering out to see what had caused the disturbance.

The butterscotch puppy was attached to the chain again with the lock in place, but her water bowl was full and a well-gnawed bone lay on the ground.

I was earlier this morning than I'd been the first time I'd come across her. The owner had most likely left recently. Did he return during the day? Impossible to tell.

Should I call nine-one-one?

Not yet. She had water to drink and a bone to chew. On my way back, I'd stop by and re-assess the situation.

Raven and the puppy were playing, the puppy nipping at Raven's wagging tail and darting away, as far as the chain allowed her. They moved in circles, a butterscotch and black whirlwind, stirring up the dust. At present all was well.

I told Halley to sit and watched them for a while. Finally I said, "Come, Raven."

Of my six collies, Raven was the slowest to obey me. She didn't want to leave her small playmate. As for myself, I could watch dogs at play all day but didn't have endless time to while away at the blue house.

Still, I was loath to tear myself away. The puppy was so pretty, so fluffy, like a roly-poly little butterball. At the moment she was determined to take a bite out of Raven's tail. She was certainly lively this morning and appeared to have put on weight.

Wait! Roly-poly butterball? This change couldn't have happened in a day's time.

As Raven sidestepped away from her, realization struck in the form of a thunderbolt. This looked like a different puppy. What was going on here?

~ * ~

Some people claim that at this age all collie puppies look alike with tipping ears, sparkling eyes, and little rope tails. To an extent this could be true, especially if the puppies were of the same lines.

I raised my voice. "Here, Butterscotch-girl!"

As she halted her game to answer the new call, I noticed something I'd overlooked until now. The first puppy had a full white collar. This one had a distinctive marking, an oval patch of butterscotch-colored fur high in the middle of her chest. It looked like a golden ornament holding a snowy shawl in place.

In all other ways, except for the additional weight, the two puppies were identical.

Did the absent owner have two puppies then? If so, where was the first one, the full-collared little girl I'd called Butterscotch? In the house? Not likely. If she were, she'd be jumping on the window sill, wanting to join in the fun. Not dead, I hoped. But also not on the premises.

The mystery deepens.

I ran my hand over her wriggling body. She stuck her nose in my pocket. I'd forgotten about the kibble. Raven and Halley sat and watched as I offered her a few kernels. The puppy gobbled them up and looked for more. I brought out a generous portion and held my hand under her mouth.

The way to a dog's heart is through her stomach.

It bothered me that I had no idea who the negligent dog owner might be. Maybe Crane would have luck with his inquiries, or perhaps the nearest neighbor would know something about the situation at the blue house.

I gave a gentle tug on Halley's leash and called Raven again. This time she came to me, and we moved on.

~ * ~

At the next house, set far back from the lane, nicely-spaced trees created an illusion of a rustic brown mansion hidden in woods. Vibrant annuals interspersed with silver mounds decorated the façade, and a homemade swing, consisting of ropes and a board, hung in a three-branched maple. The first story windows were open, and two large baskets sat on the front porch. In front of a detached garage, a sleek beige Impala soaked up the morning sun.

No one was home.

Making a mental note to return later in the day, I returned to the lane. Rounding the next curve, I found a small silver-haired woman in jeans and a blue and white striped shirt watering new plantings, sunflowers, around her mail box. She looked up with a broad welcoming smile as we approached.

"What beautiful collies!" she said. "I've seen them before on their walks, but never up close. Can I pet them?"

"They'd love that," I said. "The black and white is Raven, and Halley is the tricolor."

While the dogs basked in this unanticipated affection, the woman said, "I'm Georgina Lasenby. We moved in over Memorial weekend."

"Welcome to Foxglove Corners," I said. "You'll love living here."

"I do already."

I introduced myself. "My husband and I live in the last house on this side of the lane."

This was a natural lead-in to my rehearsed speech. "Have you ever noticed the incomplete construction up my way? Just before you reach Squill Lane?"

"Those houses are going to be beautiful," she said. "Do you know when they'll be finished?"

She must not have looked at the development closely, not have seen the fallen boards and debris.

"Never," I said and gave her the background. "They would have been, but the builder abandoned the development and left town. My friend and I are trying to collect enough signatures to have them demolished."

I added a few anecdotes detailing the atrocities that had taken place amidst the ruins. "As it stands, it's a constant danger."

"I'd be happy to sign," she said. "My husband and I moved to the country to get away from violence."

I handed her a pen. "There's something else. Do you ever hear a puppy barking in the blue house next to you?"

"I've heard something from time to time. It could be a puppy."

"As far as I can tell, she's left alone most of the day, sometimes without water."

There was no point adding my suspicion that there were two puppies at the house until I knew more about the situation.

"I belong to the Lakeville Collie Rescue League," I added. "We're concerned about her well-being."

Georgina frowned. "I met the owner a few weeks ago. His name is Jonathan Brooks. The family lives downstate. They haven't moved in yet. How could they keep a dog there?"

"Did you notice anyone else? Someone walking the puppy, maybe?"

"I've seen a blond man in a uniform walking these pretty collies and another one."

"That's my husband, Crane," I said. "We have four other collies, so we take turns walking them in threes."

"Six in all? My goodness. That's a full house. Er—dog house."

"I adopted some of my own rescues," I said. "Well, I'd better be on my way. Ready, Raven?"

Like collies the world over, mine were loath to leave this new source of attention. Halley rose reluctantly, but Raven leaned in for one more caress.

"I've seen another man in front of that house a few times," Georgina added. "He was taking pictures. He has blond hair, too, and is quite handsome."

"Are you talking about Mr. Brooks?" I asked.

"No, another man. He drives a little orange Volkswagen."

"That's odd. If he's the puppy's owner, you'd think he'd need a larger car. I pointed to Halley and Raven. "Collie puppies grow into big dogs."

Blond man, orange Volkswagen, seen at the blue house. This picture-taking man must be the puppies' owner.

Gotcha, I thought. *Well, maybe not yet, but I will get you.*

Georgina and I said our farewells, and we walked on with Raven in the lead. I couldn't have been happier. I had three signatures on my petition and, I hoped, knowledge of the person I'd been hoping to meet. I had no doubt the meeting itself would follow. I just had to visit the blue house at the right time.

Seven

By the time I brought my day's signature collecting to an end, I had added five more names to the petition, told and retold the story of the abandoned construction, and was ready for a new activity, even coming home and starting dinner.

I was baking a ham and planned to fry slices of breaded eggplant, a new vegetable dish that Crane and I both liked. And a pie. We needed a pie. Blueberry. I reached for the flour canister.

At four-thirty, I happened to glance out the bay window just as a yellow car parked behind my Taurus. It had a streamlined body and long white fins, the kind only seen on vintage automobiles. Well, this was obviously vintage. With those magnificent fins, it looked as if it could blast off into space any moment.

Out stepped a familiar figure, Foxglove Corners' premier fox hunter and perennial bachelor, red-haired Brent Fowler. For Brent, this vehicle was a stunning departure. As a rule, his many cars were new, pricy, and snazzy. For an added touch, he wore a shirt the color of spring dandelions.

The dogs were going wild, leaping at the window and falling over one another at the front door. Even timid Sky. Brent was a favorite with them, and I was sure they knew the identity of the visitor before he'd stepped out of that amazing car from yesteryear.

He stood in the vestibule in a crush of wagging tails and nudging noses, greeting each collie by name.

"I love your new car," I said. "Or should I say your old car?"

"Isn't she a beauty? It's a Plymouth Belvedere, circa 1958. It looks like it just came out of the showroom."

"Did you restore it yourself?" I asked.

"Not me."

Foolish question. Brent had an army of aides and employees. What with his many enterprises, he relied on outside help whenever possible. I couldn't see him making rust of the past disappear and wielding a paint brush.

"I'm taking her to the antique car show over in Maple Creek next month." He sank into his favorite rocker and patted his knee. Misty lost no time in leaping into his lap. "It sure smells good in here. What's cooking?"

"Ham and blueberry pie," I said.

"No wonder the Sheriff is always in a hurry to get home."

I smiled. Was that a compliment? I chose to think so. "I hope my food isn't the only reason. Can you stay for dinner? There's plenty."

"That's why I came," he said. "I ran into the Sheriff earlier today at a diner. 'Stop over for dinner some time,' he said. So here I am. That's one reason, anyway."

"What's the other one?" I asked.

"We've got trouble. Someone is out to get Lucy."

"I take it she told you about the statue?"

"We don't have secrets, Lucy and me," he said. "She took me into the woods to look at it."

"Did she tell you everything?"

"About the statue in her book? Yes. She's really freaked out. I've never seen her like this. So what can we do to help her?"

"I wish I knew," I said. "Solve the mystery, I guess."

"That's your department."

"I can think of a few explanations for the collie statue. But why it appears after Lucy writes about the girls discovering the same kind of statue in the same kind of place—that's uncanny, to say the least."

"Lucy has an event over at the library this weekend," Brent said. "Now she's talking about cancelling it. That'll just be giving in to this statue thing. Whatever it is."

"What kind of event?" I asked.

"She's supposed to talk about writing to a bunch of kids and sign copies of her book, *Devilwish*. There'll be refreshments and a photographer to take pictures for the paper."

Lucy hadn't told me about that. I knew she rarely promote her books or even discussed them, preferring to write and lead a quiet life. She already had an impressive audience for her work. I was surprised that she had agreed to a library event, but perhaps Miss Elizabeth Eidt, the librarian, had talked her into it. Miss Eidt could be very persuasive and was in a position to know exactly how popular Lucy's books were with young people, especially girls.

"If Lucy doesn't show up, there'll be a lot of disappointed kids," I said. "And I can't think of a single reason why she should be afraid to appear in public."

"That's it, Jennet. She's afraid. She doesn't think this statue, turning up the way it did, is a coincidence. I don't either. She's waiting for the other shoe to drop. We have to help her."

"I said I would. I intend to. But what can we do?"

He shrugged. "For starters, convince her to go to her event. Be there in the audience."

"Of course. We can give her our support. Only…"

I frowned. "Only I wish I understood what was going on."

~ * ~

The ham with its pineapple glaze was a success. The pie even more so. After dinner, we sat in the living room drinking coffee and talking about the collie puppy (or puppies?) at the blue house.

Crane was surprised by my revelation that there were two puppies instead of one, and both of them chained to a tree. "That's double abuse."

"I can't say the puppy I saw today was starving," I said, remembering how she had gobbled the kibble. "Most growing pups are good eaters."

That was certainly true of Halley, the only one of our collies I'd known as a puppy. I knew there were dogs, of course, who were fussy eaters. Just like babies. Perhaps that was why Butterscotch was so thin compared to the other. I had to find a name for the roly-poly pup I'd seen today. Broken Collar? No. That would imply that she had an actual broken collarbone. Butterball? That reminded me of a turkey. Ornament?

No, no, and no. I had to come up with something better.

"What about the empty water bowl?" Brent said. "It's criminal to leave a dog without water especially on a hot day."

"Jennet can't keep on taking care of other people's dogs," Crane added. "We can't assume the owner returns periodically to fill the bowl."

"We have to find him then," I said. "A blond man. Handsome." I cast a glance at my husband, the lamplight shining on his fair hair. "That describes you, Crane."

"That isn't funny, Jennet," he said.

Misty jumped off Brent's lap and returned moments later with her plush goat. At one time it had been missing, somewhere in the house. Sometimes I wished she had never found it. Brent tossed it into the dining room and laid his hand on Sky's head. She was never far from him, although she didn't presume to climb on his lap.

"Let me work on it," Crane said. "How many handsome blond men can there be in Foxglove Corners?"

"You and Georgina Lassenby might have different ideas of handsome," I pointed out. "Look for an orange Volkswagen. I've never seen one—anywhere. Find the car and you'll find the man."

"I'll look, too, and, Jennet, how about going over to Dark Gables with me tomorrow?" Brent said. "I'm worried about Lucy, and I think it'd be a mistake for her to stay away from the library. It's too much like hiding, and that isn't good."

It also wasn't like her not to honor a commitment.

"Let's do that," I said.

It was regrettable that two problems had cast their shadows on our bright summer. A pair of collie puppies who were quite likely chained to a cruel or clueless owner and a strange occurrence bedeviling a woman who made her living crafting horror stories for young people.

"I wonder about that other shoe," I said. "When it drops, what form will it take?"

Eight

We entered the woods of Dark Gables, Lucy, Brent, and I. Sky padded along in Lucy's wake, excitedly sniffing at all the wondrous, unfamiliar scents.

The day was overcast, the way beneath the trees dark and vaguely menacing. Mosquitoes and myriads of tiny insects thronged the air. It was incredibly humid. Already my cotton shirt felt damp.

The statue hadn't moved. I'd half expected it to be gone, vanished in the same manner it had most likely appeared. Silently, mysteriously.

No such luck.

"It doesn't look threatening," Brent said, walking slowly around the circumference. "It's just a hunk of concrete. How could it hurt you, Lucy?"

"It's not the statue I'm afraid of. It's that I wrote about something out of the ordinary and here it is. A figment of my imagination took on a tangible form and landed in my backyard. That is, in my woods."

"When you put it like that it *is* creepy," I said. "The next time you should imagine a chest filled with gold and precious stones."

They didn't appreciate my humor.

"Come away, Sky," Lucy said, an unaccustomed sharp edge in her tone.

"She may be picking up the scent of the person who left the statue here," Brent said.

Lucy sighed. "I don't know, Brent. I just don't want my dog near this thing."

With a curse, he swatted a mosquito away. "Now that I look at it carefully, there's something about the eyes. They look evil."

That was the kind of comment Lucy might make.

"How can a collie possibly look evil?" Lucy asked. "They're the sweetest, gentlest of dogs."

"It's just an impression," he said. "Jennet, what do you think?"

"I don't see it." I stepped back and came in quick contact with a tree trunk. "No, they're just eyes. The sculpture is clever. It's very lifelike."

"Too lifelike," Lucy murmured. "All it needs is color."

"Have we seen enough?" Brent asked.

"More than enough."

"Let's go back to the house then," I said. "I have an idea I'd like to run by you."

It had come to me this morning while I lay in bed sketching a plan for the day. I had a feeling that Lucy would reject it. Still it was an idea. Nobody else had one.

I told them about it when we were inside the house, safe from attacking bugs. We sat in Lucy's sunroom over lemonade and cookies. No tea for Brent. He didn't believe in the power of the leaves.

"What if the statue has been there for years, Lucy?" I said. "Since before you bought the property? Let's say you saw it a long time ago when you were a newcomer to Foxglove Corners but for some reason it slipped out of your mind."

"Straight into my subconscious?" Lucy asked.

"Something like that. So when you sat down to write *The Stone Collie,* your subconscious reminded you of it."

"I like that idea," Brent said.

Obviously Lucy didn't.

"Well, it isn't viable. First, I have an excellent memory. If I'd seen the statue before, I would remember it. Second, I don't make a habit of walking in the woods. They're part of my scenery. My inspiration."

Brent was incredulous. "You've never explored your own property?"

"A little," she admitted. "But only the fringes. I've never wandered that deep into the woods. I wouldn't have gone this time if Sky hadn't run away with that chicken carcass. And, Jennet, your idea doesn't explain how the statue got there in the first place."

I was aware of that, and I disagreed with Lucy. She might believe she remembered everything she'd ever seen, everything that had ever happened to her, but our minds keep some secrets from all of us. Nothing else made sense.

"Now," I said, "about your commitment to talk at the library. I think you should keep it. Think of your readers, how they must be counting on a chance to meet you and ask questions about writing and have you autograph *Devilwish.*"

"Besides, Miss Eidt will be upset if you bail," Brent added.

Lucy looked down at her cookie. They were, as usual, store-bought macaroons but nonetheless good.

"I guess I should go," she said.

"Good. Brent and I will go with you."

She signed, obviously not entirely convinced but nonetheless acquiescent. "With you two in the audience, what can go wrong?"

~ * ~

Lucy's library event was scheduled for Saturday at three o'clock. That morning I stopped at Clovers, ostensibly to buy extra

44

desserts for the refreshment table. I also wanted to talk to Annica, my young partner-in-detection who worked at the restaurant part time while taking English courses at Oakland University. Annica was a vivacious redhead with a penchant for bright colors and unique earrings. They were strings of seashells today, and her dress was blue, the color of lake water. She already had a light tan.

I selected my dessert—a dozen chocolate cupcakes with fudge nut frosting—and settled down in the best booth at Clovers with a view of woods across Crispian Road. I ordered a cup of coffee and a cupcake for myself, just to make sure they were good.

Annica joined me, not having had her morning break yet.

"What's new?" I asked as I cut my cupcake into quarters to make it seem to last longer.

"Nothing much. I'm descending into the Middle Ages with Chaucer this summer. I've had one date with Brent. Just one. But the summer is young."

Annica had a long-standing crush on Brent Fowler. And who could blame her? She made no secret of her desire to mean more to him than a casual date. Alas, on his part, Brent had no inclination to settle down with one girl when so many vied for his attention. He liked his life as it was. As he should.

"We need a new mystery to liven up the summer," Annica said. "Nothing dangerous like the last one. Just something new and tantalizing."

"As it happens, I have one. Maybe two."

I told her about the stone collie statue but didn't mention Lucy's fears. Nor did I tell her about the puzzling connection to Lucy's new book. That is, for now. Even without the enhancements, the statue made a captivating story.

"I'll bet it's a pet's grave," she said. "Someone buried a collie there and brought the statue to mark the site."

"In another person's woods?"

"They weren't always Lucy's woods, were they?"

I had to think for a moment. "She bought the house and acres some time ago."

"There!" Annica said. "We still have a mystery. Why doesn't Lucy just dig beneath the statue and find out what's there."

I'd never thought of that. I suppose Lucy hadn't either. But it was June. Unearthing a grave would be possible. If we discovered an animal skeleton buried under the statue or even human remains, the mystery would be solved.

Well, not quite. I reminded myself of the statue in Lucy's book. That was the real mystery, the one that defied detecting.

I longed to tell Annica more but felt I should ask Lucy's permission first. After all, except for Brent and myself, no one had any idea what her work-in-progress was about.

"You said you had two mysteries," Annica reminded me.

"There's a collie puppy being chained to a tree in a vacant house on Jonquil Lane. She's often left without water, and... This is going to sound strange. It appears there are two of them, almost identical except for one distinctive marking and a few pounds."

"Who's leaving her there?" she asked.

"We don't know yet. I have one clue, though. The owner may be a handsome, blond man who drives an orange Volkswagen."

"Orange Volkswagen! I saw one the other day in Clovers' lot." She frowned, apparently trying to call back an elusive memory. "I thought it was a weird color. Way too bright. But I don't recall seeing any handsome blond man in the restaurant. You bet I'd notice that."

"Unless there are dozens of orange VWs in town, we may be able to find him."

"Then what?" she asked.

"Confront him. Ask him if he knows that puppies can play in their water bowls and spill the water. Tell him how often puppies need to be fed. And educate him about chains. I can't imagine what makes anyone think a dog can thrive on a chain."

"That all sounds dangerous. Most men don't like being lectured."

"It's my duty. I'm in Collie Rescue, remember. And I'm dying to know what happened to the first puppy I saw, the little skinny one."

"Let me help," Annica said. "Looking for a handsome man sounds like fun. An odd colored foreign car—not so much. But I'll do it."

"That'll be great. What time are you off today?" I asked.

"Two-thirty."

"Do you have any plans for this afternoon?"

"Read another Canterbury Tale—in old English."

"How would you like to go to the library with me at three? Lucy Hazen is giving a talk and signing her books."

"Today? I'd love to. I know her stories are for kids, but I love them. She's such a great writer. I don't know why they don't make her books into movies."

I didn't either, but I imagined Lucy wouldn't care for the attendant notoriety.

"I'll pick you up after work, then."

Lucy would appreciate the additional support and perhaps I'd obtain her permission to tell Annica about all the aspects of the stone collie mystery. Suddenly I had high hopes for the library event.

Nine

The Foxglove Corners Public Library was an elegant old white Victorian that was once the family home of Miss Elizabeth Eidt. Some years ago, she had donated the house to Foxglove Corners for a library and now served as the head and only librarian, with the help of her young assistant, Debbie.

I sometimes wondered if there was another library in the state of Michigan quite like it. Twenty-first century advances lay lightly on our hometown institution. Miss Eidt had a computer in her office and even knew how to use it, but she still maintained physical files of newspaper clippings and a card catalog.

One could find the newest bestsellers in the library, along with books that were very old indeed, among them first editions of books in a series like the Bobbsey Twins and Judy Bolton with their beautifully illustrated covers. She was constantly on the lookout for Gothic novels, which she knew I loved, and she gave a place of honor to Lucy's books, even when no event was scheduled.

Miss Eidt regarded the library as if it were still her private home, although she owned and lived in a small house not too far from the Corners. She and Debbie took care of the grounds and did all the planting—tulip bulbs in the fall for spring color and annuals in the summer. Consequently the library was one of the most pleasant places in Foxglove Corners to while away an afternoon.

We arrived with five minutes to spare, Annica and I; and Lucy with Brent in his vintage yellow Plymouth.

Miss Eidt's black cat, Blackberry, sat in a wicker chair on the porch, fixing the visitors with her inscrutable jewel-eyed stare. She was completely at home inside or outside the library. This was unusual because Blackberry had been a wild cat. At one time Miss Eidt didn't want her staff to encourage her with food, but somewhere along the way and with little fanfare, Blackberry had become Miss Eidt's pet. She'd named her Blackberry in honor of Judy Bolton's cat.

Brent held the door open for us, then for the sundress-clad young woman behind us who was shepherding three little girls in their Sunday best to the event.

Inside, a sign proclaimed:

Welcome, Miss Luzy Hazen!

Foxglove Corners' Own Author

Books signed, questions answered, writing secrets revealed, refreshments

"How nice," Lucy murmured.

"Aren't you glad you didn't skip out?" asked Brent.

"Hush," she said.

"I'm sure glad I came." Annica hadn't known ahead of time that Brent was going to escort us. "I'm going to buy a copy of *Devilwish* and have it autographed," she added.

"I'm glad you came, too, Annica," Lucy said. "Keep your money. I'll be happy to give you a copy as a gift."

Lucy wore her traditional long, black dress, brightened with gold chains and bracelets that made a jingling sound when she moved her arms. She believed in looking the part of a horror story writer. Of her idea of one, that is. I'd seldom seen her in any other color.

Miss Eidt came bustling around the main desk, smiling broadly. She also had a favorite way of dressing: pastel suits (pale green today), lacy blouses, and pearls in multiple strands. Occasionally she added a jeweled barrette in her silver hair. Librarian, mistress of the house, hostess of the day's celebration, she was also my good friend.

"This is for your refreshment table, Miss Eidt, from Jennet." With a mischievous wink, Brent handed her the box of cupcakes. "A dozen chocolate cupcakes. I think they're all there."

She took the box, a puzzled look on her face. "Why shouldn't they all be there?" Miss Eidt had no sense of humor.

"Welcome! This is going to be a wonderful day." She indicated the rows of seats, already filled with chattering young readers, their faces turned to Lucy. "Thank you so much for honoring us with your presence, Lucy."

"Thank you for having me."

Before we drowned in expressions of gratitude, Miss Eidt led Lucy to a long table stacked with copies of *Devilwish* and flanked with tall vases of flowers, the kind of giant bouquets one can find in farmers' markets.

Still holding the box, Miss Eidt introduced Lucy, and applause broke out. In truth no introductory remarks were necessary. Although Lucy led a quiet, private life at Dark Gables, her photograph adorned the backs of all her books, always the same pose—Lucy in black holding a book on her front porch.

The crowd quieted instantly. Why couldn't my classes come to such impressive order?

"Today I'm going to tell you a little bit about *Devilwish*—behind the scenes," Lucy said. "I had fun writing it, and I'm going to share that fun with you."

I settled back in the chair which was less than comfortable.

We were off to a good start.

~ * ~

"Hi, Jennet."

The breathless voice belonged to Jennifer. My young friends from the lemonade stand, Jennifer and Molly, slipped into the aisle seats next to me. The girls loved my collies. Whenever I walked the dogs down Sagramore Road to the lake, they made a huge fuss over them. Jennifer was so enamored of the breed that she had asked for and received a collie puppy for Christmas last year.

Apparently they were also enamored of Lucy's books. Each girl held a copy of *Devilwish* as if it were a priceless treasure. The books looked new… straight-from-the-bookstore new.

"Talk to you later," whispered Molly as somebody behind us said, "Be quiet!"

Lucy was saying, "I've often been asked to reveal the secret of becoming a writer. Assuming you have talent and the desire to write, there's only one. It's perseverance. Can anyone tell me what perseverance means?"

Molly raised her hand. "I know! It's never giving up."

"That's right," Lucy said. "It means you never give up on a story or an attempt to have it published. No beginnings without endings. No manuscripts in desk drawers…"

For the moment I let my mind wander to my own unfinished manuscript, a non-fiction book about the ghosts of Foxglove Corners, the ones of which I had first-hand knowledge.

When I'd first come to Foxglove Corners, I'd seen a phantom Christmas tree in the vacant house next to the animal shelter. That was only the beginning. My last ghost had wandered the snowy fields of River Rose, trying desperately to go home. Or, more likely, to let people know what had happened to her.

Then there was the ghost who walked the halls of the Spirit Lamp Inn endlessly, searching for her friend who had disappeared during a short overnight stay. And the dogs. The snow dogs who haunted Lost Lake.

My material was fascinating, and it was all true.

I wasn't letting my work-in-progress languish in a drawer. I wanted to write an entire book and had run out of material. That meant I needed more inexplicable happenings, more ghostly apparitions, another 'thin air' disappearance or two.

Now that summer was here, I resolved to take another look at my manuscript. Perhaps there was something supernatural about Lucy's stone collie statue. If so, I'd have another unique tale to tell. Provided I solved the mystery.

I brought my attention back to Lucy. She had started out on a calm, self-assured note, as if she spoke in front of an audience every day, but I knew her well. She appeared agitated. Something had upset her. She looked pale, and she stammered over a few words that were simple to pronounce.

What had changed? Something in the audience? I didn't think so. A quick look around revealed attentive expressions. A few people were taking notes. A woman at the end of our row, for instance, the lady with short brassy curls and lime green earrings. She was scribbling in a stenographer's notebook. Everyone else was focused on Lucy.

Lucy was talking about her fascination with Stephen Vincent Benet's short story, *The Devil and Daniel Webster,* when she was in her high school English class.

"Luckily Jabez Stone averted his fate because he had a good lawyer. The best. Daniel Webster. Centuries earlier, Doctor Faustus wasn't so lucky. I thought that teenagers, like me and my friends in that class, would fantasize about having everything their hearts desired. So why not make a bargain with the devil? If it were possible."

Why not? I suppressed a smile. But those high school boys and girls didn't have a Daniel Webster to defend them and in all likelihood didn't have a concept of eternal damnation.

Still, the lure of treasures coveted by the young was strong. A date with the cute boy in Biology class, a career on the stage, a prettier face, popularity...

Teenagers tended to live in the moment and not think about consequences.

Lucy seemed to have recovered, but I noticed that she avoided looking at the left side of the room. It was almost as if there were someone there, or something, that she didn't want to see because if she did, she would lose her composure completely.

Ten

"What's the matter with Lucy?" Brent never made an attempt to lower his voice, not even in a library. "She looks like she saw a ghost."

Remembering the library's secret room, once haunted by a spirit named Marja, I said, "Maybe she did."

But I didn't think that was the case. Whatever had frightened Lucy was made of flesh and blood, not vapor, and he or she or he had been sitting on the left side of the room. She, I decided. The majority of Lucy's audience consisted of young girls.

And whatever, or whoever it was, appeared to be gone now. Lucy sat at the table, making light conversation with her readers as she signed their books. Her color had returned with a vengeance. She'd gone from pale to rosy. She seemed to be enjoying herself, but it could well be a clever act.

"We'll find out soon enough," I said. "Now I'm hungry."

The buffet table beckoned: tea, coffee, and lemonade with a variety of cookies, brownies, and small cakes. Brent had to wait for Lucy, of course, and Annica and I were in no hurry to leave the comfortable air-cooled library for the hot muggy afternoon that awaited us outside.

Besides I, too, was curious to know what had unnerved Lucy.

I glanced at the line of readers waiting to have their books autographed. Jennifer and Molly were almost at the table. Behind them I saw the woman with the brassy hair and lime green earrings who had been taking notes during Lucy's talk. Her sundress was lime green, too, long and floaty. She looked like a waterfall of Jell-O or Key Lime filling.

Miss Eidt walked by, sipping tea from a delicate china cup. "It went so well. I'd love to have another event."

"For Lucy's next book," I said.

The bedeviled one.

"I'm going to ask her as soon as she's through signing copies." So saying, she drifted back to the table.

"Lucy's talk was so inspiring," Annica said. "I wonder if I should try my hand at writing. Something besides research papers."

"Do you have the talent and the desire?" I asked.

"And the permanence?" added Brent.

"Perseverence."

"Yeah, that."

"I think so, but I have to get my degree first," she said. "School and work take up all my time."

"Your day will come," I assured her.

Brent scooped up a cupcake decorated like a daisy. "I wish I knew what happened to spook Lucy."

Jennifer and Molly bounded up to us, books in hand. The girls were growing, looking like young women in their skinny jeans and pretty ruffled tops. I imagine their lemonade stand days were behind them.

"Now I have every single one of Lucy Hazen's books," Molly said. "I can't wait to read this one."

"I asked her if she was ever going to write about a collie," Jennifer added. "She has one. I saw their picture."

"What did she say?" I asked.

"That I might be surprised. There might be a collie book in her future."

Jennifer made a face. "I don't think a collie would fit in with all those zombies and vampires."

"Lucy can make it work," Molly said.

Little did they know.

~ * ~

We stepped out into a fiery embrace of summer heat. Blackberry the cat had disappeared and the Corners swam in a light haze.

"Let's not go home right away," Lucy said. "I need to unwind. To talk."

I scanned the Corners. Nothing had changed since the morning I'd taken an exploratory tour of my new home. There was the late nineteenth century building proclaiming itself the Foxglove Corners Post Office. There the fire and police departments, probably dating from the same era. Zoller's General Store was open for business, and the Ice Cream Parlor had a new blue and white awning.

"How about going to the Ice Cream Parlor," Annica said. "If we hurry. Everyone else has the same idea."

Brent quickened his pace. "My treat. Those chocolate cupcakes made me thirsty."

We crossed the street, and he chose a cafe table outside, boldly apprehending a fourth chair from another one. "Your orders, ladies?"

We all chose scoops of ice cream in different flavors. When Brent came back, carrying a tray with ice cream and iced water, he said, "Now Lucy. Explain why you lost your cool in there."

She picked up a plastic fork and swirled it around of a scoop of coconut ice cream.

"Everything was going well until... I looked up and saw Cassandra and Madeline in the audience."

"Who are they?" Annica asked.

Lucy took a deep breath. "You're not going to believe this."

"Try us," Brent said.

"They're characters from my book. Come to life."

"From *Devilwish?*"

"No, from *The Stone Collie*. That's the book I'm working on now."

I stared at her. This might happen in a Stephen King novel, but not in one of Lucy's stories. Not to Lucy.

Annica said, "How is that possible? Unless you used real models."

"I didn't. I never do. They're my own creation. Cassandra and Madeline both have blonde hair. Madeline's hair is lighter and longer. Cassandra envies her. Cassandra wears her hair in one braid. She has freckles across her nose. She tries to cover them with powder. Madeline wears make-up. She likes bright pink lipstick.

"The girls are sisters. They resemble each other slightly, but Cassandra is convinced that Madeline is the pretty one. I named them. I had a doll named Cassandra when I was a little girl, and Madeline was my cousin."

"You've just described Anygirl," I said.

"Yeah." Brent finished his ice cream. "All teenaged girls look alike."

Annica cast him an indignant glance. "No they don't."

"So," I said, "you saw two blonde girls, one with long hair wearing bright pink lipstick, one with a braid and freckles."

"Sitting together. I couldn't believe my eyes." Lucy closed her eyes as if to shut out the sight. "Then Cassandra waved to me. She knew me. There was something sinister in that wave. After the talk, I looked for them. They weren't there."

"I can see why you're such a good horror writer," Annica said. "What you describe is positively weird. Storybook people can't come to life."

Nor could a stone collie statue, described in a writer's first draft, appear in the author's woods. No matter what I'd said about Anygirl, it seemed as if the other shoe had dropped.

Annica didn't know about the statue in Lucy's book because I considered that was Lucy's story to tell. Surprisingly, Lucy gave Annica the background, told her how she'd written about the sisters discovering a statue days before she found the same kind of statue in her woods.

"You can see why seeing those girls, my characters, threw me out of my orbit."

Annica said, "Jennet and I are going to team up and find out where that statue came from, how it could turn up after you wrote about it... And those girls... I can't explain them."

"Ghost girls." Brent hummed the *Twilight Zone* theme. "Let's go back and ask Miss Eidt if she remembers seeing them."

I didn't think that was a good idea. Miss Eidt would want to know why we were asking about them, and I didn't think we should take her into our confidence yet, if at all. She was impressionable and would be certain to worry.

"Let's wait until we know what we're dealing with," I said.

"Definitely," Lucy added. "This is my problem. If it were known, people would think I was crazy. Crazier than they do already."

"No one thinks that," I assured her. "If anything, they envy you."

"It's *our* problem, Lucy," Brent said. "Never think you're alone. I'll try to find out who those girls are."

"How?" I asked, thinking of how many girls had long hair and freckles scattered across their noses. If only Lucy had noticed more distinctive characteristics.

"I have ways," he said.

Sometimes Brent sounded a lot like Crane. They had been spending too much time together.

"When I find them, I can guarantee their names won't be Cassandra and Madeline," Brent added. "Seconds anyone?"

Lucy's ice cream lay in her dish, a melted pale mess with bits of coconut in it.

She looked away from it. "I don't feel very well."

"I'll take you home," Brent said quickly. "And Lucy, we're all proud of you. You faced down your fears."

"But look what happened."

"So far, nothing happened," he said.

Nothing yet. Two strange coincidences that could perhaps be explained, the second easier to understand than the first. Lucy had placed herself in a position to imagine connections. Hence, the girls who looked like her characters.

Still...

In spite of the heat of the day, I felt a chill. A foreboding?

Yes. A strong feeling that worse was to come, bringing more dropped shoes for Lucy down the road. Because we had pledged her our support as friends, there'd be more trouble for us.

Eleven

It was another hot morning. Only Candy and Misty were interested in walking, and even Misty had second thoughts. She retrieved her Frisbee three times and flopped down in the shade of the porch with her tongue hanging out.

Across the lane, Camille was in her garden watering her plants with a hose. Twister, her black Belgian shepherd, and Holly, the black collie, were playing in the stream of water, dashing back and forth. Holly was trying to bite it. Canine fun.

These two had never known thirst since coming to live with Camille.

How was the puppy—or how were the puppies—at the blue house? I thought about them as I shepherded my five into the house, wishing the little ones could break free from their chains and play with other dogs.

What to do on a hot day when I had a free morning and nothing planned but making dinner and taking a brief look at my spirit manuscript?

Gather more petitions? I decided to wait for cooler weather. Already I had acquired a sunburn on my arms. Not an attractive golden glow like Annica had, but a tender sheen of red.

Decrying the need for an extra covering, I slipped a sheer white blouse over my tank top and set out on the day's jaunt.

To her dogs' chagrin, Camille turned off the hose and waved. I crossed the lane and found myself showered with droplets of water as two energetic canines shook themselves dry.

Camille was the only person I knew who could work in her garden and hold on to that crisp, rustic look achieved by pairing a long denim jumper with a white shirt, rolled up to the elbows. Every silvery hair on her head was in place. If only I could say the same for myself.

Get used to it, I told myself. *It's going to be a long, hot summer.*

Impatiently I undid the top button of my blouse. Already the material felt damp.

"How beautiful your garden is," I said.

Camille's flowers were always spectacular. The yellow Victorian had the same exposure to sun as my house, but somehow Camille's plants always grew taller and fuller. When they blossomed, the colors were vibrant rainbow shades, even the pale columbines, and their blooms even lasted longer than mine.

Of course her garden had been in existence when mine was still a field.

Still, I always thought there was something magical about Camille's flower beds. Some plant food with a secret ingredient. If so, Camille never shared the secret, although in all other ways she was unfailingly generous.

"If you're not in a hurry, come in and sample my pineapple coffeecake," she said. "It's just out of the oven. I'm including the recipe in my new cookbook."

"You're baking in this heat?"

"Sure. We have air conditioning and ceiling fans."

"I'm going to check on the situation at the blue house," I said. "But I can always spare a few minutes for your coffeecake."

I followed her inside, dodging dogs who somehow understood Camille's invitation and counted on being included in the sampling.

"How did Lucy's library event go?" Camille asked as I sank into a chair in her cozy blue and white country kitchen where the sun shone through the collection of cobalt glass on her windowsill, again creating magical color.

Camille didn't know about the strangeness that had touched down on Dark Gables, about the coincidence of the collie statue and the girls whom Lucy believed were characters from her new book. As I had with Annica, I'd hold off on informing her until I'd secured Lucy's permission.

"It went fine," I said. "Lucy has lots of fans. I think they were all there."

"In this heat?"

I smiled. "Miss Eidt has air conditioning too."

"Of course. She'd have to with all the people who visit the library."

Twister and Holly watched in fascination as Camille brought two dessert plates out of the cupboard and cut into the coffeecake cooling on the counter. "You're not going for a walk, I hope? It's almost ninety already."

"Only down the lane a way," I said. "I've been checking on the collie puppy every day. Seeing she has water and food."

"The poor baby," Camille said.

"Babies, maybe."

I told her about my suspicion that there had been two pups at the house at one time and my fear that something had happened to the first one. Butterscotch. I hadn't come up with a name for the second pup yet.

"That's even worse," she said. "Their wretched owner won't be happy until they're dead."

"That won't happen if I can prevent it," I said.

Camille put water on to boil for tea. Hot tea went best with coffeecake, even on a stifling summer morning.

"Speaking of the owner, have you seen an orange Volkswagen on the lane?" I asked.

"No, and I think I'd notice a sight like that. Is it important?"

"It might belong to the puppies' owner. If I could get the license plate number..."

"I'll be on the lookout for it," Camille said. "Anything to help catch a dog abuser."

With Georgina and Camille watching the lane and Annica checking out handsome blond men at Clovers, sooner or later, I'd be able to confront the man who either didn't know how to treat his dogs—or didn't care.

~ * ~

She was happy to see me, the little puppy with the butterscotch marking on her chest. Wagging her tail and yipping frantically, she bounded toward me as far as the chain allowed her.

The bringer of food and water.

Her bowl was empty, and there was no trace of the bone.

"Let's get you a nice drink," I said, holding the bowl under the faucet. "Cold, clean water."

She lapped it eagerly and licked the empty bowl. Hot morning, no water, definite abuse. I refilled the bowl and reached for my phone.

It wasn't there!

Impossible! It was always there. I never left the house without it.

I checked both pockets. All I found were my key and a crumpled tissue.

I'd planned to call nine-one-one. Check the temperature. Take a picture.

You can still do that.

I'd just have to go back home.

Disgusted with my carelessness, I retraced my steps. Back up the lane, around the curves, past the Linton house where white sheets billowed in a gentle wind. Soaking up dust and morning heat. Eyes on the lane, hoping the phone might have fallen from my pocket, an unlikely occurrence. I didn't remember taking it, remembered only slipping on the sheer white blouse.

Raven watched my approach from the front yard where she had been lying half in sun, half in the shade of the porch. Tilting her head, she barked once.

Back so soon?

She rose, stretched, and ambled up to me. It was too hot for dashing. The other dogs were barking inside the house. Misty's and Candy's faces appeared in the bay window.

Raven followed me as I let myself in the side door and waded through my enthusiastic welcoming committee. The dogs knew I'd broken the pattern. I should have been away longer.

And there was the phone on the kitchen counter.

Finally I could dial nine-one-one, and, my mission accomplished, take the time to drink a glass of iced water.

~ * ~

The dispatcher assured me that she'd send someone to the house on Jonquil Lane, which I described as blue and vacant before remembering that another house fit the same description. Not another house with a collie puppy chained in the backyard, though.

"I'll be there, waiting," I said.

I'd lost about a half hour. Not enough time for the puppy to drink all her water or spill it again.

Somewhat refreshed, I retraced my steps once again after deciding not to drive.

As I approached the blue house, I saw flashing strobe lights. Parked where a future driveway would be was a bright orange Volkswagen.

Good. The villain had been caught in the act.

Voices drifted out from behind the house. They weren't angry. Not defensive, but conversational. Almost cordial. One was familiar.

Since when did my one-time nemesis and Crane's good friend, Lieutenant Mac Dalby, respond to animal abuse calls? I couldn't believe the sight that greeted me. The puppy was still chained, but she had access to two bowls, one filled with fresh water, the other heaped with kibble. A plush duck and a red tug-of-war toy lay on the ground within easy reach.

Over this idyllic scene presided a tall man who was indeed handsome. Tall, lean and bronze, a virtual Viking. And blond. Impassive features might have been carved in granite. His eyes smoldered with an emotion that could have been resentment.

"Hello, Jennet," Mac said. "You had some concerns? Everything seems under control here. Little Pepsi looks okay to me."

"This is the first time..." I swallowed over the dryness in my throat and started again. "Every time I've seen this puppy, her water bowl has been empty. I've never seen food set out for her. The chain... Puppies should never be chained and left alone. No dog should."

"Pardon me, ma'am," the blond man said. "As you can see, I don't have a fenced yard yet. What's better? A puppy run over in the road or a chain? I only tie her up when I'm at work."

He bent down to stroke Pepsi's head. She didn't recoil from him.

"We can't be too careful," Mac said. "I had to break a window to free a setter locked in a car yesterday."

"That's why I don't take Pepsi with me," the man said.

I still didn't know his name.

"Are you satisfied, Jennet?" Mac asked.

"This situation isn't ideal," I said, adding, "I belong to the Lakeville Collie Rescue League. We look out for the collies in our area."

"I assure you, Pepsi doesn't need rescuing."

"Do you have another puppy?" I asked.

"Just Pepsi."

"Did you ever? In this house, I mean."

"No," he said.

A blatant lie.

I felt there was more to be said, that what Mac saw didn't reflect the reality of the situation. That the blond man had perhaps anticipated a visit from a law officer and arranged the scene as carefully as one would set out props on a stage to give the desired impression.

But how could he have known anyone would call nine-one-one today? I couldn't prove anything, not even the existence of the skinny, full-collared puppy, Butterscotch.

Where did that leave Butterscotch?

It was best to retreat. For now. Not that I intended to drop the matter.

"Drive you back to the house, Jennet?" Mac asked.

Why not? I didn't think I could make the trek up the lane again. Besides I wanted to talk to Mac privately.

"Thanks," I said. "I'll take you up on the offer."

Giving Pepsi a farewell pat, I walked with Mac to the cruiser.

Twelve

"He's lying," I said as Mac navigated the cruiser around the curves and up the lane.

"About what?"

"I saw another collie puppy chained in that yard a week ago. She was thinner than Pepsi and had a full white collar."

"So does Pepsi."

Mac slowed to let a fox cross the lane. In a heartbeat the little creature disappeared in a field of tall Queen Anne's lace.

"No, she doesn't," I said. "Didn't you see the light mark on her chest? It looks like a brooch."

He glanced at me. "That little patch?"

"The other pup didn't have a marking like that." Breaking the pause that followed, I said, "If you don't believe me, Sue Appleton saw her too."

"I didn't say I didn't believe you, Jennet. What happened to that other puppy then?"

"I wish I knew."

"I'll keep an eye on the man," Mac said without a hint of his trademark condescension in his voice. That was what I'd hoped for, that the police would be aware of the puppy, to monitor her conditions.

"What's his name?" I asked.

"Drummond. Zachary Drummond."

"Did you find out if he owns the house?"

"He says he's the homeowner's brother-in-law."

I frowned. "He probably has permission to use the yard then. And the house too?"

"I assume so."

"If," I pointed out, "he's not lying about that. To my knowledge, only one person, a neighbor, has seen Jonathan Brooks."

I was silent for a moment, wondering if Butterscotch had been inside the house all this time. I considered it unlikely. If so, she would have barked. What had happened to her then? I wished I had an answer for Mac's question.

"You're not satisfied," Mac said.

"Not entirely. Are you?"

"I don't like to see any dog on a chain. Dogs need human companionship. Joanna and I have a collie, Kinder. She's always with Joanna."

"I agree. To withhold company from a little puppy is inhumane. They need to be socialized."

"About the fence," Mac said. "Drummond told me he's having an invisible fence installed next week."

"In my opinion they're not as safe as one made of wood or chain link. Training is the best of all."

"I'll keep an eye on the place," Mac assured me.

"I will, too."

"Don't make a pest of yourself, Jennet. You'd be trespassing on private property."

Ah, there was the condescension. It was so much a part of Mac Dalby's make-up that I'd almost missed it.

"Sometimes the Rescue League has to be persistent," I said. "I have no intention of forgetting about Pepsi."

We had reached the house. Raven, who had come back outside when I did and reclaimed her place in the shade, ambled up to the cruiser. It was still too hot to run.

"Thanks for checking, Mac," I said.

As he drove away I wondered how long Zachary Drummond would remain at the blue house. How long Pepsi's water and food would last and if, back in the shade of the weeping willow, she was lying close to her toy duck.

~ * ~

Among summer's gifts are the long free hours I could fill in any way I pleased. I didn't have to think of school, and I could read for pure pleasure. After a light lunch of cold ham, biscuits, and iced tea, I took three dogs for an abbreviated walk and turned to my spirit book.

Every supernatural experience I'd had since moving to Foxglove Corners had a chapter of its own, in which I described the phenomenon in detail and updated the reader on recent events, if any. In most cases, once the ghosts were happy again, they went back to whatever plane they inhabited. At least they tended to retreat from the view of the living.

The secret room of Eidt House, for example. Although the library had been Miss Eidt's childhood home, she had never known about the room sealed off in the hope of containing a restless spirit. That had been before her time, before the Eidt family owned the house.

The room still existed, at one time open to the public as a curiosity. Miss Eidt had long since closed and locked the door. I would be surprised if she ever crossed the threshold. She was too fearful. Still, she kept the room intact as a shrine of sorts.

Those were the ideal conditions to spawn another supernatural manifestation.

A stray thought drifted into my mind. If Lucy's characters, Cassandra and Madeline, were ghosts, they had come to a place that welcomed their kind.

I whiled away the afternoon hours reading my chapters. They had already been revised and proofread. Someday, I felt certain, the book, finished and published, would be flying off the shelves. Like Lucy's *Devilwish*.

I might have a chapter titled 'The Stone Collie' or one about characters in a book who come to life.

The long stretch of quiet came to an abrupt end with the chiming of my phone.

It was Lucy, who was usually too busy writing during the day for idle conversations.

"Is anything wrong?" I asked.

"No, not really," she said. "I just feel uneasy. All this hot weather. It's going to storm soon. You can almost taste it in the air."

I glanced through the bay window at a clear blue sky with fluffy white clouds. Spruce Road wasn't so far from Jonquil Lane, but weather conditions can change rapidly. Then again Lucy might be talking about a foreboding.

"I wanted to thank you again for coming to the library yesterday," she said. "You and Annica. She's such a sweet young lady."

"She is," I said. "Have you been writing?"

"Rewriting. I changed the appearance of Cassandra and Madeline. Now they're identical twins with short dark brown hair. Cassandra has no reason to envy Madeline now that Madeline is her mirror image. Also, I lost the freckles."

I didn't know what to say. Did Lucy think changing a few details would make the girls from the library audience disappear? If she did, that meant she must indeed believe that what she wrote would by some strange alchemy become reality.

This wasn't good.

"Are you going to keep the stone statue in the book?" I asked.

"Well, yes. It's still there, as of this morning."

"You mean you went into the woods again?"

"I just took Sky for a little stroll."

Through the woods?

This was Lucy, who claimed she had never before walked in her own woods. I feared she was deluding herself, but we all cope with our fears and adversity in different ways.

"Can you come over for tea again soon?" she asked.

It was, I considered, a plea for help. If not help, then for company.

"Tomorrow morning would be good," I said. "Let me bring the refreshments this time. I have extra blueberries. Would you like a homemade blueberry-banana bread?"

"That sounds heavenly."

"It's a date then. Maybe the storm will blow away the statue."

She couldn't really believe that.

"We can hope," I said. "I'll see you soon."

No sooner had I ended the call then the phone rang again. This time it was Annica.

"He's here right now," she said. "Eating a BLT. I saw that orange Volkswagen when I pulled in the lot. He's a doll," she added. "Shall I try to make conversation with him?"

"It couldn't hurt," I said. "But do it naturally. We don't want him to suspect we're spying on him."

"I'll be super natural. It'll take some doing, though. He's Marcy's customer, not mine, and she whispered to me that she'd like to go out with him. He isn't wearing a wedding ring."

"You'll manage," I said.

It had been a good day. We were getting closer. Now, we could only hope Lucy was wrong about the coming storm.

Thirteen

The storm slammed into Foxglove Corners during the night. Thunder exploding directly overhead and intermittent crashes in the woods drove the collies from their favorite sleeping spots to the upstairs hall where they huddled together for protection.

It was safer there.

I could only hope Pepsi was inside the blue house or another one, not left on a chain without protection from the elements.

A particularly loud thunderbolt that sounded as if it could break through the roof woke me. Crane woke too, then promptly fell asleep again. Out in the hall, one of the dogs whimpered. Sky, probably. The other collies weren't afraid of thunderstorms, as a rule.

Lightning scissored across the room. Maybe we weren't so safe.

I lay awake, listening to the rain pound the windows and thinking about Lucy's feeling that a storm was imminent when the skies were clear.

'You can almost taste it in the air,' she had claimed.

Strange. But then Lucy had a strange side—or she'd listened to the weather report which I often neglected to do in the summer. Sometimes it was difficult to know when Lucy was speaking metaphorically.

Finally I fell asleep and woke to a cooler temperature. Glancing out the window, I saw a fresh-washed world. Leaves dripped raindrops, and a large tree blocked Jonquil Lane. No doubt others had fallen in the woods, but this one was going to be a problem.

When I came downstairs, Crane was already in his uniform, badge pinned to his shirt, gun belt strapped on, ready for the day. The dogs were eating breakfast in their individual bowls. They didn't look up. Crane poured me a cup of coffee.

"Sit down," I said, bringing a carton of eggs out of the refrigerator. "Is French toast okay?"

"Perfect. That'll give me energy to move that fallen tree out of the way."

"Or you could wait for Brent or Gilbert to help you. Chances are no one will be driving on Jonquil Lane today."

"Won't you be going out?" he asked.

"Oh, yes, to visit Lucy."

That meant I had to bake blueberry-banana bread. I yawned. I didn't feel like baking but couldn't pass off a treat from the Hometown Bakery as my own, and there were no baked goods in the freezer.

I made an extra piece of French toast and sat down to eat with Crane.

"Lucy believes something weird is going on," I said. "After she saw those girls in the library, she changed the descriptions of her characters."

"That's over the top."

"It doesn't sound like Lucy." I drenched my French toast with syrup. "I'm going to try to reassure her that she isn't living her horror story."

Candy, always the first to finish eating, nudged me with her nose. In her book, French toast was tastier than dry kibble, but if I shared my breakfast with the dogs, there'd be none left for me.

Seeing that I wasn't responding to her plea, Candy moved to Crane's side.

"You'll have your work cut out for you." Crane slipped her Candy a piece of crust.

"I should just make French toast for all of us," I said.

~ * ~

The buzz of a chain saw greeted me as I approached Dark Gables a little later. A towering maple had crashed into the front roof of the house. A piece of the gutter hung free. Shingles and broken branches and leaves lay in the mud. One of the windows, high on the third floor, was boarded over.

Two men were hard at work sawing wood into manageable pieces. They'd need a crane to lift the tree trunk off the ground.

Lucy, all in black, opened the door. Sky slipped out to investigate the unaccustomed noise. Lucy called her back, a note of barely suppressed panic in her voice. Sky came reluctantly.

"I'm so sorry, Lucy," I said. "Your beautiful house."

"It can be repaired."

"Who are the good Samaritans?"

"My neighbor and his son. They came over early this morning, eager to help. I'm blessed. In one way. In another…" She shrugged.

I handed her the loaf nicely wrapped in tinfoil. "Here's our dessert."

"It's feels—good. Nice and warm."

"Fresh from the oven," I said. "It'll taste good too."

Lucy led the way through the dim hall to the back of the house, to the sun room and into the light.

"I'm having the roof fixed next week," she said. "It'll take longer to replace the window. It's not easy finding a contractor. The storm did a lot of damage in the area."

She seemed to have a grasp on the situation, but I wondered. Her eyes had a haunted look. I'd seen it before.

"What else is wrong?" I asked.

"You're not going to believe this."

She'd said this before, after the library event.

"What is it?"

"There's a storm in my book. I just finished the chapter yesterday. The aliens conjure up a severe thunderstorm as proof of their power. It caves in the roof of the girls' house."

"Well..."

It seemed suddenly chilly in Dark Gables, even in this sunlit room. I couldn't wait to drink a cup of Lucy's steaming tea. What could I say?

"Those are nasty aliens." I added, "At least the tree didn't cave in your roof."

"No, just dented it. But this is another coincidence. I write about storm damage. My house suffers."

"Oh, Lucy."

She truly believed this. And she loved Dark Gables. How sad to think you had caused harm to your house.

"We have a tree down on Jonquil Lane," I said. "Crane and his Uncle Gilbert moved it out of the way. You just said there's a lot of damage in Foxglove Corners."

"According to the morning news. I don't see this as a coincidence, though."

"You'll make yourself crazy," I said.

She might not have heard me.

"This is the third coincidence, Jennet. The collie statue, Cassandra and Madeline, and now this unnatural storm."

"It wasn't unnatural," I said. "Thunderstorms are common in the summer. If they're severe, they cause damage. Flooding and worse. Don't write about a tornado," I added.

"The aliens could have done that, too."

For a moment, just a moment, I relived the horror of the tornado that had brought me to Foxglove Corners.

"That's a powerful book you're writing," I said.

"It's doomed. I should throw it away."

"Oh, no."

Lucy filled the electric teakettle and murmured her admiration for the blueberry-banana loaf which did look fantastic. "I'm making coffee for the men," she added.

Meanwhile, I searched my mind for something—anything—I could say to set her mind in a different direction.

"I honestly think this is just a run-of-the-mill coincidence," I said. "But I have an idea. You could write a test chapter. Make it as realistic or outrageous as you like. Then sit back and wait to see what happens. Maybe nothing well."

Miraculously I'd found the one idea that appealed to Lucy.

"That could work," she said. "I'll do it today."

"You'll see. Whatever you write won't be repeated in your life."

At least I hoped it wouldn't.

She actually looked better, less drawn, and we sat down to enjoy our blueberry-banana bread and tea while the buzz of the chain saw stole in through the open window. Somehow I'd managed to dispel the aura of gloom that had settled over Lucy. All was well.

For the moment.

Fourteen

On my way home from Dark Gables, I stopped at Clovers for coffee. They had stuffed cabbages on the menu, one of Crane's favorite dinners. With a second blueberry-banana bread on the counter, it looked as if I'd have a few more hours free this afternoon.

The restaurant had a grand total of five customers. The owner, Mary Jeanne, was on vacation, and Annica and her fellow waitress, Marcy, looked a trifle bored and were trying gallantly to hide it.

Annica poured my coffee and a cup for herself and sat across from me at a booth with a view of the woods. I told her about Lucy's latest setback and her fear that her fictitious storm had somehow caused the damage to her house.

"That's impossible," she said.

"Lucy believes it."

"Poor Lucy. We promised her we'd solve the mystery of the stone statue, and we still don't have a clue."

Fleeting images of a fallen tree on a roof and a boarded window slipped into my mind. Suppose the three so-called coincidences were connected? Suppose a fourth coincidence was even now on its way?

Start with the statue, I thought.

"I did an Internet search for collie figurines and statues," Annica said. "There are hundreds of them available in all sizes."

"How will that tell us who left the statue in Lucy's woods?" I asked.

"It won't, but if we find a match, we'll know it's modern."

"I had the impression it had been there for years," I said.

Annica stirred sugar into her coffee vigorously. "We have to check out that statue again and take pictures of it."

"The woods will still be wet. It poured last night."

"I can't go today anyway," she said. "I have a class after work. How about tomorrow early? Before noon?"

"That'll work. It's a date."

"After we do that, let's drive over to Maple Creek. There's a nursery there that sells lawn ornaments. It's called Greenspires. They have a collie statue. It costs two hundred and fifty-nine dollars, and it isn't even painted."

Who would pay that much money for a statue, then hide it in the woods? Only somebody who wanted to spook Lucy. I liked my idea better, that the stone collie had been in the same place for years.

"I'd like one for our front yard, but I don't want to pay that much," I said.

"No, you could buy a real collie for that. By the way, how's the little collie puppy at the blue house doing?"

"All right, I guess. I saw Mac's cruiser on Jonquil Lane this morning. He promised to keep an eye on the house. I checked when I drove by, and Pepsi was there. She had water and food. I didn't see the orange Volkswagen or I wouldn't have stopped."

"All's well then," she said.

"Except I still don't know what happened to Butterscotch. Drummond denies he had another puppy. I don't believe him because both Sue and I saw her. Luckily she'll be easy to identify with that full white collar."

"Maybe he took the first one back to the breeder?"

"And traded her in? Like a car?"

"Well that's better than thinking she died. Maybe she did, though. Don't they say that collie puppies sometimes fail to thrive?"

"When they're first born, yes. Some of the poor babies just don't have the will to survive. They don't fight."

But that hadn't been true for Butterscotch. To be sure, she hadn't appeared to be as robust as Pepsi, but she hadn't looked sickly either.

Unless, of course, Drummond had starved her or let her die of dehydration.

But why would any man do that—unless he was a dog-hating sadist? And then turn around and buy another puppy who looked like her? It didn't make sense.

Mac's daily presence on the lane ensured that Drummond wouldn't mistreat Pepsi. No man wants to be slapped with a fine and possible jail sentence. Still, I couldn't stop thinking about Butterscotch. She was a side mystery but nonetheless an important one, and as a member of Collie Rescue, I had a duty to investigate. Duty aside, I wanted to know her fate. If she still needed help, I was eager to provide it.

"I'll see you tomorrow bright and early," Annica said. "Try to come up with a Step Two so we can solve the statue mystery."

"Don't you mean Step One?" I asked.

~ * ~

Later that day, Sue Appleton called me. She had two unexpected cancellations and wanted to know if I'd like to go signature collecting this afternoon.

"I'd rather go some morning while it's still relatively cool," I said.

A weak excuse, but it seemed as if I'd already had a long day, and it was getting hotter out.

"I missed a few houses on Jonquil Lane," I said. "No one was home. I'll try them later. Where should we go next?"

"I'll get my map of Foxglove Corners and figure out new routes for us."

"We don't want to go too far from Jonquil Lane," I said. "People are more inclined to support a change when it affects them."

"True, but having that eyesore spoils the look of our countryside. So what day are you free?"

I glanced at the calendar. Not tomorrow. I'd already made plans with Annica.

"The day after tomorrow, if you don't have lessons," I said.

"I won't—in the morning. Oh, I saw Lieutenant Dalby's cruiser, and he stopped to talk. He told me about Pepsi and how he's going to drive by that house every day. Do you think Drummond ever had another puppy?"

"Sure. We both saw her."

She hesitated. "Well, I don't know, Jennet. Maybe it's the same pup, like he says."

"That can't be," I said. "Don't you remember Butterscotch has a full white collar? Pepsi has a gold marking on her chest."

"I can't be a hundred per cent certain that Butterscotch didn't have that same mark," she said.

I hadn't expected this.

"I can," I said. "Then there's Pepsi's appearance. She's slightly heavier than Butterscotch."

"It's so hard to know for sure. If only we could see them together."

That, of course, was impossible at the moment.

"I'm going to assume that Butterscotch and Pepsi are two different puppies," I said.

Because I was certain, and it grieved me that somewhere in Foxglove Corners there might be a puppy in distress. Just because there was no trace of Butterscotch at present didn't mean she didn't exist.

Hadn't existed?

The truth was elusive, but I was determined to find it.

~ * ~

Darn. I wished I hadn't talked to Sue. Until she'd shared her doubt with me, I'd been certain there had been two puppies at the blue house, albeit not at the same time.

Now I wondered. Did Butterscotch really have a mark on her chest?

You took pictures of her, I reminded myself.

I checked the camera roll on my cell phone. There was Butterscotch, but I'd been focused on capturing an image of her empty water bowl. She was turned away from me. I enlarged the picture and still couldn't tell if she had a mark in the middle of her chest. She didn't look quite so thin to me.

It looked to me as if she had a full white collar.

Trust your instincts.

They told me not to believe Zachary Drummond.

At one time, he had owned both Butterscotch and the pup he called Pepsi. When questioned, he'd lied. Why would he deny owning Butterscotch? I could think of only one reason. She was dead, and he'd been responsible.

But how could I prove it? And, more important, if I was wrong, how could I find out if Butterscotch needed my help?

Fifteen

The woods were still damp after the storm. Did they ever dry out in the perpetual dark beneath the trees? I found myself shivering as we made our way across vines and forest debris that had melded to the ground.

Woods, I thought, like snow, are best viewed on a canvas. In a painting one could have all the beauty and none of the misery. Like mosquitoes. I was collecting a few more bites, thanks to this woodland excursion.

"It's just ahead," Lucy said, holding a long branch aside for Annica, who had already tripped once.

We had no difficulty navigating the path through the woods. It looked as if it had been trampled repeatedly by two feet and four.

Lucy might have read my mind. "I come out here every morning with Sky."

"Why?" Annica asked.

"To see if there've been any changes."

"Like?"

"If the statue has been moved—even a fraction of an inch."

By the aliens, I assumed.

"And has it?" I asked.

"It appears to be in the same place. Only..." She broke off. "It looks lighter and brighter after the rain. Sometimes I think it kind of glows."

When we reached the clearing, I examined the stone collie from all angles. It looked cleaner, yes. Glowing? No.

"I'm beginning to see why Brent said Stony has evil eyes," Lucy murmured.

Annica cast me a surreptitious look. "Stony?"

"I didn't want to keep calling it the stone collie or the statue."

But by naming the statue, wasn't she giving an inanimate object a dollop of humanity? In other words, owning it? I decided not to mention my misgivings. "Stony it is then," I said.

Both Annica and I took our pictures with our phones. We stood as close to the statue as possible, then moved away. I took one of Lucy and Sky, too, posed with Stony.

"Why do you want more pictures?" Lucy asked.

"We're going to check out similar statues at Greenspires in Maple Creek," Annica said.

Lucy smiled. "Do you think you'll find one with evil eyes that glows?"

"You never can tell," I said.

~ * ~

We emerged from the woods, all of us glad to be walking in the sun. Sky dashed ahead of us, seizing her opportunity to roll in the grass.

Lucy's fallen tree had been transformed into neat stacks of logs waiting to be picked up by neighbors who wanted free wood. The third story window was still boarded over.

"Let's have tea," Lucy said. "Annica, would you like me to read your tea leaves?"

"You can do that?"

"She's amazing," I said.

Annica leaped at the chance of a glimpse into her future, and soon we sat down to cups of hot tea and Lucy's signature grocery store cookies.

I guided Annica through the steps necessary to prepare a cup for reading and sat back to enjoy her wide-eyed anticipation.

Lucy peered into Annica's cup. The charms on her gold bracelets jangled as she turned it slowly. "Your wish will come true, but not right away," she said, pointing to a leaf shaped like a heart—sort of. "You'll have to be patient. I see a new romance…"

Having your tea leaves read was always more fun if there was a chance of love in your life.

Annica's eyes shone. A wish come true and a heart. She must be thinking of Brent Fowler. I was a little puzzled as Brent and Lucy were close. Lucy couldn't possibly have missed the signs of Annica's interest in Brent. Annica was never subtle. By rights, anyone would think she would discourage Annica.

Well, some women would, but not Lucy, and perhaps I had misread the nature of her relationship with Brent.

"I see an award," Lucy said. "An honor. You're attending college, aren't you?"

Annica nodded. "I'm majoring in English literature."

Lucy saw symbols of additional good fortune in Annica's cup. Then she turned to me. "Jennet, is your cup ready?"

I handed it to her, drained, with patterns that had formed on the pristine white surface inside the cup.

"Uh, oh," she said after a moment's perusal. "There may be trouble ahead."

Did I believe this? Of course not. Not entirely. Then how to account for the sudden racing of my heartbeat?

"What kind of trouble?" I asked.

"I can't say for certain. It looks like a perilous journey. You'll come to crossroads…"

"I'm not planning on taking a trip," I said.

"Maybe it's a metaphorical one."

"That's no fun," Annica said.

"Crane and I often talk about going to Tennessee to visit his relatives, but we don't want to leave the dogs. We'll probably stay in Foxglove Corners till the day we die."

Annica fed Sky a piece of her cookie. "Think metaphorical," she said. "Then you won't have to worry about dogs."

I agreed to forget about the perilous journey.

Suddenly Lucy said, "I wrote my test scene yesterday."

"Can you tell us about it?" I asked.

"Certainly, but first…"

For Annica's benefit, she explained my idea to add a scene to her book and see if it would be repeated in real life.

"Cassandra and Madeline find a strange object made of some kind of metal on their porch. It's shaped like a ball and keeps changing color. They have no idea what its purpose is or who left it there. We know it was the Voltarians."

"Let me guess. You haven't found a strange object on your porch."

"Not yet."

"That kind of object would be hard to duplicate," I pointed out.

"This proves the other stuff that happened is just coincidental," Annica added.

"I hope so, but there's still time."

When had Lucy grown that pessimistic? She was no stranger to gloom and doom, but generally she was able to see through to the happy end.

"On that note, we'll leave," I said. "I'll let you know what we find at Greenspires. Keep us updated on developments here, Lucy."

She promised to do so.

~ * ~

The statue of a tall, scantily clad male with a remarkable physique greeted us as we veered right to a section of Greenspires given over to lawn decorations. He looked like a Roman god.

"Wow!" Annica said. "Imagine having him in your front yard."

"I can't. He belongs in a formal garden, in a mansion. Look at the price tag!"

"He costs nine hundred and fifty dollars," Annica said. "He looks a little like Crane."

I took a closer look. "No, he doesn't."

"Imagine him with a deputy sheriff uniform on."

I did. He wasn't Crane, but he did look familiar. Vaguely.

"Let's remember why we're here," I said.

"Collie statues. Right."

We found them. The collie that resembled Lucy's statue wore a red 'Sold' tag around its neck. It wasn't as cleverly wrought as the one that kept a lonely vigil in Lucy's wood. It wasn't realistic. No one would ever look at those stone eyes and see a glint of evil.

Three smaller collie statues were nicer and less expensive. I considered buying one until I saw a pint sized dinosaur. It made me smile. I could imagine it in my flower bed, dwarfed as the plants around it grew taller.

"Lucy's statue didn't come from Greenspires," Annica said. "What now?"

"I'll buy this dinosaur," I said, lifting the small sculpture. It was heavier than it looked. About twenty pounds.

"How cute! You can call him T-Rex." A sudden note of excitement entered her voice. "Hey, Jennet, look! It's the statue. It came to life."

"What"

Visions of a collie statue bearing down on us with bared fangs leaped into my mind.

Annica lowered her voice. "Over by the evergreens. That man."

I looked.

What had caught Annica's attention was no statue but Zachary Drummond frowning over two weeping shrubs that appeared identical. He was close enough to hear our voices but appeared focused on his selection.

"That's Pepsi's owner," I said. "What a coincidence."

That was why the god statue had looked vaguely familiar to me.

"He's cute. Too bad he's a jerk."

"I'm going to say hello," I said, walking toward the shrub display even as Annica reached out to grab my arm.

"Hello," I said. "Do you remember me? I'm Jennet Ferguson, your neighbor."

He inclined his head briefly, no look of welcome in his eyes. "A nosy neighbor."

I let that pass. "How's your little puppy?" I asked.

"Fine."

I couldn't mistake the venom in his voice. He turned from me, lifting the taller of the two shrubs, and stalked away to the outside cash register.

Darn. Well, did I expect him to be civil? He probably assumed I was the one who had informed Lieutenant Dalby about his treatment of Pepsi.

"Why did you do that?" Annica asked.

I shrugged. "To make him aware of me, I guess. I'm not going away as long as I have doubts about Pepsi—and Butterscotch."

"He's not going to make it easy for you," she said. "Are you going to buy the dinosaur?"

I'd forgotten about it.

"Oh, yes."

It had a price tag of twenty five dollars, which I considered reasonable.

On our way to the cash register, Annica picked up a potted red geranium. "For my balcony," she said.

Drummond had completed his purchase and was on his way to the car. The orange Volkswagen stood out in a lot filled with neutral colored automobiles and trucks. He had parked closed to the door. I watched him shove the evergreen into the passenger's seat.

He didn't look back.

Sixteen

The sun was hot on my back and shoulders as I set the stone dinosaur carefully in the trunk of the Taurus so the sculpture wouldn't be damaged if it fell over when I stepped on the brakes.

"With regard to Lucy's statue, we're back to square one," I said. "I don't know what to do now except to wait for what comes next."

"That's no fun. What would a real detective do?"

"I have no idea."

Annica settled herself in the passenger seat, and I turned on the ignition and the air conditioning. "You're not waiting for Lucy to find an alien ball on her porch, I hope."

"No, but there'll be something else. Lucy's test scene didn't convince her that what she writes has no connection to real life."

I pulled out of Greenspire's lot carefully. There were an unusual number of customers, probably procrastinators who had let Memorial Day slip past them without doing their summer planting.

"It's too nice a day to go home and read," Annica said. "I finished *Jane Eyre* and *Wuthering Heights*. Now I have to read *Doctor Thorne*. It doesn't look very appealing."

"What would you like to do?"

"Aren't we close to River Rose?"

She referred to the once-thriving collie kennel now in limbo with the collies gone and their mistress dead.

"Pretty close, yes."

"Let's drive by and see how it looks in the summer. Then we can stop for coffee or ice cream."

"Good idea."

I had written about the haunting of River Rose, but wanted to give the reader an idea of what it was like today with the mystery solved and the spirit of the ghost of the woman in white at rest. I anticipated acres of rampant weeds and gloom and a silence so deep it almost seemed to hold muted sounds. Dark woods rising up to touch a summer sky. A sense of uneasy peace and waiting.

The kennel sign was gone. I had seen it swinging in a strong wind, dripping with icicles, and stilled on a windless day as if held in place by an invisible hand. Who was responsible for removing it? Who would have the right?

"I wonder what happened here," Annica said as I turned into the driveway leading up to the kennel building and the house. "Everything looks nice."

It was like travelling into the past. We parked under a tree and beheld a strange sight. Someone had mowed the grass, whacked the weeds out of existence, and generally neatened the place. The kennel building glowed with a fresh coat of paint, sunny yellow to match Rosalyn's ranch house. The porch was swept clean of last fall's leaves, and a ladder leaned against a side wall.

"It's like Rosalyn came back," Annica said.

"That's impossible. She's buried in a proper cemetery. Maybe an heir has surfaced. It looks like someone is planning on moving in."

"Someone with dogs?" she asked.

"Or some use for a kennel."

It would be a crime to tear down the building that had housed generations of tricolor and blue merle champion collies. Rosalyn had equipped it with bathing and grooming facilities and even a television, claiming that the dogs like to watch *Lassie* reruns and *Animal Planet.*

The windows in the house were closed, though, and there was no car in the driveway and no outward sign that anyone was inside. I felt certain we were alone. So certain that I snapped a picture with my phone.

"I want to find out who's moving in," I said.

"How are you going to do that?"

"I've met one of Rosalyn's neighbors. Maybe she knows. I'll pay her a visit, but not today. It's getting late."

"Do we have time to stop for ice cream?" she asked.

"Sure. We'll find a place in Maple Creek."

"Good." She sat back as I turned the car around and repeated, "I wonder what happened here."

Life was filled with surprises. Whether the change at River Rose was a good or bad one remained to be seen.

~ * ~

Brent had found Cassandra and Madeline, the girls Lucy believed had come from her book. Rather, he and Lucy had found them.

We listened to his story the next day over coffee on the porch. Even in this different location, Misty and Sky lay close to him, looking for pats. The other dogs had fallen into a light sleep, and Raven had come out of her house to join us inside.

"How did you accomplish that?" I asked.

"Miss Eidt said that ever since Lucy's talk, kids are constantly checking out her books. So Lucy and I have been showing up at the library every day at different times. Today we got lucky."

"Meaning you found the girls?"

"They were at that display Miss Eidt has of Lucy's books. Turns out they're big fans."

"So there's nothing supernatural about them," I said.

"They're as normal as any kids. They're friends, not sisters. Pam and Cecy. It's just like I said. All teenaged girls look alike."

To be on the safe side, Lucy had changed the descriptions of her characters. I could practically see the mysteries that bedeviled her melting away. Except for the mystery of the stone collie. Where had it come from? Who had placed it in the woods in a location where it might never have been discovered? And most important, why?

That mystery was as real and elusive as ever.

"Is Lucy easier in her mind now?" Crane asked.

Brent shrugged. "You know Lucy. She's relieved, yes, but still not completely convinced. She's writing again. That's good."

"I didn't know she'd stopped," I said.

"She didn't go so far as to set the book aside. She just wasn't working on it."

But now she was, and I assumed no mysterious object had landed on her porch, or I would have heard about it. Could all possibly be well at Dark Gables?

"She's back to juggling aliens and mysteries," Brent said. "She still doesn't know what to do with that stone collie."

"Nobody does," Crane said.

What more could we say?

"I ran into Zachary Drummond at Greenspires today," I said. "He wasn't very friendly. Barely civil. He called me nosy."

"You are," Brent said.

I bristled. "Only when a collie's welfare is at stake."

I told them about our visit to River Rose and the change at that formerly haunted place.

"So now the worst is over," Brent said. "We can all rest and enjoy the summer."

I nodded, taking a long, satisfying look at the beauty that surrounded me. My new lawn ornament sitting in a bed of red carnations. The yellow Victorian with its gardens of vibrant flowers, the quiet lane, and the woods beyond that held no secrets.

Not lately anyway.

Best of all, it was still June.

Seventeen

Summer lay gently on Foxglove Corners. A warm sun smiled down on verdant fields and woods and lakes. Flowers bloomed heir hearts out, and the air held a light pleasant scent. The golden days passed slowly like fragments from a dream.

For some, summer peace was an illusion. The blue house on Jonquil Lane remained unoccupied. I detected no sign of an invisible fence, nor of the new family that was supposed to move in.

For Pepsi, very little changed. She still languished on her chain, but now a bowl of water and a dish of food lay within her reach. She didn't seem particularly unhappy. Only lonely. Only overjoyed to see me, as if she seldom came into contact with another human.

I never saw Zachary Drummond. More telling, the shrub he'd purchased at Greenspires was nowhere in sight. Where had he planted it?

Elsewhere in the county, four teenagers perished in an alcohol related accident. A young boy drowned while swimming with friends, and Lime Lake claimed a victim when a novice pilot crashed his plane.

Sometimes, I reflected, it was best to stay home, walk with the dogs on Jonquil Lane, and take an occasional trip to Clovers for take-out.

But no one can hide from life or fate or whatever name you choose to give the force that governs our life's events.

"Something else happened, Jennet." Lucy's voice on the phone held a note of suppressed panic. "It's truly frightening."

"Something with the statue?" I asked.

"No... Yes. At this point, I don't know. I just know I'm afraid."

"Do you want company?"

"I'd appreciate it, if you can spare an hour or so."

I glanced into the kitchen. I had a casserole ready for the oven, salad makings in the refrigerator, and cloverleaf rolls (my own) in the freezer. I'd planned to bake pies but I could pick up dessert at Clovers.

The dogs had been walked. I had no plans except to sit on the front porch and enjoy the scenery and the weather.

"I'll be there," I said. "Whatever happened, don't worry. We'll figure it out together."

She thanked me, and I ended the call, curious and a bit apprehensive. What would I find at Dark Gables?

I gave the collies fresh water and biscuits and set out for Lucy's house.

She was waiting for me on the porch with Sky lying at her feet. All of the wood from the fallen tree was gone, and the broken window was whole again, shining in the sun. On a side table, I noticed a stack of paper. A manuscript?

All in black, bedecked in gold jewelry, Lucy looked pale again, almost haunted. This wasn't good.

"What happened?" I asked, petting Sky and sitting in the porch's matching wicker chair next to Lucy.

"Did you read about the plane that went down in Lime Lake the other day?" she asked.

"I did. That's close to home."

I never admitted it, not even to Crane, but I had a great fear of death dropping down from the sky, of funnel clouds forming, and airplanes crashing into houses, killing innocent people who never dreamed they were in danger.

"I wrote about it," she said.

"You mean you used the incident in your book?"

"Not exactly. I wrote about a similar plane crash days before it happened. Maybe I'll still find a color-changing ball on the porch. Who knows? Maybe it was there one day, and Sky took it away."

"How did a plane crash fit into your story?" I asked.

"The Voltarians arranged it."

"They're getting deadly."

"It was a fictitious lake, of course," she said. "Loam Lake. I took the name from that play, *The Importance of Being Ernest*. Lord Loam, remember?"

I nodded. 'Loam' was disturbingly close to 'Lime.'

"In my scene, the pilot spots an Unidentified Flying Object. It startles him, and that's what causes the crash. It was the aliens in their spacecraft. The pilot survives and explains what happens, but nobody believes him. No one else saw the UFO. The Voltarians are able to make it invisible."

"That's different," I said.

"Yes, it is. The real life pilot didn't survive. We don't know what caused him to crash into Lime Lake yet."

"Well, I'm sure it wasn't Voltarians," I said.

Lucy sighed. "It isn't over at all, Jennet. I allowed myself to think it was when we found the girls and my test scene didn't happen."

"I wish I knew what's going on."

"It's that statue," she said. "That stone collie. It all started the day I found it in the woods. No, the day I began writing this book. It's laid a curse on my life."

I didn't know what to say. In a sense, I agreed with her. Before that, life for Lucy had been serene and uneventful. What, I wondered, had changed? What had caused the change? Certainly not beginning a new book.

"I just wish I knew how it was going to end," she said.

~ * ~

Later, while we drank our tea in the sunroom, I quizzed Lucy about her book.

"What's going to happen next?"

"I write a short barebones outline," she said. "I know that the Voltarians are dangerous. Their scientific advancements are superior to ours, but the planet Voltar is dying. They're searching for a new world to colonize, one with fresh water and forests and a hospitable climate."

"Like earth," I said.

"Like earth," she repeated. "The aliens that the girls will encounter are an advance team. Think of them as scouts."

"What will they do with the people? With us?"

"Eradicate them. That's their diabolical plan."

"Which will be thwarted by two heroic girls," I added.

"That's *my* plan, after a series of frightening incidents. I may omit the test scene with the alien ball."

"So far you've had a severe thunderstorm and a plane crash," I said. "What comes next?"

"A pandemic. I haven't written that part yet."

Sitting in Lucy's airy sunroom, I'd almost forgotten I was listening to the plot of an unfinished book. What if a mysterious disease began to spread in Foxglove Corners? Lucy would believe she was responsible. Everyone's life would be affected. Mine, Crane's, even Lucy's.

"Don't do that," I said, envisioning overflowing hospital corridors, patients burning with fever, overwhelmed doctors and hopelessness. "Write about something pleasant like gold coins falling from the sky."

Lucy smiled. "That wouldn't go with my theme."

"Well," I said, "just write what you planned then. Take a chance. Storms are common in summertime. To a lesser extent, so are plane crashes, especially small planes piloted by amateurs."

"And in the words of our friend, Brent, all teenaged girls look alike."

I couldn't help but laugh.

"I'm thinking of changing the girls' descriptions back," Lucy said. "I liked what I wrote the first time. Now that I know there's nothing unnatural about the lookalikes in the library, it doesn't matter."

"Speaking of descriptions, what do these Voltarians look like?" I asked.

"Like you and me, like anyone. But that's the appearance they assume to deceive us. Actually they're sort of like..." She paused, trying to find the best words. "Like grayish white blobs."

"Ugh."

"I don't plan to reveal their appearance until the end," she said. "I want the reader to think anyone could be one of *Them*."

"In your book, they're the ones who placed the stone collie in the woods. That doesn't help us solve the mystery."

"Not at all."

"How much of the book have you written?" I asked.

"Over half, but I'm considering abandoning the project and moving on to something different. Maybe that's the answer."

"It might be. Is that what you want to do, though?"

"Sometimes."

I wouldn't like to see Lucy do that. In a way, I felt there was no connection between the events in Lucy's story and the incidents that happened in everyday life. But did I really believe that? When I was in Lucy's company, the impossible became commonplace, and doubts assailed me.

"Whatever you decide, don't write about a pandemic," I said. "Please."

Eighteen

I was so affected by Lucy's plan to include a pandemic in her book that I almost forgot I had to buy a dessert at Clovers, almost drove past Crispian Road.

Of course I didn't believe a pandemic could spread in the peaceful hamlet of Foxglove Corners and from there to far-reaching places. It was the stuff of science-fiction and horror stories.

Still, what if it did? What if, throughout Foxglove Corners, pesky summer colds turned into cases of influenza and imperceptibly into something else? Something deadly.

"I feel as if a malign being is looking over my shoulder, reading what I write and making it happen," Lucy had said when we parted.

"Then take my advice. Write about something wonderful like a shower of golden coins or a treasure chest of precious jewels."

Double rainbows or pink waterfalls or ever-blooming flowers. The list was endless.

Lucy had shaken her head. "That wouldn't be true to my story. The Voltarians didn't come to earth to bring wonder."

But she'd promised to rethink the pandemic sub-plot.

The sight of the bright green clovers that adorned the border of the little restaurant drove gruesome thoughts out of my mind. Five minutes later, I stood in blissful air-conditioning at the dessert carousel contemplating a selection of fresh-baked pies and cakes.

"Try the peach pie," Annica said, coming up behind me. "This is Peach Week."

In keeping with Clovers' theme, she wore a charming dress with a square neckline and a pattern of tiny bouquets against a silky peach background. It had a vaguely old-fashioned look, which was out of character for the flamboyant redhead. For once her earrings were sedate, pearls set in silver.

"We have peach muffins," she said, "peach-walnut bread, and peach tarts still in the oven. They're all made from California peaches. It's too early for Michigan's. These were extra sweet, though."

"I'll take a pie."

"How about a muffin with coffee for now? I'll join you."

How could I resist?

"Your neighbor, that Drummond jerk, was in for breakfast," Annica said. "He ordered a ham dinner to take out. Do you think it's for Pepsi?"

"More likely for himself."

I'd never seen anything in Pepsi's food dish except dry kibble. Of course, dogs usually gobbled down their toppings first.

"What are we going to do about the statue?" Annica asked.

"I wish I knew. I haven't been able to help Lucy, and she... Lucy needs help."

I'd started to say that she was sinking deeper and deeper into her fantasy, and I was afraid for her mental health. But I didn't want to gossip about my friend.

"I was thinking," Annica said. "Suppose we set up one of those surveillance cameras in the woods? Then if anyone goes near the statue, we'll have his picture. Brent would know how to do it."

"We could," I said.

And we'd most likely end up with images of a bird scrounging for food at the base of the statue or a fox scampering by. On the other hand, maybe we'd catch a person up to no good. It was better than doing nothing. I wished I'd thought of it.

"Let's do it," I said.

While Marcy managed the lunch crowd, we sat with coffee and muffins and planned our next step. Naturally it involved contacting Brent.

There was a method to Annica's madness.

~ * ~

Anyone who has ever lived with a collie puppy is familiar with that feverish, high-pitched collie yipping that seems to go on forever. Anyone can tell when there are two yipping voices instead of one.

I heard the racket as I neared the blue house. Fortunately I didn't see the orange Volkswagen, so I turned into the space that would one day be a driveway. And behind the house I found Butterscotch.

Like Pepsi, she was chained. Quickly I noted details. Two chains, one dish half filled with kibble, one bowl of water with a leaf floating on the surface. Seen together, Butterscotch was the thinner of the two. Not dangerously thin but fragile. She was smaller boned with the full white collar I remembered and bright eyes

The two puppies resembled each other so strongly, I thought they might be littermates.

"Where have you been?" I asked Butterscotch, coming closer in order to pet each puppy.

Mac should see this. I wondered if he was still driving by the blue house.

Well, he'd hear about it.

I took pictures of the two chained puppies, their food and water containers, and a small red ball that had rolled out of their reach.

Who gave a ball to a puppy unless he was there to play with her?

Then I called Mac and knelt down to roll the ball for the puppies.

It was a small rubber ball with a bell inside and bone-shaped holes for baby teeth. I rolled it from Butterscotch to Pepsi and watched them fight over it.

I longed to scoop up both of them up and take them home, but the same conditions that existed before hindered me. Locks I couldn't break and a charge of dognapping.

Wait for Mac, I told myself.

Before long I heard a distant siren. I went out to Jonquil Lane to meet the cruiser and accompanied Mac to the back of the house.

"Trespassing again, Jennet?" he asked. But there was a twinkle in his deep blue eyes.

"I told you there were two puppies," I said as Butterscotch and Pepsi continued their happy yapping. "You have to fine Drummond. Arrest him. Do something. There are two dogs and not enough food or water for one."

Mac took charge of the ball and tossed it to Butterscotch, but Pepsi intercepted it.

"Playful pups," he said. "Hot out today." He wiped his forehead.

"Especially for little creatures wearing fur coats."

"They don't have enough water for one good drink," he said.

"And it isn't fresh. Check the perimeter. See if you get shocked."

"Did you?"

"I don't have to. I know Drummond never had an electric fence installed. You, however, obviously need proof."

I hadn't meant to challenge him. Baiting an officer of the law is often counterproductive. But Mac was nonplussed.

He strolled along the property line and announced, "You're right. There's no fence."

"What are you going to do?" I asked.

"Break the lock and take these little ones to the station. When Drummond shows his face, I'll arrest him for animal abuse."

"He'll say they have food and water, and he's using the chains because there was a delivery problem at the fence company."

"Let him say whatever he wants," Mac said. "He'll have to jump through hoops before he gets these babies back."

"Please don't let that happen. I don't trust the man."

"Don't worry, Jennet," he said. "I'll take care of it."

I knew I could relax. Mac loved collies. He'd had one when he was a boy, and his wife, Joanna, had brought her collie, Kinder, into the marriage. He wouldn't fail Butterscotch and Pepsi.

As for Drummond, he would get his just desserts.

As for me, I'd made another enemy.

Nineteen

As far as anyone knew, Zachary Drummond never returned to the blue house on Jonquil Lane. Nor had his orange Volkswagen been seen in the neighborhood or at the Corners.

Pepsi and Butterscotch, re-christened Cola by the officers, were still in the custody of the Foxglove Corners Police Department.

How would they have fared if Mac and I hadn't intervened? Had Drummond meant that little bit of food and water to last them forever? Surely not. It was unthinkable.

Sue Appleton was more charitable when I told her about the latest development. "Maybe he was in an accident. He might be in the hospital or dead."

I didn't think so. In my opinion, he'd abandoned the collie puppies, and we still didn't know where Butterscotch—no, Cola—had been all this time.

Sue thought Pepsi and Cola should go into Rescue, but Drummond's disappearance was too new. Mac still hoped he would return. He wanted to fine him or arrest him for putting the puppies' lives in danger. In other words, to make an example of him.

"We'll get them in foster homes eventually," Sue said.

"In the meantime, it looks like Foxglove Corners has another disappearance."

"No one is looking for Zachary Drummond. Except Lieutenant Dalby."

"It would be better if he'd stay missing," I said. "Then the puppies could have loving homes and people to take good care of them."

The blue house remained unoccupied. Even Crane didn't know why the Brooks family hadn't moved in yet.

"Maybe your information was wrong," I said.

Crane remained optimistic. "They may still show up."

"Then we can find out if Zachary Drummond was really related to them and if he had permission to use their property."

Until then we had one more mystery, but there was no urgency in solving it. The puppies were happy at the station, enchanting hardened officers with their antics. Mac took them home at night and talked about training them and adding them to the force's one-dog K-9 Division.

I was happy for them but in a way sad. I'd looked forward to visiting them. To me nothing is more appealing than a baby collie.

"I wish we could have another puppy," I said to Crane.

"Six is our limit," he reminded me. "Besides, Misty is still pretty much a puppy if you want chewed furniture and bratty behavior."

"Raven lives outside. We only have five in the house."

He smiled at me, his frosty gray eyes suddenly warm. "What color would you like?"

"Tricolor," I said so quickly I realized the thought of adding to our collie family had been with me for a while.

"Make out your Christmas list, honey," Crane said.

"It's only June."

I knew Crane. He thought that by December I'd forget my impulsive wish.

Maybe he was right.

"Okay," I said, "if you make out yours, too."

~ * ~

The next time I saw Brent, which was the following day at dinnertime, I told him about Annica's surveillance idea.

"I'll do it," he said. "Annica has a good head on her shoulders. A pretty one, too."

"Should we tell Lucy what we're doing?" I asked.

"Sure. Why not? It'll be in her woods."

"I thought it might add to her apprehension."

It was bound to. So far she hadn't mentioned the possibility of intruders on her property. From now on, she would look over her shoulder every time she trekked into the woods to see if the stone collie was still there.

I hoped we'd have some success. A human mischief maker would be easier to catch than the malign being she envisioned reading over her shoulder as she wrote her story.

"Except, why would anyone pay a secret visit to a statue?" I said.

"Maybe we'll catch our visitor leaving something else there."

"What's happening to Lucy can all be explained," Crane said. "Like that plane crash. Investigators suspect human error. The pilot was young and inexperienced."

"Or weather," I said. "Or a combination of the two. Remember…the plane went down in a thunderstorm."

"There was no mystery about the girls in the library," Brent reminded us. "It was all Lucy's imagination."

"We're left with the statue in the woods," I said. "I've thought and thought but can't begin to imagine who left it there or why."

"Wouldn't it be great if we caught one of those Voltarians on tape?" Brent said.

"But they'll look like humans, according to Lucy," I added. "Or maybe the camera will pick up blobs."

"You two are starting to scare me," Crane said. "Don't forget. Lucy writes horror fiction. We live in the real world where so far nobody has seen a creature from outer space."

"No one's forgetting," I told him.

Except maybe Lucy. Perhaps next she'd start believing in her own aliens.

~ * ~

July ushered in another hot spell. The collies lost interest in long walks in favor of fresh water and lazing around in the air-conditioned house. Sue suggested that we resume gathering signatures for our 'Raze the Construction' petition, driving to the new routes she had mapped out for us. Then she decided it was too hot for such activity.

Pepsi and Cola, still in the custody of the FCPD, were thriving, and one steamy morning, Miss Eidt called to tell me she had found three vintage Gothic paperbacks in good condition at a yard sale.

"They were seventy-five cents apiece," she said. "I don't think they were ever opened."

Nothing could lure me out on a hot day like the prospect of new Gothics to read.

"I'll stop by this morning," I said.

"Good. I wanted to talk to you anyway."

Uh oh. I knew that tone, and those words were often a prelude to trouble. What had happened now?

At the Hometown Bakery I picked up a dozen freshly baked cinnamon rolls and drove to the Corners where the old white Victorian-turned-library drowsed in the heat of the day. Even Blackberry had forsaken the porch for a place inside near the floor fan.

Miss Eidt looked cool in her pale aqua suit with a flower of the same material and color on her lapel. She accepted the cinnamon rolls happily and promptly plugged in her new electric teakettle in her office.

"Debbie can handle the crowd," she said...the crowd consisting of about a dozen quiet browsers.

"What did you want to talk to me about?" I asked as she cut the string on the box, exclaiming over the white-frosted bounty inside.

"Lucy," she said. "Or rather, Lucy's books. Ever since she gave her talk, I can't keep her books on the shelves. Did you notice my special Lucy Hazen display?"

I hadn't, having gone straight to Miss Eidt's office.

"It's as bare as Mother Hubbard's cupboard. Kids keep asking for *Devilwish* or any of Lucy's other books, and I don't have them. I keep ordering more and still can't keep them stocked."

"But that's good, isn't it? It means Lucy's work resonates with our kids. I always knew that."

"I thought so, too, at first, but lately I'm beginning to suspect that something's off kilter. I ordered a dozen copies of *Devilwish* four times. You won't find a single one on the shelves."

I took a sip of tea. "Could Debbie have shelved them in the wrong place?"

"Never."

"What are you suggesting? A surplus of thieving horror fans?"

"I'm not sure. To my knowledge, no one has ever felt the need to steal one of our books. Why should they? All they have to do is check them out." She betrayed her agitation with a twirl of her signature pearls. "I wish that were the answer. I simply don't understand what's happening in my library."

"I'll look," I said.

"I was hoping you would."

After finishing my tea, I strolled out into the library. First I checked the Lucy Hazen display, a cardboard carousel that looked as if it had just been assembled. It was empty.

I moved on to 'New Arrivals,' 'Michigan Authors,' and 'Fiction' with no luck. Then, on an impulse, I wandered into the non-fiction section, thinking someone—surely not Miss Eidt or Debbie—had mistakenly shelved one of Lucy's books in with paranormal texts.

Miss Eidt was right. All of Lucy's books were gone. Miss Eidt had a sizeable waiting list for them on her desk and six of each of Lucy's paperbacks on order.

What was going on?

This could be simply explained as a direct result of Lucy's talk, combined with her longstanding popularity in her hometown.

But I felt strongly that it was something more.

Twenty

At Miss Eidt's desk, I picked up my Gothic novels—two Victoria Holts and one Katherine Wigmore Eyre.

"These look brand new," I said.

"They're almost a half century old."

"They must have been kept under glass." I gazed at the evocative covers. A young woman in a long dress running away from a castle-like mansion, the background colored in greens and blues. "And look at these prices. Ninety-five cents. A dollar twenty-five."

"Times have changed." Miss Eidt fussed with her pearls again. "Did you find any of Lucy's books on the shelves?"

"Not a one." I slipped the Gothics into my shoulder bag, eager to go home and start reading. "I have an idea, Miss Eidt. When your new order comes in, why don't you keep the books behind your desk? That'll give you some control."

Blackberry had leaped onto the counter from which position she kept her green jewel eyes fixed on the library patrons.

"Blackberry can serve as an additional safeguard for the books," I said. "Too bad she isn't a dog."

Miss Eidt brightened. "I like your idea."

"Or you can tie bells around the books," I said, hoping to divert her with a ridiculous suggestion. "Like belling the cat."

"Then you don't think there's anything weird going on?" she asked.

I hesitated before speaking. Surely Lucy wouldn't have confided in Miss Eidt about events in her unfinished book turning into real life happenings.

"I think Lucy's stories are irresistible," I said. "Kids love them and decide to keep them. Or maybe they're just forgetful."

"Not every single kid. Not every book."

"Well, no. After all, aren't readers, young and old, supposed to be the cream of the crop?"

"The point is they're not checking them out," she said. "If they were, I could contact them."

I didn't know what else to tell her. "Maybe this will die down in time, and you can display them again."

Miss Eidt sighed. "I hope so. I've always been so proud of showcasing our hometown author's works."

I wondered if this mini-mystery involving Lucy tied in with the other strangeness in her life. Offhand, I didn't see how it could.

"Excuse me, Miss Eidt?"

The voice was strident, the face familiar. I wondered where I'd seen the woman before, then remembered. There was the brassy hair and neon color, a green tank top tucked into a baggy denim skirt. She had been at Lucy's library event taking notes. She had a notebook in a flap of her handbag and held a pair of gaudy sunglasses in a tight grip.

"May I help you?" Miss Eidt asked.

"I'm looking for a book by Lucy Hazen. *Devilwish*. Do you have it?"

"Not at the moment." Miss Eidt reached for her waiting list. "May I add your name and phone number to my list? As soon as a copy becomes available, I'll call you."

"What happened to your Lucy Hazen display?" she asked, pointing to the empty cardboard carousel.

"Lucy's books are quite literally flying off the shelves," Miss Eidt said.

Neon Top ignored the list. "My daughter's birthday is coming up in a few days. I guess I'd better buy a copy at a bookstore."

"Perhaps that would be wise."

"Thanks—for nothing. By the way, it's unsanitary to let a cat lie on the counter."

The woman glared at Blackberry and left in a huff.

Why would anyone be upset over such a small matter?

Miss Eidt dropped the list in her drawer. "What a rude woman!"

"I find it odd that she wants to check out a library book for her daughter's birthday," I said. "You'd think she'd go straight to a bookstore."

"The world is full of odd people, I'm sorry to say," Miss Eidt said. "Even the ones who patronize our library. Happily, they're in the minority. I'll take your advice about keeping the new books out of sight, Jennet. Anyone with a hand behind the main desk will certainly attract my attention or Debbie's."

I left the library with a sense of satisfaction. We'd solved Miss Eidt's immediate problem, to a degree, even though we still didn't have an answer to the mystery of the vanishing books.

~ * ~

Brent and Lucy joined us for an impromptu pizza dinner that evening. It was a welcome change from our usual fare, perfect for a warm summer day. We ate on the front porch while the day wound down and the heat gave way to a cool breeze. Country quiet surrounded us and six collies hoping for handouts.

It seemed that, for an hour or two at least, all the troubles in the world were fading with the day.

Brent had set up his surveillance equipment in the woods with Lucy's knowledge and approval. He'd ended up with several minutes of a tranquil woodland scene presided over by a stone collie statue and visited by a lone blackbird.

"No suspicious activity," he said as he tucked into a piece of my homemade blueberry pie. "Not even a curious fox. I was hoping for a kind of story."

"Or a Voltarian," I added.

"It has no plot," Lucy said with a hint of her old humor. "If only the statue could talk."

Crane passed Lucy the next piece of pie. "Don't wish for that, Lucy."

"Please keep the camera going or running or whatever it is you do, Brent," Lucy said. "The footage only reflects one day and night."

Brent agreed. "Until we're sure no one is trespassing on your property."

Lucy laid her hand on his arm and the chains on her gold bracelets stirred to life. "I can't thank you enough, Brent. You've made my troubles your own."

"That's what friends are for," he said.

I said, "We're with you, no matter what happens."

I had made a decision not to mention Lucy's disappearing books for the moment. No doubt she would discover it herself on her next visit to the library.

I believed that a connection existed between the disappearing books and the other occurrences, even though I couldn't see it at the moment. Some malign force was at work, moving stealthily behind the scenes, although not hovering over Lucy and reading her work, as she imagined.

Our job was to identify and stop it.

~ * ~

After that night I enjoyed two days of summer peace. I sat on the porch for long stretches of reading time with a glass of lemonade at my elbow. *The Lute and the Glove* was new to me. Or if I'd once read it, I'd forgotten the story, and it captivated me with lush descriptions and gradually mounting horror.

Life cooperated. The phone didn't ring, no one came over, and few cars traveled on Jonquil Lane, making it easy for me to steal away into an English manor house haunted by a pair of Elizabethan ghosts.

This is why I wanted to live in the country, I told myself, pausing to drain my glass and refill it from the pitcher on the side table.

Of course on my first day in Foxglove Corners, I never imagined I'd be joined one day by five additional collies and the man of my dreams who would be home soon.

Which meant I'd better start dinner.

The harmonious notes of my phone drew me away from the English haunting.

"It's happened again," Lucy said.

The nature of peace is that it comes and goes. I steeled myself to hear the latest news.

Twenty-one

I drove to Dark Gables the next morning, not knowing what to expect. All Lucy would tell me over the phone was, "You have to see it for yourself, Jennet."

So I did. What I saw was a blue object lying in the center of a round wicker table from which Lucy had removed everything else. It looked like a small cone or a giant carrot. Or a piece broken off from a larger object.

Enlightenment eluded me. "What is it?" I asked.

"It's a horn," Lucy said. "I found Sky playing with it on the front porch. She was reluctant to surrender it. In fact, she came close to growling at me, but I prevailed and placed it on the table, out of her reach. It came from a unicorn."

I sank into the nearest wicker chair, wondering if the strain or the heat had finally overtaken Lucy. Was she referring to a unicorn statue? I hoped so.

"But the unicorn is a mythological creature," I said.

"I know that."

"You'd better explain. Start at the beginning."

"All right. In my new chapter, the Voltarians are trying to trap Madeline. They know she collects unicorn figurines because they can look into her mind. They create a blue unicorn. Madeline sees it and tries to capture it, but it's a holograph."

"How do unicorns fit in with planet-hungry aliens running amok and making planes crash?" I asked. "Are you sure your story isn't getting away from you?"

"Maybe it is. That scene wasn't in my original outline."

She dropped into the other chair and gazed out at her front yard where the fallen tree had been. "I'm in such a muddle with all that's been happening. It's a wonder I can write at all. Anyway, I finished the scene two days ago. Yesterday I found Sky trying to chew a unicorn's horn. So you see, the curse is still alive. It just took a little time off."

"I'm sure there's another explanation."

I touched the object, expecting it to be as cold as a fossil. To my surprise it had soaked up the warmth of the day. Like the stone collie, it seemed to have a glow.

Or was I becoming as delusional as Lucy?

"You don't really believe that," I said.

"I don't know what to think except it's all part of the same diabolical plan. Someone is trying to drive me out of my mind."

"Let's examine this logically. What would a horn from an animal feel like?"

"I don't know. Hard probably. Rough." She took the horn from me. "Like this."

"A real horn wouldn't be blue."

"We're talking about unicorns here," Lucy said.

Oh dear. Where had logic gone?

"What else has horns?" I asked.

"A goat, any number of animals, the devil, a satyr…"

"And a statue of any one of those," I said. "This may have been broken off a sculpture. It isn't particularly heavy. The wind could have blown it here. Then Sky found it and carried it to your porch."

"That's possible, I suppose."

"But you don't think so."

"No, I don't. You'll notice it has no scent. Nothing to attract a dog except the blue color."

Hoping to add a bit of levity to what was becoming a grim conversation, I said, "Maybe it's the Voltarians' version of a color-changing ball."

Lucy wasn't in a mood for levity.

"My writing used to be so easy," she said. "I'd have a plot outline in mind, I'd sit down and write the book and send it to my publisher. None of this weird stuff ever happened."

"Just be thankful none of your vampires came to life."

"I guess I should be grateful for that."

"Well, from now on, be careful what you write," I said. "What does Brent make of it?"

She attempted a smile. "That the unicorn is a mythological beast."

"What else?"

"That I'm going bananas."

"And?"

"When he looks at it, he doesn't see a horn. Just something Sky dragged in from the woods. His guess is that it's made of plastic and there's no way it can be harmful. But I don't want Sky chewing on it. She's formed a regrettable attraction to the thing."

That was strange, but not inexplicable. Sky probably thought it was a toy. *Her* toy because she'd discovered it. No dog likes to part with a favorite possession. Consider Misty with her beloved toy goat.

At the moment, Sky was lying at the top of the porch stairs, watching the object warily as if she feared it would disappear.

"In other words, this horn is nothing to worry about so you can put it out of your mind," I said.

"According to Brent. In my book, the color ball was a time travel device. I don't know the significance of the horn, but I have the feeling it has some kind of power and purpose, of course. Then there's the usual question. How did this person know I had written about a unicorn?"

"A holograph," I added.

Lucy covered the horn with one of the paper napkins she kept in a basket. "Let's have some tea, Jennet. My throat feels scratchy. I hope I'm not coming down with one of those wretched summer colds."

I followed her inside, Sky in our wake. I was glad to escape from the heat to the cool house and was dying for tea, cold or hot.

I swallowed, wondering, realized my hand had strayed to my own throat. A sore throat...

Was this the way a pandemic would begin?

~ * ~

"What's Lucy's latest problem?" Crane asked later that afternoon.

I gave the stew a brisk stir and turned down the heat. It was good to be home in my own kitchen where I could count on things being what they seemed. Usually.

"Nothing lethal. She thinks one of her fictitious unicorns came to life and lost his horn in her woods. She believes this horn or whatever it is has some power. Next I'm afraid she's going to search the woods for a unicorn."

"That's crazy," Crane said.

"The real problem is that Lucy is letting these events affect her. They're clouding her thinking. Pretty soon she's going to see dire significance in everything that happens."

"Lucy needs time away from her writing. You can only live so long in a make-believe world."

If it were only that simple!

"Then there's the matter of her books vanishing from the library," I said. "She doesn't know about it yet. Thank heavens."

When she found out, there would be more drama, more angst. More mystery laid at the door of the rapacious Voltarians.

"Something's going on, that's for sure," Crane said. "A unicorn loose in Foxglove Corners. That's a first."

"I'm going to look for a blue sculpture missing a horn in Lucy's woods."

"Not alone." His voice had the anticipated frosty edge.

"No, I'll take Annica with me."

"Go ahead and look for your sculpture, but I think you should focus on Lucy's books being stolen from the library," Crane said. "To me that suggests Lucy has an enemy. Could be someone is jealous of her success."

That was something to think about, but I saw a major flaw.

"If this person's reaction is to get rid of Lucy's books, he's deluded. A book in print can live forever. All Miss Eidt has to do is keep ordering more. She's already done that, and she's going to take my advice and keep the new ones out of sight. Remember, Lucy's books are in all the bookstores. It's not so easy to steal from them these days."

"I'll admit I'm stumped," Crane said.

So was I, but, unlike Crane, I was not going to admit it. I'd never yet let a mystery defeat me, and I wasn't going to start now.

Twenty-two

I heard the dog barking as I approached the blue house on Jonquil Lane. An ear-splitting, impervious, yet heartrending sound, it called to me.

Shades of *déjà vu*. It was like taking a step back in time. For a moment it was as if I had never confronted Zachary Drummond, as if he'd never left Pepsi and Cola one last time, thereby forfeiting his right to call them his puppies. As if Pepsi and Cola weren't safe in Mac's care.

It had to be another dog, and, of course, I had to stop and investigate. If the orange Volkswagen had been parked in front of the house, however, I would have formulated a Plan B.

I didn't allow myself to think that Drummond could return at any moment, angry and dangerous. I simply parked, got out of the car and walked briskly to the back yard.

The house was still vacant. It reminded me of one of the mansions in the abandoned construction that hadn't yet succumbed to complete deterioration. Not in appearance, though; in atmosphere. An aura of despondency hung heavily over the roof like a dark low-floating cloud, and except for the barking dog, all was steeped in silence.

This was not a happy place.

The dog didn't sound happy.

But she seemed to be. I found her secured by a chain to the weeping willow with a bowl of kibble and a pail of water within reach. She was a pretty sable at the adorable awkward stage with a long body, ears that she would grow into, and the brightest, most expressive eyes imaginable. She was wagging her tail wildly.

Come play with me!

She wasn't too thin, so not starved, and neatly groomed, so not neglected. But she was chained. Obviously there was no invisible fence around the property. Plans to install one had been a delaying tactic.

This was Zachary Drummond's work, no doubt about it. I let my imagination create a scenario. Too cowardly to face Mac, accept his punishment, and get his puppies back, Drummond had simply replaced them with a new collie, a little older.

Another female, no doubt intended to be the third in the foundation of a backyard breeding operation. Except he'd forfeited the first two.

She was the color of honey.

"Honey," I said softly and offered her my hand to sniff. I guessed I was going to name all of Drummond's dogs.

She flattened her ears and continued wagging her tail and barking

Play play play.

She had nothing to play with. No toys, not even a rag rope or a chewed bone. Not even a stick lying on the ground.

I cursed the fate that let Drummond possess this little treasure. He had provided food and water, but only the lacy fronds of the weeping willow for shelter from the scorching sun. Nothing else a dog needs.

The chain was damning evidence of his disregard for a dog's feelings.

Honey's presence proved Drummond was still in the area. But

where did he stay? In the house that showed no sign of occupancy? I didn't think so, although at one time he had had a key.

Well, that was a separate mystery. All I could do was keep checking the house and watch the road for a bright orange Volkswagen.

Reluctantly I went back to the car and left a message for Mac. He should know about this.

With the Taurus' windows open, the sound of frenetic barking followed me longer than it would under normal circumstances.

~ * ~

My destination was Clovers where centerpieces of red, white, and dyed blue carnations heralded the Fourth of July holiday.

Annica, who loved to complement the restaurant's décor whenever possible, was dressed in a white-trimmed red dress. Her earrings were tiny glittering flags, and she wore a bracelet heavy with patriotic charms. Add her red-gold hair, and she was Independence Day personified.

I'd scarcely given the holiday a thought, and here it was... Tomorrow? Yes, tomorrow. Crane would be on duty, and these days, with our canine family, neither one of us cared for fireworks.

At one time it had been different. I smiled at the cherished memory of our first date. We had driven to a picturesque town up north for a picnic with fireworks and a tour of the town's historic houses. I was already falling in love with Crane, but for a long time afterward I was unsure of his intentions. Fortunately they'd been honorable, and we were living our happily ever after with six collies who didn't like loud noises.

"What are you doing for the Fourth?" Annica asked as I settled myself in my favorite booth, which had just become available.

"Warming up a Clovers dinner and baking a blueberry pie," I said. "I see you have your famous barbecued ribs on the menu."

"And they're scrumptious. They'll be even better tomorrow."

"What are your holiday plans?" I asked, knowing Clovers would be closed.

"Reading," she said. "I couldn't wade through *Doctor Thorne*, so I gave up on it and moved on to *Bleak House*. That's Dickens. It's readable."

"Aren't you going backwards?"

"The professor doesn't care about chronology. Just so we read all the novels on the list. I may never return to *Doctor Thorne*."

"How would you like to go on a hike in Lucy's woods with me tomorrow?" I asked.

"With all the bugs? Only if there's a good reason."

I couldn't resist. "We're going to hunt for unicorns."

"Seriously."

I told her about the holograph unicorn in Lucy's book and the horn that had appeared on her property. She drew her own conclusions.

"So it's happened again."

"Lucy thinks so. I'm hoping to find a statue of a blue-horned creature that lost its horn," I added.

"In the woods? That's like looking for a needle in a haystack."

"I'm guessing Sky found the horn fairly close to the woods' edge. Ever since she ran away with a chicken carcass, Lucy has tried to keep her close to home."

"That's okay, then."

"I told Crane I'd ask you," I said. "He doesn't want me to go alone, and I don't think Lucy will be up to a search."

"Mmm." Annica placed a glass of iced water in front of me and took out her order pad. "Will Brent be there?"

"I doubt it. He usually barbecues at his barn on the Fourth and invites his workers."

She sighed. "I guess it'll be more fun than staying inside reading."

"Good. We'll go early. Around ten-thirty."

"All right," she said, "but I thought unicorns only came out in the moonlight."

~ * ~

And mosquitoes came out in the morning. I'd taken the precaution of wearing jeans, a long-sleeved white shirt, and boots. Still they found me.

Annica, who was similarly attired, didn't seem to be bothered.

"I sprayed on a bug repellant," she said.

"Ugh. I hate that stuff."

My wrist began to itch. I wasn't fond of Benadryl either.

"Let's hope we don't meet up with bees," Annica said. "Enough stings can kill you."

Bees. Another deterrent.

With that unhappy thought, we trudged on, our eyes watching the ground. So far we hadn't seen anything that didn't belong in a forest.

"Sky could have found that horn anywhere," Annica said.

"That's true." I spied a stump ahead and brushed it free of nature's debris. "Let's rest for a moment."

"Do you suppose someone threw the horn on Lucy's porch?" Annica said. "Someone like that enemy you talked about."

"It's possible."

"In which case, we're wasting our time out here."

"Well…" I rose, running my hand through my hair to make sure nothing had landed on my head. "It was worth a try. Should we go a little farther or are you getting tired?"

"Yes to both," she said.

Lucy had invited us back to her house for tea, which sounded tempting at the moment.

"Five more minutes," I said.

A spate of staccato booms shattered the silence. Four... Six...
The very leaves seemed to tremble.

"Firecrackers!" Annica said. "I wonder who's shooting
firecrackers out here?"

"It's coming from the east."

A minute passed and more booms followed.

"Maybe it's thunder," Annica said. "I can't see the sky. The
trees are in the way."

"And maybe it's gunfire," I said. "Let's get out of here."

~ * ~

The trek back to Dark Gables seemed interminable. I had time to
doubt my initial thought. Ever since the shooting in my classroom
and its frightening aftermath, I had been gun shy. It was the Fourth
of July, after all. Fireworks could easily be mistaken for gunshots.
It made more sense that revelers were celebrating with firecrackers
than that someone had been shooting at us in the woods.

I emerged from the woods grateful that my only souvenirs were
mosquito bites. The sky was growing dark, the sun hiding behind
sullen clouds, the air thick and muggy.

Lucy opened the door. Sky, ears flattened, stayed well behind
her mistress.

"Did you hear the fireworks?" Lucy asked. "We never have
them out here. Poor Sky." She gave Sky a reassuring pat. "Did you
find anything?"

"Nothing," I said.

"The noise scared the unicorn away," Annica added.

Lucy's fleeting smile faded. "I don't think there's a real unicorn,
Annica. I was hoping you'd find a statue with a broken horn."

We followed her to the sunroom. "Shall we have tea outside or
in here?" she asked.

"Inside," I said. "It looks like rain."

"What's going to happen next in your book?" Annica asked as Lucy plugged in the teakettle.

"The Voltarians are going to capture Madeline. Cassandra will look for her sister and may fall into their trap as well."

That sounded ominous. Next we'd hear about the disappearance of a teenaged girl.

"Why don't you write about something fun?" Annica asked.

"Like an overflowing treasure chest," I said.

"In this kind of novel, I'm going to save the good for the ending."

"Well, then, you don't have to worry. Everything will come out right."

"Somehow I don't think that's going to happen," Lucy said.

Twenty-three

The rain came and went during the night, and the morning promised a perfect summer day of warm breezes and sunshine. Feeling carefree and happy, I walked up Jonquil Lane with Halley, Sky, and Misty...destination Sue Appleton's horse farm.

Sue would want to know about Honey, the new collie at the blue house. We'd have to make sure Honey didn't end up like Pepsi and Cola before their rescue without sufficient food and water.

When Mac had investigated, there was no sign of the third collie, only the chain. And no sign of Zachary Drummond. I might have anticipated that.

As we passed the abandoned construction, Misty tried to turn left onto a makeshift path overgrown with a noxious vine. With a firm grip on her leash, I directed her back to the lane.

What was the appeal of the crumbling ruin of unfinished mansions?

I could guess. From a dog's viewpoint, a world of new scents to explore, wonders hidden in shadowy corners, and nesting animals. There was plenty to attract a curious canine, and plenty to convince me to keep walking. The memory of every frightening thing that had ever happened in these doomed acres seemed to live on.

I hurried the dogs on to Squill Lane. Recent events had driven the 'Raze the Construction' petition out of my mind. After the

Fourth of July, summer always seems to be on the wane. By the end of the month, if not sooner, stores would bring out dark clothing and 'back to school' supplies would fill drug stores shelves.

Summer had only just begun, or so it seemed. When school started again, there would be no time for extra activities.

I had added names to my petition, of course, without canvassing country roads. Lucy, Miss Eidt and Debbie at the library, along with a few concerned readers, and at Clovers, Annica, Marcy, and Mary Jeanne, the owner. But I didn't have enough signatures to convince anyone in authority that the ruins were a constant hazard, not to mention an eyesore. Neither, I suspect, did Sue.

We found Sue outside with her horses and dogs, all of them enjoying the glorious morning. She had a pretty new foal to be admired and fussed over. After the animals had greeted one another, she invited us to rest on her shady front porch.

Sue agreed with me about the lull in our petition project. "We've let it fall by the wayside. Tomorrow should be nice, and I'm free in the morning. How about hitting the road again?"

"That'll work. Did you map out new routes for us?"

"Three of them," she said. "There's a new community just off Spruce Road. It's called Diadem Estates. You can start there. I'm taking Castle Court near Sagramore Lake."

"People who live so far from Jonquil Lane might not be as enthusiastic as our neighbors," I said, "but we all have a stake in keeping our surroundings free of blight."

Woods and lakes and neatly maintained houses like the yellow Victorian and the newer structures built in Victorian style. For their sake, I was willing to give up hours of leisure time. I figured somebody had to do it.

"I took a new batch of pictures of the ruins," Sue said. "I nearly broke my neck tripping over a beam I didn't notice."

"If the area is cleared, in no time the trees and plant life will grow back," I said.

And I wouldn't expect ghosts to leap out at me whenever I walked past.

That was a bit of an exaggeration, but Lucy believed the environment could hold the imprint of an evil deed for years. Perhaps forever.

If that were true, ghosts had indeed made their home in the ruins of the failed development. The sooner we sent them on their way the better.

"What will be done about Drummond's new collie?" Sue asked.

"I'll keep checking on her," I said. "I can take the dogs walking by the blue house every day."

"The way he just replaced Pepsi and Cola... Do you know what I think?"

I nodded. "All females. All young. Unspayed. He wants the dogs for breeding. They're a commodity to him."

"Unfortunately we can't stop him."

"But we can make sure he doesn't abuse them."

Sue sighed. "In a year or so, we'll have unwanted puppies trickling into Rescue."

She painted a dismal picture. Unfortunately it was a realistic one. We'd managed to save Pepsi and Cola from the life Drummond planned for them. Now how about Honey?

~ * ~

Diadem Estates was a new development of houses built in different styles with paint so fresh it glittered in the sunshine. The lawns were green and lush, and the landscaping consisted of small shrubs and colorful annuals on the ground and in hanging baskets.

I left the Taurus on Old Fox Trail and made my way down Diadem Lane, garnering a respectable number of signatures. At last I came to a house that wasn't part of the Estates. Obviously it had been on its acres long before the newcomers, like Camille's yellow Victorian on Jonquil Lane.

This house had nothing in common with Camille's elegant Victorian, though. It was made of dreary gray stones and surrounded by a dispirited overgrown garden. Instead of facing forward as most houses do, it sat at an angle, presenting its west side to Diadem Lane. A high black iron fence enclosed house and grounds, and a sign 'Beware of Dog' warned away solicitors and passersby.

I was neither. Opening the gate, I walked up to the dark massive door and rang the doorbell.

Immediately a woman's voice thundered out into the deep silence to the accompaniment of angry barking. "Go away! You are trespassing on private property! You are not wanted here. Don't come back."

Well, that message was clear enough.

In my quest for signatures, I had encountered barking dogs, indifference, and people who pretended not to be home but never hostility. I wondered why the occupant went to such lengths to discourage visitors. A bad experience, perhaps? Something to hide?

I wasn't about to stay to find out. Hastily I walked back to Old Fox Trail, and, having completed my canvass of the new houses, drove away from Diadem Estates. I had acquired fifteen signatures, which was a respectable showing for an afternoon's work. But as I drove away, I kept thinking about the unwelcome message that had emanated from the stone house.

There was a story there. Unfortunately I would never know it.

~ * ~

Because I was so close to Spruce Road, I made an unplanned stop at Dark Gables. Lucy and Sky were relaxing on the front porch.

Usually at this time of day, Lucy would be at her desk writing, and Sky would be with her.

Sky sprang up, barking a welcome, and Lucy stood, her full black skirt moving in a soft breeze. "Jennet, what a surprise!"

"I was in the neighborhood," I said. "No, really. For signatures for my petition."

"I was hoping to see you. I'm feeling a little down today."

"Did something else happen?" I asked.

"Yes, but I guess it's been happening all along. I just didn't know about it. Did you know Miss Eidt doesn't have a single one of my books in the library?"

"That's what she said. You're a popular lady."

"If it were only that. I look on it as another way to erase all traces of me from Foxglove Corners."

"Oh, I don't think so."

"What do you think then?"

"That kids read your books and don't want to part with them. I'll be charitable and suppose they don't realize it's stealing."

"Miss Eidt ordered new copies of all my books," Lucy said.

"She'll keep them out of sight. That should take care of the problem."

"It's giving in to them."

"By them you mean...?

"Not my readers. They aren't behind this. It's somebody else. I'm going to visit the bookstore at Maplewood Mall and see if they have any of my books," she added.

"Don't overreact, Lucy," I said softly, although I knew that if they were my books, I'd do everything within my power to get to the bottom of the problem.

"Then it'll be something else. Like the unicorn's horn. I put it in the trash. I didn't want to look at it anymore and didn't want Sky to have it."

As if discarding the horn would change whatever mischief dogged Lucy.

"I've decided to set *The Stone Collie* aside at least until this is over," she said. "Assuming it will be over someday."

"Oh, don't do that. You'd leave Madeline in the hands of the Voltarians?"

She smiled. "And Cassandra on the brink of capture. I can always go back to it. You were right about the pandemic, Jennet. I just thought about adding it to the plot and caught one of those twenty-four hour bugs. Heaven knows how. I rarely leave the house."

"Germs are in the air. Everywhere."

"Kind of like those pesky aliens."

I was happy to see that Lucy had retained a dollop of her sense of wry humor and even happier when she suggested tea. That meant tea leaf reading. She wasn't entirely down. Still, she was deeply concerned about the disappearance of her books from the library, as she should be.

This summer seemed to bring one mystery after another and drop it at my feet.

Oh well, solving mysteries kept life interesting. Leonora should be home from her vacation soon. I was looking forward to her input and her help.

For now I put another visit to the library on my 'to do' list.

Twenty-four

After talking to Lucy, I decided to make another search in the library for Lucy's books. Some of them might have been returned.

Life, however, intervened. Sue called to remind me of our next League meeting the day after tomorrow for which I'd have to prepare a report. Misty refused to eat her dinner. Just as I was about to make an appointment with the vet, she perked up and wolfed down a jumbo-sized biscuit. Meanwhile, I ruined my beef stew by salting it twice.

Back to the drawing board. We'd have spaghetti and meatballs. I'd rinse the meat and set it aside for the dogs. Tomorrow was another day.

The next morning I woke to the wail of a high wind. Crane's side of the bed was empty, and a delicious smell of bacon wended its way up the staircase.

I couldn't walk the dogs until the wind died down, which meant I had most of the morning free.

I dressed quickly and joined Crane in the kitchen where the lure of bacon overpowered my senses. Crane was in his uniform ready for his shift. The dogs were restless, pacing and whining, except for Sky, who had taken refuge under the table where she lay trembling. Through the window I could see branches whipping about in the wind. A scattering of leaves had stuck to the pane. It was a wild morning.

"The dogs were out already," Crane said. "They don't like the wind."

"Neither do I…not when it's this strong."

I called Sky but she didn't venture out from her shelter. Giving in, I reached down to give her a reassuring pat.

Crane had been busy. The table was set for breakfast with plates of bacon and glasses of orange juice. He was beating eggs for French toast. I had the most thoughtful husband in creation, but, really, cooking was my job. I took a fresh loaf of white bread out of the breadbox.

"Did you hear the crash?" he asked.

I had, now that I remembered, but thought it was part of a dream.

"There's another tree down in the lane," he said. "They're predicting gusts of up to sixty miles per hour."

It would only get worse then. I turned away from the window.

He stepped away from the stove to pour coffee into our mugs and sat at the table. "Were you going out today?"

"I was," I said. "Just to the library. Nothing important. I guess I'll stay home."

And find something to do? Clean house? Think again.

"I don't want to see you crushed by a tree," he said.

"What a gruesome thought."

But I'd been out walking in similar wind storms at the risk of being blown off my feet. Also high winds spooked the dogs. I guessed I would be homebound.

Misty screeched as another tree fell across the lane, but Candy ran to the living room to investigate the crash through the bay window.

The wind was fairly howling. It sounded like a tortured soul being propelled around the house, which made me think of Lucy.

"You be careful too," I said, taking over the French toast making.

"I always am."

I dipped the first slice of bread into the egg mixture and hoped the wind wouldn't cause any more damage.

~ * ~

In late afternoon the winds died down, and an eerie silence descended on the lane. Could it be trusted? Whenever the wind acted strangely, I worried about tornadoes.

I stepped outside, scanning the sky for signs of an additional weather onslaught, but it looked clear. From my vantage point, I could see Jonquil Lane newly littered with downed branches, assorted debris blown out of the woods, and, of course, the fallen tree.

The dogs were whining, anticipating my decision. Which three would enjoy the first walk of the day?

Halley, Gemmy, and Misty. Sky, who was a breeze to walk, still lay under the oak table.

I leashed Gemmy and Misty and turned on the lane, in the opposite direction of the tree. Raven emerged from her house and trotted after us. A longer than usual rest had energized the dogs.

As we passed the abandoned construction, I glanced quickly at the ruins to see how they had fared in the wind storm. A tree had fallen here, too, squashing a portion of a wall that had managed to remain upright throughout the months. The remains of the unfinished mansions were as forbidding as ever, and I heard a suspicious rustling in the shadows.

Misty tried to lead us into the ruins as she always did. As always, I tugged on her leash until she fell into step with her sisters, and we walked on.

The lane needed a thorough cleaning. Twigs, branches, leaves, pages torn from newspapers, candy bar wrappers, empty soft drink containers, half a sandwich—that wouldn't last long—and half a paperback book in the middle of the lane.

I brought the dogs to a stop and stared at it.

It was a terribly mutilated book. I recognized the colors on the cover, then the title. Lucy's *Devilwish*.

The book had been torn in two, the half tossed in my path as if by a vicious hand. A heavy black X defaced the cover, and the pages were discolored. Not from an earlier rain. The damage might have been caused by a greenish liquid that saturated every page but didn't obscure the print. I had no idea what it could be.

"Stay," I told the dogs and picked the book up.

It felt damp and gritty. I slipped it into the empty plastic bag I carried to clean up after the dogs. It could be evidence of something. Of what I didn't know yet. Besides, for Lucy's sake, I didn't want to leave it lying in the lane.

~ * ~

Back home, I examined the book more closely. Possibly this was one of the library's copies, although it had no identifying stamp and the back half was missing. I leafed through it, looking for a name on the flyleaf or notes in the margin but found no sign that anyone had ever read it.

Had someone bought a copy of *Devilwish* merely to destroy it?

Naturally I had no intention of telling Lucy about my discovery, but as soon as possible I was going to return to the library. This could be one of the stolen books. If the new copies Miss Eidt ordered had arrived, was my plan to keep them out of sight working?

Leaving the *Devilwish* half in its plastic wrapper, I sat at my desk and reviewed all the strange happenings that had changed Lucy's life. First and perhaps strangest, the discovery of the stone collie statue in the woods, followed by the appearance of the two girls who resembled her characters at the library event. Brent had accounted for that anomaly.

Then tree that had damaged Dark Gable's roof. Easily explained. Lucy was not the only one in Foxglove Corners who had lost a tree. The blue horn. Not so obvious but perhaps innocuous. Finally the continuous parade of Lucy's books out of the library door.

Now that I viewed them from a distance, only the stone collie was truly a mystery. As for the missing books, perhaps here on the lane I had uncovered a clue that suggested a motive. Lucy had spoken of someone wanting to erase her existence from Foxglove Corners. Could she be right?

If so, she had an enemy, and it certainly wasn't a Voltarian. A real person hovered over her shoulder, figuratively, of course, waiting to turn her writing into personal disasters.

With this unsettling image, my thoughts came to a halt.

Because I was already sitting at my desk, I started writing my report for the Rescue League meeting. Heading the list was Honey, the new collie Zachary Drummond had installed behind the blue house.

Maybe after I had given my mind a rest, I would turn to Lucy's dilemma again and see something I'd missed.

Twenty-five

The wild winds of yesterday gave way to a glorious, calm summer day. Puffy white clouds moved lazily across a pure blue sky, and the air was fragrant with floral scents.

What is so rare as a day in June? Make that July.

I walked the dogs, stopping every now and then to toss manageable debris from the lane into a plastic bag. Later I planned to treat myself to a morning at the library. Later still, I'd attend the Rescue League meeting.

Enjoy the hours of sunshine and warmth, I thought, as I drove to the Corners. The days were flying by. All too soon we'd be in August, which meant school was waiting in the wings.

Dreary thought. I loved having free time to arrange my activities to suit my mood.

At the library, Miss Eidt had brought out the cardboard carousal again. In its new carnation it featured books by Michigan authors.

One of the paperbacks stood out because of the cover's soft pink and green colors. *Cherry Blossom Love* by Lily May Hill. A lightweight romance, I decided, by an author with a made up name.

Lucy wasn't in the line-up. How unfair, but until we solved the mystery of the disappearing books, it was best to keep her work out of sight.

I found Miss Eidt with a woman at a low section of shelves beneath a window. I recognized the brassy-haired, neon-clad woman who had wanted to check out *Devilwish* for her daughter's birthday and been so rude when informed it was unavailable. Her lime sundress had an eerie glow in the dim corner.

"That won't do," I heard the woman say. "Like I told you, I need one with pictures of clothing from all periods of American history."

It seemed to be reunion day at the library. Molly and Jennifer emerged from the stacks, dressed in jeans and pastel tops. Each girl carried three books. Collie art graced the covers of the ones in my view. The girls had apparently discovered Albert Payson Terhune.

After we'd greeted one other, I asked, "How is your new puppy? I'm afraid I forgot her name. Spice? Sugar?"

"Ginger," Jennifer said. "She's growing. Ginger is almost as big as your collies."

"I see you're reading one of my favorite authors," I said.

"There's a whole shelf of collie books by him," Molly added. "He's cool."

Neon Dress turned around, a disapproving frown creasing her face. "Be quiet. Don't you know this is a library?"

Miss Eidt's heightened color betrayed her annoyance. "They're not disturbing anyone. You'll love those books, girls. I used to read them when I was young."

"The same ones?" Jennifer asked.

"It's possible."

I remembered that when Miss Eidt had donated her family home to the town for a library she'd included books from her own collection.

"Excuse me, Miss Eidt. I believe you were helping me."

"There are several costume books back in the Theater section," Miss Eidt said to the woman and smiled at us as we moved toward the circulation desk. "I'm holding a book for you, Jennet. You're going to love it."

To my dismay, Brassy Hair followed us, clutching an oversized volume, the kind that seemed to exist primarily to adorn coffee tables.

That was quick, I thought. Or was she just nosy?

"Are you girls having a nice summer?" I asked.

"So far," Molly said. "We're going up north to our cabin in August. Jennifer and Ginger are coming, too."

"That'll be fun."

"We joined Miss Eidt's summer vacation book club," Jennifer added. "It's just for kids. We read a book a week and talk about it every Friday."

"Are you reading *Bruce* or *Treve*?" I asked.

"No. These books are just for us. It's Lucy Hazen week. We're reading *Devilwish*."

Wherever I turned I seemed to bump into *Devilwish*, although there were no copies in the library.

Debbie was on duty at the circulation desk. At present she was helping a girl with long pale yellow hair. The girl's dark green dress was long, a maxi, with a pattern of tiny flowers.

Miss Eidt sailed past the desk and beckoned to me. "Do you have time to join me in my office for a moment, Jennet?" she asked.

"Sure," I said and almost stepped on Neon Dress's toeless sandals. I didn't realize she was standing so close behind me.

"Sorry," I said, and to the girls, "I'll see you around. Enjoy your books."

"We're going to stay awhile and read," Molly said. "It's so nice and cool in here."

Miss Eidt's office was the coziest place in the library, part office and part kitchen. She had an apple cinnamon coffeecake and a tattered paperback, *To See a Stranger,* which she presented to me as if it were a treasure. As indeed it must be.

"I read it in one day," she said. "I found a box of old Gothics, about thirty, at an estate sale for five dollars. I'll share them with you, but I want to read them first."

She plugged in the teakettle and cut us each a slice of coffeecake. "I'm thinking, Jennet, if you give me a copy of your petition, I can ask some of the people who come to the library to sign it."

"That would help," I said. "Sue Appleton and I don't have enough signatures to convince anyone to level the construction."

I told her about my recent visit to Diadem Estates and how I'd been warned away from an old stone house that wasn't part of the development.

"That doesn't surprise me," Miss Eidt said. "I know the house you're referring to, although I wonder who's still alive to care."

I took a bite of coffeecake. Delicious. "Care about what?"

"The old scandal."

"What happened?"

"A most unusual old murder," she said. "It happened ages ago, but we don't have to rely on my memory. There's a book about it. We should have a copy. When we're finished, I'll find it for you."

"Who was murdered?" I asked.

"The Gorham family's daughter, Barbara. It's the strangest case. There didn't seem to be a motive, and no one was ever arrested for the crime. It's a perfect mystery for you."

"I'm intrigued, but I'm up to my neck in mysteries this summer."

"Such as?" Miss Eidt looked up from her teacup with interest.

"Such as Lucy's missing books."

"Oh, of course. By the way, the replacements haven't come in yet."

"Tell me about your new reading club," I said.

"I approached some of the kids I see on a regular basis with the idea of forming a book club just for the summer and assigned Lucy Hazen's *Devilwish* for our first read. I hoped someone would give herself away. They're all girls," she added. "Most of them bought their books at Lucy's library event."

"Have you had any luck?"

"We have our first meeting this Friday."

I wasn't sure what Miss Eidt hoped to accomplish. I almost told her about the defaced half copy of *Devilwish* I'd found on the lane but decided it was irrelevant. For now. Although I trusted Miss Eidt's discretion, I'd hate for Lucy to learn how someone had treated her book.

I ate the last bite of coffeecake and accepted another slice, a small one. Between Miss Eidt, Camille, and the dessert carousel at Cloves, I was going to gain weight if I hadn't already.

When we were finished, Miss Eidt said, "Let's go find that book about the murder. Who needs to read Gothic novels when we have real life mysteries in our midst?"

She carried the cups and plates over to a small sink. "I hope that unpleasant Jacelyn Holland is gone."

"Who's she?"

"That woman who wears the sundresses in the outrageous colors. She's the most unpleasant person I've ever met, and she's always here with some new request, demanding prompt attention. I guess she has no other life."

I had a name for Brassy Hair then, but hoped I wouldn't have to use it. She didn't sound like the kind of person I'd want to know.

When we left the office, though, Miss Eidt's nemesis was gone. No one lingered at the Circulation Desk except Blackberry, who looked immensely bored with her life. She wore a new collar with sparkly red stones.

A thought flitted through my mind but evaporated before I could grab it. It had something to do with...

"See you, Jennet," Molly said as the girls swept by us. "We're off to the Ice Cream Parlor."

On a day like this, that was a good idea.

Twenty-six

Collies were coming into Rescue at an alarming rate. Sue Appleton was running out of foster homes and responsible adoptive families. At present Sue had six collies in her home.

"We just placed three and have four more," she said. "We won't lower our standards. Our goal is to find good forever homes for our dogs. Not everyone who wants a collie is prepared to take care of one properly."

Too many collies, not enough homes. This was hardly news, and here was new member Dinah, a bubbly young woman with a brown ponytail, proudly showing off her six newborn tri's and sables. This was Dinah's first litter. She'd always wanted to have collie babies. To her they were the dearest of God's creatures. She hoped to get a good price for them.

On the surface, that was reasonable, but at the same time disturbing.

"My Thalia was bred to a Canadian champion," Dinah said. "So if you ladies want a show prospect puppy or know someone who does…"

She drew an envelope of pictures from her purse and passed them around to a chorus of ohs and 'how adorables'. I took a sip of ginger ale and rested my hand on the soft head of the magnificent blue merle who had chosen to lie at my feet.

River Rose Icemaker, known as Icy, had found a permanent home with Sue after a tragic turn in his young life, but I flattered myself that he remembered me and our time together in Rosalyn Everett's woods.

Collies don't forget people who have been kind to them.

Sue was frowning. Any minute she would continue talking.

I knew what she was thinking. My thoughts were similar. We were a rescue league, not a breeders' club. We didn't think of our dogs as a commodity but as a sacred trust.

Andrea, another new member who had been quiet until Dinah spoke about her litter, had a litter of her own. She was keeping one of her males.

"You have to be so careful when you choose a buyer," Andrea said. "I learned that lesson the hard way. My pups were nearing the three-month mark when this gentleman came along out of the blue and fell in love with two of my little girls. I sold them both to him, and he promised to keep in touch with me. But he gave me a false number. Probably a false name, too. And he seemed so nice."

Sue held on to her frown. No one else said anything, but disapproval was thick in the air.

I remembered Icy living in the wild through a bitter winter and Sparkle, our tri-headed white collie who had been rescued only to be lost again. Happily both collies had landed in wonderful homes. They were among the lucky ones.

"I watched him drive off with my babies," Andrea added. "I wonder what became of them."

They could have ended up anywhere, I thought. Then... Two sisters? Could it be...?

"Were they sable and white?" I asked.

"Why, yes. They were the sweetest little things."

I searched for my phone and hit camera roll.

"Do these puppies look familiar to you?"

As she viewed the images, the color seemed to drain from her face. "Yes. Yes, they do. My Linnet has this same ginger-colored mark on her chest. What a coincidence." Her voice trailed off. "Could these be my puppies?"

"Notice the chains," I said.

"What are you trying to say, Jennet?"

"These puppies were kept on chains without adequate food and water in my own neighborhood. Most of the time no one was home with them. You know what a hot summer we've been having."

Andrea's voice broke. "You said *were*?"

"They're fine now. I took these pictures and called the police. They're currently in the custody of Lieutenant Dalby of the Foxglove Corners Police Department. We call them Pepsi and Cola."

I glanced at the other members. "That was part of my report. Pepsi and Cola are safe now, but there's another collie, Honey, a little older, in their place. We're keeping an eye on her. The owner has been elusive. By the way, his name is Zachary Drummond, if he approaches anyone wanting a young unsprayed female rescue. He's tall, blond, and quite good looking."

"Can I see them?" Andrea asked. "To be sure?"

"I don't see why not."

"If they are Andrea's pups, do you think she can get them back?" Sue asked.

"I'm not a lawyer. Right now they're legally Drummond's property."

"He paid me twenty-four hundred dollars for them. I'm willing to refund his money, of course. He said his name was John Brown," she added.

John Brown indeed.

Emma Brock, one of our long time members, said, "A sale is a sale. Drummond may not be willing to part with the puppies."

"But if he bought them under false pretenses…" Andrea sounded desperate.

"He doesn't have them at the moment," I reminded her. "As it is, he's in hot water, facing a fine. At least."

"He wants them for breeding," Emma said. "To make money."

Andrea's voice took on a defensive note. "He didn't say that."

I felt the last of my patience slip away. "Of course. He wouldn't."

"He told me he grew up with a collie just like Linnet."

"As Andrea says, she's learned her lesson," Sue said.

"There's another lesson in the puppies' story," I added. "Be aware of what's going on in your own neighborhood. The house where I found Pepsi and Cola is unoccupied at present. We think Drummond is using the yard without the owner's permission."

"What about the dog who's there now?" Emma asked.

"I'll have an update on Honey the next time we meet."

"If anyone has room to foster a rescue, talk to me before you leave," Sue said.

It seemed to me that she singled out Dinah and Andrea for her request. Well, that was okay. The League was devoted to education along with rescue. God forbid a puppy bred by one of our own members would end up in Rescue one day.

~ * ~

Lucy had another dilemma, once again a development I had to see to believe. All she said on the phone was, "This was is different. I feel threatened again, but I don't want to call the police."

"Why not?

"Because it's too terrible."

A half hour later, I stood in front of Lucy's house surveying the mess on her front porch. It looked as if a flock of dark birds had landed in the midst of her wicker chairs and tables and died there.

Lucy, clad in her signature black, and Sky stood in the doorway unmoving like two figures in a tragedy.

I climbed the stairs and saw that the birds were paperback books, dozens of copies of *Devilwish* with heavy black X's defacing their front covers. Some of the books looked as if they had been soaked in water or some other liquid. Some pages were ripped. Others had burnt edges.

"I didn't move them," Lucy said. "I couldn't."

She had been crying. Sky, sensing her distress, nudged her hand, offering a collie's unique brand of sympathy.

"Well, we have to eventually," I said.

"My books," Lucy whispered. "All my books."

"These could be the missing books from the library."

I couldn't just move them aside with my foot to make a path for myself. Instead I picked some of them up and set them on the table. I had room to pass then, and I'd clear the rest before I left.

But what would we do with them?

"When did this happen?" I asked.

"They weren't there when I went to bed. I heard Sky barking in the night but didn't get up to investigate. She usually barks at deer and night creatures."

An enemy who worked in darkness then. A coward.

"This is terrible," I said.

I followed Lucy inside and she closed the door with unnecessary force. Shutting out evil.

"But you're right," I said. "This is different, and it tells us there's nothing supernatural about what has been happening. We need to look for a human agent."

She nodded. "I didn't write remotely anything like this. In fact I haven't written anything in days."

"That's terrible, too, Lucy. You're a professional. You can't let these ugly incidents bring your career to a halt."

"Somebody hates my books," she said.

Impulsively I hugged her. "Your books are wonderful, Lucy. They're filled with vampires and werewolves and zombies and other weird creatures, but you also write about courage and guilt and repentance and forgiveness."

"I've tried."

"And kids love them. You've had ample proof of that over the years. Just look at how many people came to your library event."

"That's true," she said. "But somebody hates me and I can't help worrying about what's going to happen next."

Twenty-seven

"We have to do something to help Lucy," Brent said that night as we made ourselves comfortable in the living room. "She's worried about what's going to happen next."

He had joined us for a roast beef dinner, invited by Crane who had run into him at the Lakeside Diner. Brent had just come from visiting Lucy and was enraged at the latest blow delivered to her.

I looked around at the familiar scene. Our friend in the chair he invariably claimed as his own, my husband, our dogs always with us. I couldn't imagine any malign force attempting to alter our world.

"I agree," I said. "But what?"

Brent patted his knee, and Misty leaped into his lap, all sixty pounds of her.

"First we'll give her damaged books an honorable burial. We're having a bonfire at Dark Gables tomorrow. Can you bring the marshmallows? And the graham crackers and chocolate?"

"You're turning it into a party," Crane said.

"Why not? Lucy needs cheering up."

"And then?" I asked.

"We find out who's harassing her. Lucy thinks she's the object of somebody's hatred. I think her books are the real target."

"That makes sense," I said, remembering the dark black X's that defaced their covers.

'X' for condemned?

"Some nutcase thinks her books are dangerous," Brent added.

"A nutcase with money. Whoever dumped those books on Lucy's porch parted with about two hundred dollars just to make a point."

"Maybe they weren't all new," Crane pointed out. "Could be you found the missing books from the library."

"You're right. Not all, though. I checked."

"Lucy didn't do anything to deserve this," Brent said. "She's such a good person. Do you know she sends money to Letty and Lila Woodville at the Foxglove Corners Animal Shelter every month? She donates her books to shelters for abused women and kids and to children's hospitals. She funds a grant for aspiring young writers. There's more."

"I didn't know that," I said, "but it doesn't surprise me."

"I wonder if the person behind this book trashing is the one who left the horn on her property. And maybe the collie statue, too. Who knows?"

"I don't see how a statue in the woods ties in with the attack on her books," I said.

"Lots of weird stuff has been happening to Lucy. Maybe the books are only a part of it."

"We can eliminate the tree that fell and the girls at the library event. The horn? Lucy jumped to the conclusion that it was a unicorn because of something the Voltarians did in her story. I have another thought. Who or what else has a horn?"

"The devil?" Crane said.

"Exactly."

"*Devilwish*," he said. "Our perpetrator has zeroed in on that book."

The image of all the ruined paperbacks piled on Lucy's porch like mounds of dead blackbirds leaped into my mind.

"That's true. Most of the vandalized books were *Devilwish*, but not all of them."

"What's *Devilwish* about?" Crane asked.

"It's the story of teenagers who make a bargain with the devil for frivolous favors, then try to get out of it."

"Our vandal objects to Lucy's use of Satan, then," Brent said.

"The problem is who's to know what another reader will object to?" I said. "I've read many of Lucy's books. They all have upbeat endings. If she portrays a battle between good and evil, good is always victorious."

"We have to anticipate what this person will do next," Brent said.

"How could we?"

He shook his head. "Lucy used to be able to look into the future sometimes. She says now all she sees is a blank. She's taking this personally."

"Well, she should," I said. "It *is* personal."

"She's afraid someone may harm her or Sky or try to do damage to the house. I suggested she have a surveillance camera installed but she doesn't want something so modern in her home. So I'm going to offer to let her borrow Napoleon."

Napoleon was Brent's faithful guard dog, a gigantic, intimidating animal with a good heart. He would do whatever Brent told him to do.

"I wonder how he'll get along with Sky," I said.

"Just fine. They've already met. But nothing we do is really helping, is it?"

"I wouldn't say that. A festive bonfire will lift Lucy's spirits. I think it's a good idea, Brent. It just seems a little like book burning."

"That's what it is," Crane pointed out. "These books have already been destroyed. We're not the book burners here."

"I'll get the marshmallows and other stuff together," I said.

"Lucy's buying the hot dogs and buns. We'll have fun."

And we'd be sending a message. Unfortunately, Lucy's tormentor wouldn't be there to hear it.

Not having the ingredients for s'mores in the house, I took a quick trip to Blackbourne's Grocers the next morning. As was my habit, I stopped at the blue house on Jonquil Lane.

I didn't like the deep quiet that surrounded the place.

The back yard was empty. No food, no water bowl. No Honey.

What had happened to her?

I could think of only one answer. Drummond had moved her somewhere for some reason that eluded me. Every now and then, Pepsi and Cola had disappeared from the blue house, too, only to return.

So don't be too concerned.

Good advice, but I couldn't take it.

Obviously Drummond had another location. He slept and ate elsewhere and perhaps kept other young female collies there. How did an empty house on Jonquil Lane fit into his scheme?

Somehow I had to find him and assure myself that Honey was safe. I could only guess at her age, but I suspected she might have had her first season, might already have been bred.

The thought of innocent collie babies born to make money for their owner tormented me. I saw them, sweet and winsome and ultimately unwanted by their unwilling owners, in a steady parade toward the Rescue League or Animal Shelter. I could almost see Drummond counting his hundred dollar bills with glee. All that mattered to him was making a profit.

The pictures were too painful to sustain.

The weeping willow cast shadows that seemed to fill the entire yard. That wasn't possible. If I were Lucy, I would say that the unnatural darkness on the hot morning was a sign of coming disaster.

Think about marshmallows and chocolate and graham crackers, I ordered myself. *Imagine sending Lucy's ravaged books to a better place.*

Feeling bereft, I walked back to the lane. I couldn't do anything about the situation at the moment, and I had grocery shopping to do.

~ * ~

Coincidences are common in fiction and occasionally in life, but more often found in fiction.

At Blackbourne's, I steered my cart into the baking aisle, wondering how many packages of marshmallows I should buy. Ahead of me stood the man who had recently filled my thoughts, Zachary Drummond. He wore Levi's and a moss green vest, and, I had to admit, was very handsome.

I moved my cart closer. He had an impressive supply of barbecued spare ribs from the hot food case in his cart and enough beer to satisfy the thirst of a good-sized party. He appeared to be checking out the cooking oils.

What stopped me in my tracks, though, was the gun belt strapped to his waist, plainly visible.

We weren't in the Wild West, for heaven's sake. Didn't anyone else notice that he was armed? Was I the only one shocked by the sight?

Quickly I tossed eight packages of marshmallows into my cart and steered it toward Drummond just as he reached the end of the aisle. I had almost overtaken him when I realized I'd walked into a confrontation. Coming to a standstill, I listened.

Grayson, Blackbourne's manager, was talking quietly to Drummond, apparently telling him he would have to leave.

"We don't allow firearms in the store. It's always been our policy."

"I have a right to arm myself," Drummond said. "Did you ever hear of Open Carry?"

"You're not bringing a weapon into my store," Grayson countered. "There's no need. Someone might get hurt."

"I have my rights," Drummond said.

"So do my customers."

They had drawn a crowd, a sea of curious faces. No one came too near the antagonists. In fact, from where I stood, I could see the front door. It seemed that an inordinate number of shoppers were hurrying to the parking lot as if they feared the argument might escalate into gunfire.

The papers were filled with stories of madmen opening fire in public places. But this couldn't happen in Blackbourne's on a sunny morning in Foxglove Corners. Could it?

Of course it could.

So you'd better back up. Talk about courting danger.

"What's the trouble here?"

A new voice, deep and authoritative, entered the fray. A young man in a navy blue uniform stepped out of the crowd. Firemen were a familiar sight in the store, as members of the Foxglove Corners Fire Department shopped in the store every day for the groceries they used for cooking meals at the station.

"No trouble," Drummond snapped. With a muttered curse, he gave his cart a push, right into Grayson's path. Grayson jumped out of the way just in time to avoid a collision.

"I'm going to find another place to take my business," Drummond barked. "Don't think this is over. It isn't. Not by a long shot."

His audience gave him a wide berth as he stamped out of the store, leaving his filled cart behind.

"All right," Grayson said. "Excitement's over. Everybody, carry on."

Grayson was a good actor, but I could see that he was shaken. He and the fireman were engaged in a subdued conversation at the bread section.

I was a bit shaken myself. I knew that volatile, gun-toting man. I'd challenged him about his treatment of his collies. I'd threatened him. Good grief!

It was a great effort to gather the rest of the party supplies and take my place in line at the register. All anyone could talk about was the gunman.

I wished Mac could have been there.

Twenty-eight

The flames licked the air, raising the temperature around Brent's bonfire by several degrees. I stepped back to join Lucy, who stood watching the conflagration with Sky on one side and Napoleon on the other.

Contrary to expectation, the bonfire did not cheer her. Her long black dress and silky cardigan reminded me of Halloween and all sorts of grotesques that belonged to another season. I suspected that Brent's plan had backfired, that she regarded the burning of her books as a second ravishment.

"I haven't had toasted marshmallows since I was a kid," I said to lighten the atmosphere. "You can't build bonfires in Oakpoint. Well, you can, but you'd be breaking the law."

"That's one of the many advantages of living in the country," Lucy said. "No one can tell you what to do on your own land."

Apparently satisfied that the fire was under control, Brent joined us. "Do you know how to make s'mores, Jennet? I forgot to ask."

"Sure. Just spread melted chocolate and marshmallows on graham crackers," I said. "Or we could just toast the marshmallows."

"Let's do both."

Lucy slipped her fingers under Sky's collar. At some point, the collie had grown agitated.

"Stay," she said, then more loudly, "Stay!"

Napoleon did the opposite. With a deep growl, he dashed into the woods, bypassing the picnic table with its leftover hot dogs and other temptations.

"Napoleon!" Brent's voice boomed over the crackling flames. "What got into that dog? I told him to stay by Lucy's side."

"We have an intruder," I said.

Someone who had seen our fire and wanted to investigate? Or a person who had wandered onto Lucy's property for some nefarious purpose?

Sky whined, frantically pawing the ground. She wrenched herself out of Lucy's grasp and took off after Napoleon.

"Sky!" Lucy cried. She turned to me. "She never does that."

"Usually it's only you and Sky. Napoleon has opened up new worlds for her."

"Watch the fire, Jennet," Brent said. "I'll see what's up with those hounds."

"No, Brent," Lucy said.

But it was too late. Brent had reached the woods' edge and in a moment was lost in a tangle of vines and close-growing trees.

"Something bad is going to happen," Lucy said. "It's been quiet for too long."

"Can you tell?" I asked.

"I see a dark mist settling over the woods and feel cold. It's like a wind is coming up."

"I hope not," I said, thinking of the bonfire. In my view, the woods were clear, and it was far from cold. A savvy woodsman like Brent would never build a fire in unsafe conditions.

But Lucy's wind was unnatural, a product of her own conjuring. For myself, I was too warm. Bonfires are meant for chilly autumn days. I'd never been this near one when the temperature soared into the eighties.

Mesmerized by the dancing flames, I stared into the fire and let my thoughts wander. Fire and smoke. Burning books, devils, and tormented souls. Pitchforks... I was looking at the long-handled forks Lucy had brought out for the marshmallow roast.

Did anyone in the real world ever consider making a bargain with the devil, or was that the providence of horror fiction?

You never knew what people would do. Didn't some misguided souls still worship the devil? The Satanists?

I breathed in the smell of acrid smoke. Images of encroaching darkness overwhelmed my mind. Whoever or whatever wished to harm Lucy seemed to be present with us, watching our fire. Gloating.

Which was impossible.

The fire had done its work well, reducing Lucy's books to ashes. Here and there I glimpsed a page or charred cover that had survived the flames. It was as if they had made one last desperate attempt to escape.

Get a grip, Jennet, I told myself. *It's just a bonfire. Brent built it.*

"I wish they'd hurry back," Lucy said.

And I wished Crane had been able to be with us. He'd throw cold water on my wild imaginings and provide back-up for Brent if he ran into trouble.

Fifteen slow minutes ticked by. The ashes smoldered. Lucy shivered and drew her black cardigan closer around her body. Finally the trio emerged from the woods, Brent unfazed, and the dogs' fur covered with burrs and leaf bits. Sky's tail was wagging, a good sign. Poor dog. She didn't often have a chance to go on an adventure.

"What did you find?" Lucy asked.

"Nothing. The dogs were sniffing around the statue, but I didn't see any sign of an intruder."

"Around the statue?" Lucy echoed.

"Something must have attracted their attention," I said.

"Probably, but it was long gone by the time I got there."

"I don't like this," Lucy said.

Brent put his arm around her. "Don't be afraid," he said. "I'm here. I can stay as long as you need me."

His words seemed to calm her. I reached for a package of marshmallows.

"Time for dessert," I said.

~ * ~

Lucy wanted to go to the library.

"Miss Eidt told me she received a shipment of my books," she said. "I want to see if they're still there."

I knew the cardboard carousel that formerly showcased her work featured other authors. Lucy had agreed that her books would be safer behind the desk.

"We'll go in the morning," I said. "I'm out of reading material."

By that I meant I'd read the Gothic novel Miss Eidt had given me. I remembered she had a box of old paperbacks she planned to share with me.

The bonfire had driven thoughts of Zachary Drummond, grocery store cowboy, temporarily out of my mind. What if he came into the library wearing his gun belt? Miss Eidt wasn't used to dealing with his kind. Because it was summertime, kids flocked to the library. What was the day of Miss Eidt's book club again?

Should I advise Miss Eidt to hire a guard? Or was I overreacting? Was Drummond even a reader?

The library needed Napoleon.

"Are you working on *The Stone Collie*?" I asked Lucy.

"I haven't been. Maybe when this is over…"

She didn't define 'this.' She didn't have to.

Like Lucy, I found myself waiting for the next disturbing happening.

~ * ~

When we walked up to the library the next morning, when I saw Blackberry resting on a wicker chair, watching us with wary emerald eyes, I remembered a fleeting thought I'd had a few days ago.

Throughout the ages, black cats have been associated with the devil, to the extent that their nine lives are sometimes in danger, especially at Halloween which was months away. Still...

This thought would never have occurred to Miss Eidt, but I was sure she was careful with Blackberry simply because she had grown to love her.

An armed man in the library, a black cat in peril because of her color... Surely I was manufacturing trouble where none existed. Didn't we have enough on our plate already?

Miss Eidt appeared to be entirely free of worldly care. Instead of a suit she wore a soft peach shirtwaist dress with her favorite accessory, a double strand pearl necklace.

I'd just slip a mention of an open carry advocate in town into the conversation. Later, before we left.

Lucy's glance fell on the carousel.

Miss Eidt hastened to explain. "I can't keep your books on the shelves, Lucy."

"I know," Lucy said.

"I haven't unpacked the new shipment yet. From now on, anyone who wants to check out one of your books has to go through me or Debbie."

"I'm sorry it's come to that."

"Well..." Miss Eidt was seldom at a loss for words, but she seemed flustered.

"Let's check out the competition," Lucy said. "I may know some of these other writers."

She touched the carousel, spun it gently around. It had eight shelves, each one jammed with hardcovers and paperbacks all penned by writers in our state. Ironically she singled out the pink and green book I'd noticed earlier.

"*Cherry Blossom Love*," she said, not quite concealing her disdain. "I never read romance. All those 'happily ever afters'. They're not realistic."

"Some people would say neither are vampires and werewolves," I said. "No offense, Lucy."

She couldn't hide her blush either. "None taken. I guess I shouldn't criticize my fellow artists."

"Look," I said. "Here's another one. *Cherry Blossom Wedding*, and here's *Cherry Blossom Family*. I wonder what comes next."

All three books shared the same pastel pink and green color scheme with a beautiful young couple on the cover in a frame of cherry blossoms.

"I wonder who this Lily May Hill is," she said, scanning the back cover of the *Love* book. "It just says she's a lifelong Michigan resident. The winner of the *Golden Dove Award*. I've never heard of that."

"I think Lily May Hill is a pen name," I said. "It goes so well with all those cherry blossoms."

"It certainly fits her genre." Lucy replaced the paperback and pulled another off the shelf. "Jennet, look!"

She held a copy of *Devilwish*. A heavy black X defaced the cover.

"Here's one they missed," I said. "This connects the library with the books that ended up on your porch."

"Well, someone who frequents the library."

She opened the book, found the library stamp, and frowned. "This narrows it down. The person who's making these things happen stood right here at the carousel."

"Let's show Miss Eidt," I said.

Twenty-nine

Miss Eidt's hand trembled as she reached for the defaced copy of *Devilwish*. "Oh, Lucy, I'm so sorry."

"It isn't your fault," Lucy said.

"But it is. I should be aware of what's happening in my library." Quickly Miss Eidt whisked the book out of sight behind the circulation desk.

"How could you be aware of something so subtle? I asked.

"I wonder if all my books are marked with an X," Lucy said. "And if whoever did this marked them in the library or somewhere else."

"Have you ever seen anyone with a black magic marker near the carousel?" I asked.

"No, but kids congregated around the carousel all the time before Lucy's books started disappearing. A marker could be out of sight, in a pocket or a purse. I see lots of kids sitting at tables with pens doing schoolwork, but not in the summer."

"It's a mystery," Lucy said.

"Not one we can't solve." In truth, I had no idea how to solve it, but we had to stay positive.

"I'll have Debbie search every shelf again," Miss Eidt said. "I don't want anyone else to come across a copy in this condition."

She beckoned to Debbie, who was pushing an empty cart back to the desk.

"Debbie, will you take over for about ten minutes?"

As Debbie took her place on the librarian's high stool, Miss Eidt turned to us. "Let's have a cup of tea in my office. Jennet, I have two more Gothics for you."

Lucy seemed anxious to leave the library, but I imagined she couldn't find a ready excuse to turn down Miss Eidt's invitation.

Miss Eidt's cozy office restored an air of serenity to the situation. As she plugged in the tea kettle, Lucy sank wearily into a seat around the table. "It's one blow after another," she murmured. "When will it end?"

"Let's create a profile," I said. "Who would be likely to object to the subject matter of Lucy's books?"

"An over-protective parent?" Miss Eidt rummaged in a cupboard and brought out a package of gingersnaps. "Occasionally a mother points out a passage she finds offensive, but it's rare. I don't think most parents are aware of what their kids read or they don't care. Anyway, look what they can find on television and the Internet."

"Has anyone complained lately?" I asked.

"Not in a couple of years, and never about one of Lucy's books."

"Well, how about somebody who has an obsessive desire to eradicate the evil from the world?"

"That's impossible," Lucy said. "Anyway, why start with my book?"

"This person considers any reference to Satan evil. By the way, here's something I just realized. *Devilwish* sounds like devilish."

Miss Eidt set tall mugs in front of us and arranged the cookies on a paper plate. "Crusaders with their own agendas. Like that Angel woman who writes letters to the editor in the *Banner*. There was one just the other day."

"I don't recall seeing it," I said, "but then in the summer I don't read the paper every day. I'll have to make an effort to keep up with the news."

"She signs her letters Angela White," Miss Eidt said. "Her latest target is the movie industry, but she's ranted against salacious reading material, too. She wanted *The Grapes of Wrath* removed from the eleventh grade English curriculum at Lakeville High School."

"Did they give in to her?" I asked.

"No. She even went before the Board."

Lucy scoffed. "Angela White. Another made-up name with a message."

"Who else has a made-up name?" Miss Eidt asked.

"That romance writer, Lily May Hill," I said.

"Oh, I think that's her real name. She approached me about giving a talk on her writing career at the library. I think she got the idea from you, Lucy."

"Ah ha!" I said. "I have a new idea for our profile. Suppose our vandal is a jealous writer?"

"I don't think one author would go so far as to trash someone else's books," Lucy said.

"Trash?" Miss Eidt echoed. "Literally?"

I remembered then that Miss Eidt didn't know about the recent happenings at Dark Gables. I glanced at Lucy.

"Someone dumped a load of my books marked with black X's on my front porch," Lucy said. "Some of them had been burned or torn."

"My goodness. That's... that's harassment. It's insane. It's even worse than stealing them."

"Some of them came from the library," I said.

But how could one person take so many books from the library?" Miss Eidt asked.

"One by one. Or maybe there's more than one person involved."

Miss Eidt's face lost much of its color. "What on earth are we dealing with here?"

"More than stolen books," I said. "Do you know everyone who uses the library?"

"I couldn't possibly know everyone who comes in here. Only the regulars. Only those with cards on file."

"Could you make a list for us?" Lucy asked.

"Yes, but whoever did this doesn't necessarily have a library card," I pointed out.

For some reason, that reminded me of Zachary Drummond and the warning I'd meant to give Miss Eidt.

"All kinds of people live in Foxglove Corners," I said. "Not all of them are well meaning. Recently a man made a fuss about being allowed to bring his gun into Blackbourne's Grocers. You might start paying more attention to who comes into the library and tell Debbie to do the same."

Miss Eidt's hand shook as she poured the tea. "This is too much all at once. Where did our peaceful summer go?"

"I don't know how," I said, "but we'll make it peaceful again."

~ * ~

Before we left the library, Miss Eidt gave me two more treasures from her Gothic box, *Haldane Station* and *Nine Coaches Waiting*.

"What do you think about the Stone House murder?" she asked.

I searched my mind quickly and came up empty.

"Which murder?"

"About the cold case of Barbara Gorham. Remember the book I found for you the last time you were in the library?

I remembered then. At the time it had sounded so intriguing, and I'd recently been warned away from the stone house when collecting signatures for the petition. How could I have forgotten about it?

"I didn't get to it yet," I said. "I've been busy. Too many mysteries."

At the moment I couldn't recall where I'd stashed it. Wherever it was, the petition was inside. I was neglecting too many projects, cramming too much into my mind.

Like Blackberry.

"Where's Blackberry?" I asked.

"Isn't she outside? As long as it isn't too hot, she likes to sit on the porch and watch the world go by."

"With all these odd happenings, maybe you should keep an eye on her, too," I said.

She looked puzzled. "Why?"

"Because of their association with witchcraft," Lucy said. "Devils. Evil."

"It's probably all right, but better safe than sorry. Well, we'd better go," I said.

Now that we'd given poor Miss Eidt even more to worry about.

Better safe than sorry, I repeated to myself.

Thirty

A red-hot sun burned down on the yellow Victorian. For a moment, it looked as if the house were made of pineapple ice cream and marshmallow topping, both melting in the heat.

Camille sat on the wraparound sipping her morning beverage with Twister and Holly lying at her feet. The dogs barked their welcome as I crossed the lane.

I climbed the stairs and joined Camille in one of the wicker chairs.

"You're up early," she said.

"Always. I get up with Crane."

I gave Holly a gentle pat on her velvety head. She never forgot that once for a brief time she had been my dog. Neither did I.

"It's going to be another hot day," Camille added.

"It's been a hot summer."

So much for weather talk.

But oh, it was sweltering beyond the air-cooled rooms of my house. Crisp and smooth only a few hours ago, my sleeveless cotton blouse felt clammy.

"Do you keep your back issues of the *Banner*?" I asked.

"Until the stack grows too high. Why?"

"I want to read some letters to the editor I missed."

"Every now and then there's a real treasure," she said. "Mostly it's just politics or petty complaints. Usually I just read the editorials."

"The letters I'm looking for may lead us to the person who's been harassing Lucy."

"Hasn't that stopped?"

"No, and I have a feeling that time is running out. Something else is going to happen. Something worse."

"It's unconscionable," Camille said. "Lucy never hurt anybody. Just the opposite. Now someone comes along and brings her career to a standstill."

"She's afraid to write another scene for fear it'll happen in real life. Like a demented echo. I think her enemy is using a different approach, though. A more direct one."

"Come inside and have a cup of tea," Camille said. "The old newspapers are in the basement."

We all trooped inside where ceiling fans cooled the air. I waited in the kitchen for the teakettle to boil while Camille disappeared into the basement to look for the papers. In a few minutes she brought up about twenty *Banners*, and we divided them.

"Look for the name Angela White," I said, turning to the first editorial page.

The teakettle whistled, papers rustled. Twister put his paws on the counter, searching for sweet treats, but Camille hadn't done her daily baking yet. Holly sat at my side, watching me. Occasionally she uttered a tiny whimper.

"Here's one," I said. "Listen to this."

Today's children are steadily being incorporated into Satan's army. Schools and libraries, which should be safe and godly places, have become breeding grounds for young Satanists. Do you know what books your child is reading right this minute? What books he's exposed to? Visit your public library and the local book stores. Wake up before it's too late and godliness is leached out of the younger generation.

"It says Angela White is from Maple Creek. I wonder if the writer really lives there."

Camille shrugged. "Only the paper knows. She certainly doesn't mince words."

"Ms. White is waging a losing battle," I said. "Once kids begin to read on their own, parents have lost control. Besides, I don't think books are the greatest threat. These days more kids spend time with their electronics than reading books."

"Lucy's books are hardly salacious," Camille said.

"I'll bet this White woman has never read one. She just gathered up all the Lucy Hazen books she could find and destroyed them. What possible good did that do?"

"She wanted to make a point. She made it and made certain Lucy knew." Camille brought a pair of scissors out of a drawer. "Clip this letter, but let's keep looking. There may be more."

In all we found five letters to the editor, all variations on the same theme, all obviously penned by the same avid crusader. Angela White. She found evil in books, plays, movies, music, and even art, in particular the obscene garden statue Miss Eidt had added to the garden behind the library. I'd never noticed it.

I knew the *Banner* would never reveal the addresses of their letter writers. How, then, could I hope to find her?

Maple Creek had a sizeable population. I could look up Angela White in the directory and even online, but felt certain it was a pen name. Then, assuming I found her, what would I do? Introduce myself, accuse her of harassing Lucy, leave myself open to a lawsuit?

No, I didn't see myself doing any of the above.

My intention was to learn more about her, if possible. Perhaps I'd enlist Brent's aid. He had an impressive network of friends who always came through for him, no matter the problem.

I took the clippings home with me. Whoever she was, Ms. White appeared to have an enormous amount of time to devote to her campaign. Perhaps time to hang around the library.

Miss Eidt was already aware of the letters. She was also, unfortunately, a bit naïve, too inclined to lose herself in books while the real world went by.

I, on the other hand, had a suspicious nature. So far I'd wondered about the woman I'd nicknamed Brassy Hair and romance writer, Lily May Hill. Add to the list the woman who called herself Angela White. I had no idea what the last two women looked like.

In fact, either or both might be men.

Besides waiting for Lucy's nemesis to strike again, I decided to spend more time at the library, more time observing. Also, I'd visit local bookstores and see if they had any of Lucy's work on their shelves or if Angela White—or those sympathetic to her cause—had bought all the forbidden books in stock.

I saw Angela White as a dark figure, her face obscure, with a broom in her hand, traveling through the county sweeping up dangerous novels. She'd bring her book burning mentality to whoever would listen to her and stop at nothing to further her goals.

Meanwhile Lucy stood in her way—Lucy and her band of fictitious demons and witches and vampires.

Whether or not Angela White was the person bedeviling Lucy, a woman with such a vicious mindset was a definite danger.

~ * ~

I had been expecting Leonora to come home from her western vacation for days. Still I was surprised to see her at my kitchen door the next morning.

Tanned, all in white and apparently well rested, she greeted the collies individually and slipped into the seat she usually chose at the oak table. She had let her golden hair grow. Lightly skimming her shoulders, it caught the rays of light pouring through the window.

"I had a glorious time, but I'm so glad to be home," she said. "All last night I kept dreaming that I was still in the car."

I put water on to boil for tea and searched the freezer for the coffeecake I'd made yesterday. There it was—blueberry pecan. I unwrapped it and placed it in the microwave to defrost.

"Did you meet any interesting men on your trip?" I asked.

"A few but none to compare to Jake. Wafer and Lass were great icebreakers. Maybe I should try my hand at writing a romance."

"You'd better get started then. Summer vacation is half over." I glanced at the calendar. I could take my own advice. I, too, had a work-in-progress, my so-called spirit book, that I'd hardly touched this summer.

"What was it like traveling with two collies?" I asked.

"A trip." Leonora laughed. "The dogs are exhausted. I'm energized. What's been happening in Foxglove Corners?"

"Mystery and mayhem," I said. "But not murder, not yet. And we have a gun-toting villain and a collie in distress. Maybe more than one."

By the time I'd filled her in on all she'd missed, the coffeecake was defrosted and our tea was ready.

"Poor Lucy," she said. "That's so bizarre. I never thought anything could rattle her. Can't she use her powers to figure out what's going on?"

"They don't work that way," I said, then elaborated on my theory that Angela White, self-appointed demon slayer, was behind the trashing of Lucy's books.

"Clearly you need help," Leonora said. "You need me. Where do we start?"

"I'm open to ideas. I'm going to ask Brent to help. In the meantime, we're all waiting for what will happen next."

"What about Honey?" she asked.

"Well, I haven't seen her," I said, "and I check every time I drive past the blue house."

"I saw a lot of guys carrying guns out west," Leonora said. "It seemed natural there, but a grocery store in Foxglove Corners is the last place I'd expect to find an armed man."

She broke her leftover coffeecake into pieces. "May I?" she asked. "I can't resist those half-starved looks any longer."

I nodded. Candy was the first to reach Leonora, the first to wolf down a chunk of my cake. The others crowded around her, eager for their share of the largesse.

"I've missed you, babies," she said. "Let's make a plan for tomorrow, Jen."

"I thought I'd spend some time in the library."

"That's not very exciting."

"No, but it's a beginning. I want to see if Miss Eidt can tell me something about this romance writer, Lily May Hill. Then there's a rude woman with brassy hair. She'd make a good villain. She was acting suspicious the last time I was in the library."

"I'll go home and finish unpacking," she said. "Tomorrow we'll start sleuthing."

As she talked, I felt hopeful for the first time in weeks. Annica and I were a good mystery solving duo, but now, with Leonora, we'd be a formidable force.

Thirty-one

The next morning, Leonora and I met at the Mill House for breakfast. I had scrambled eggs for Crane earlier and had eaten only a slice of toast. But now, at a more reasonable hour, I was hungry.

"Buttermilk pancakes and bacon," I decided, closing the menu. "Grapefruit juice and coffee."

"I'm having a spinach omelet," Leonora said.

"I used to meet Crane here for breakfast every Sunday before we were married."

I glanced at the cozy décor. Green gingham checked tablecloths, wildflower centerpieces, and on the walls vintage photographs of the original mill house that gave the restaurant its name. I recalled that one of the young waitresses, Susan Miller, had a crush on Crane. Crane and her brother used to be deer-hunting pals. I didn't see her. I remembered that she'd talked about a career in law enforcement.

"How romantic," Leonora said.

"It was. In those days, I didn't have to cook at an ungodly hour."

But that wasn't fair to Crane. Sometimes he cooked breakfast for both of us.

I let the memories wash over me. Those had been happy days when love was new. I'd had one collie then—Halley—and one hope—to be the wife of the handsome gray-eyed deputy sheriff who had stolen my heart.

In one way, life in my new town that first summer had been uncomplicated but touched with uncertainty. Did Crane love me? Would we have a future together or just an endless stream of breakfasts at the Mill House and casual dates as seasons changed? Then one autumn, I received a proposal when I least expected it.

"I'd like to add to our agenda today," Leonora said, bringing me back to earth. "I've been wondering about River Rose and what's happening there."

"Nothing much, I suppose."

In truth, between Lucy's dilemma and the Zachary Drummond situation, I hadn't thought about River Rose in weeks. The last time I'd seen it, there'd been signs of improvement such as painting and a late spring clean-up of the grounds and painting. I had planned to ask Rosalyn Everett's neighbor whether she had met the new owner, but promptly forgot about it.

"Now I'm curious," I said.

I spied our waitress approaching with breakfasts on a tray and smelled the rich aroma of coffee wafting through the air.

"Let's go," I said. "Right after the library."

~ * ~

Miss Eidt's rainbow-hued annuals glistened in the morning light, having been recently soaked with water. Everything in my view was lush and green. Debbie took good care of the grounds, along with being indispensable to Miss Eidt in the library.

A pair of emerald eyes glittered from the safety of a flowering bush. Blackberry the cat watched our approach with wary eyes. She was motionless and aloof, not like a bouncing, joyful collie.

Well, Blackberry was a cat, not a dog.

Leonora veered toward the porch steps.

"Wait!" I said. "I want to check out the back yard."

"Why?"

"To see the obscene garden statue that aroused Angela White's ire."

We followed a path of broken concrete to the back yard, and I opened the gate of the white picket fence, always kept closed but never locked. From the Foxglove Corners Animal Shelter next door, the barking of several dogs mixed with the sound of splashing water.

"An obscene statue doesn't sound like something Miss Eidt would have in her yard," Leonora said.

"I agree. Let's see what Angela White considers obscene."

The library's yard contained a decades-old fountain that had been on the property when the house had belonged to Miss Eidt's family, before she donated it to the town. And there was the statue, in pieces, most of them lying in a bed of crushed blue delphiniums.

"Oh, no," Leonora said. "How did this happen?"

"Three guesses."

"The wind?"

"I don't think it was an act of God. If the wind blew the statue over, it would have landed in the grass. This looks like it came in contact with concrete—or someone smashed it with a hammer."

"Why would anyone do that?"

"I'm guessing, but Lucy's so-called salacious books are ruined, and Miss Eidt's statue is broken. I see a pattern."

When whole, the statue had been a huntress, long tresses partially hiding her bare breasts. The maiden's head had broken off at the neck. It lay in a tangle of smashed flowers surrounded by small pieces of concrete. Where her face had been was a sad, caved-in expanse of stone. A few feet away I saw a slender pale arm. The hand still held a bow.

"I wonder if Miss Eidt knows," Leonora said.

"We'll have to tell her."

I searched among the shattered bits of concrete looking for what had been the statue's face but couldn't find it.

"This damage makes me think I'm on the right track," I said. "Our enemy is familiar with the library."

"And Lucy isn't the only one on the receiving end of the vendetta, or whatever you want to call it."

I was suddenly afraid for Miss Eidt.

~ * ~

I expected her to be surprised. Upset. Angry. Anything but tearful.

When I told her what had happened to her statue, she insisted on leaving the library to see for herself. As she surveyed the wreck, she wiped impatiently at her eyes.

"It's only a statue," she said. "Just a thing. But Brent gave it to me for my birthday last month. It was so pretty. Do you think it can be repaired?"

"No," Leonora said.

I bent once again to sift through the pieces of broken concrete. "Well, if we find the face... If the pieces are all here..."

"I wonder how it happened," she said. "Do you suppose some animal knocked it down? One of those squirrels maybe? Or a deer? It was pretty heavy."

"Deer?" I shook my head. "With all the dogs next door? Unlikely."

"A fearless deer hungry for pretty flowers," Leonora said.

Miss Eidt rescued the top of a purple delphinium. "There's a herd of deer living in the woods next to the park. They don't usually venture into my yard. I just don't know."

Neither Leonora nor I believed an animal had broken Miss Eidt's statue. But as we lacked proof that a two-legged vandal was to blame, it would be kinder not to mention the possibility to Miss Eidt. Not yet, that is. Not until the idea occurred to her.

I found the arrow lying in the grass. It was largely intact; only the tip was broken.

On the other hand, it didn't sound as if Miss Eidt had read the letter describing her garden statue as obscene. She would want to know.

With a glance at Leonora, I told Miss Eidt about it.

"Surely you don't think someone did this deliberately," she said.

"It's possible."

"I don't know what to tell Brent. He was so happy to give it to me. He named her Diana."

"Well," I said. "Let's go back inside."

"And have tea and cake," Miss Eidt added.

"We just had breakfast," Leonora said.

"Tea then. Nice hot tea makes everything seem better."

Even this?

With a last look at the remnants of her statue, Miss Eidt led the way back into the library.

Debbie sat on the stool behind the desk reading a book. While Miss Eidt quizzed her, no doubt about the last time she'd seen the statue intact, I surveyed the library. A few patrons sat quietly with their materials, taking notes. Others roamed the stacks browsing for summer reading. All were female, most were young. Nowhere did I see a woman with blowsy, brassy hair.

But speaking of hair, a girl with pale yellow hair wearing a long, old-fashioned dress stood at the carousel spinning the tiers. She looked as if she'd stepped out of a western movie. She also looked familiar.

"Girls..." Miss Eidt beckoned to us.

"I need a cup of tea," she said. "Debbie watered the flowers in the back yesterday afternoon. The statue was all right then. The damage may have happened after dark or early this morning. We were busy earlier. I wouldn't have noticed if anyone slipped out of the library. Or they could have gone through the gate."

She brought down a new set of mugs, each one depicting a different flower. "I'm going to call the police," she added.

"Good. Lucy didn't tell them about the damage to her books. I wish she had."

"I suppose they can't do anything about it, but I'm not going to let it go."

"Of course not," Leonora said. "It's vandalism. That statue must have cost over a hundred dollars."

"That isn't the point. The library may belong to the public, but Diana was mine. And what constitutes obscenity anyway? There's a woman out there right now whose neckline is scandalous, in my opinion."

I smiled. At least she had a neckline. But Miss Eidt was right. A person could disapprove of a book or an artifact all he or she wanted, but no one had the right to destroy it.

Unfortunately not everybody believed that.

Thirty-two

Miss Eidt refilled our mugs with fresh tea. "There now. Wasn't that better? Have some more."

Hot tea could banish chills and settle a turbulent stomach, but it couldn't dispel the sinister currents that had invaded the library. Beyond the cozy confines of Miss Eidt's office, something evil lurked, either inside or on the grounds.

But I did feel better. Squeezing the last of the lemon into the dark brew, I took a long sip and remembered what I had planned to ask Miss Eidt.

"Do you know anything more about Lily May Hill, that romance writer?"

"Not much. She's soft spoken and gracious. You can meet her next weekend. She's talking about her books on Saturday afternoon. She has a brand new release, *Cherry Blossom Gold.*"

Copying Lucy. I was predisposed to resent her.

"What time?" I asked.

"One o'clock. She's hosting a luncheon afterward at Clovers."

How fancy.

"We'll be here," Leonora said. "I mean, there."

Soft spoken and gracious. Not the kind of woman who would whack the head off a hapless garden statue.

Still, you never knew your enemy until he revealed his—make that her—true face to you.

"Are you girls sure you wouldn't like a muffin?" Miss Eidt asked. "Debbie brought them from the Hometown Bakery this morning. They're chocolate chip."

Still full from breakfast, we both declined.

"We have another stop to make," I said. "Leonora wants to check out River Rose. There's a new owner."

"That reminds me, Jennet, did you have time to read about the Stone House murder yet?"

"Uh, no."

I hadn't even thought about it. But I'd better at least glance at it before my next visit to the library. Miss Eidt could be tenacious at times.

"I'll get to it soon." I rose. "Thanks for the tea, Miss Eidt. We'll be in touch. Make your police report and try not to worry."

I felt a brush of fur against my ankle. Blackberry had come inside with one of the library patrons, but when had she joined us in the office? Cats could be sneaky, which reminded me of why I was a dog person.

Still, I said goodbye to her. She had once saved my life.

~ * ~

"River Rose looks the same," Leonora said as I drove up to the yellow ranch house. "A little neater, maybe. Somebody is keeping the grass and weeds under control."

And a dog was barking.

Not again.

"Do you hear that?" Leonora powered down the window. The sound seemed to increase a hundred fold.

Surely it couldn't be another one of Rosalyn's collies who had eluded the police, and more importantly me, to haunt the woods. But the sound came from the freshly-painted kennel building, not the woods.

"It sounds pretty real," I said.

Except for the barking, the place looked deserted. Behind the house, dark woods rose up to a pure blue sky. The windows were closed. It must be airless inside. No garden tools lay around, no pots of flowers suggested habitation. Most telling, there was no car.

Only the lone dog barking.

Don't leave. I'm here alone.

I brought the car to a stop, and we followed the sound to the kennel, Leonora glancing anxiously over her shoulder.

"We're trespassing, Jen."

"We're investigating," I said. "We're the Rescue League, remember?"

As we neared the kennel, a face appeared in the window. A sable and white collie. Honey? I couldn't be sure. She looked like Honey.

The dog looked excited, nose pressed against the glass, ears flopping up and down. She disappeared, only to bounce up again, raking sharp nails over the window.

"Honey?" Leonora called out loudly.

"She won't know that name," I said, trying the door. It was locked, of course.

Not so long ago, I had been locked in this building myself. It had been hard enough for me to escape. A dog would have to wait for someone to let her out.

"I hope she has food and water," Leonora said.

"At least she's not on a chain."

"Do you suppose she belongs to Zachary Drummond, that he found another vacant place to keep his dogs?"

"That would be quite a coincidence," I said. "I don't think Drummond is the kind to pull weeds and mow grass. Probably other people live here and it's their dog."

But Drummond must have a key to the kennel. Puzzling.

What kind of unfeeling brute would lock a dog away from the sun on a glorious warm day when the runs were empty? It was a shame. More than a shame. A crime.

"We can't do anything except keep an eye on River Rose," I said. "Except let's see if Rosalyn's neighbor is home."

She was the woman who had heard howling last winter and seen the ghost in white that had haunted the property before Rosalyn's body was found.

Leonora opened the Taurus' door. "This place gives me the creeps. By rights, it should be deserted, but something is always going on."

"And it always involves a collie," I said.

~ * ~

As I stopped at the end of the driveway, I spied an orange Volkswagen barreling down the country road. In a second, the driver would intercept us. Quickly I turned in the opposite direction and stepped on the accelerator. Fortunately that put me on a path to Rosalyn's neighbor.

"I guess that answers my question," Leonora said.

"It's Drummond's car and Drummond's dog in the kennel. Do you think he recognized the car?"

"With our luck, yes."

"We'll be back," I said.

The neighbor wasn't home. I considered leaving a note on her door, but she might not call me. I'd rather talk to her in person. Then I needed to keep an eye on the goings-on at River Rose.

"Where to now?" Leonora asked.

"Home. We've both been away from our dogs too long."

It occurred to me that my collies were locked away from the sun, too. I'd soon remedy that. I was in the mood for a long walk in a different direction. Sagramore Lake would be an ideal destination. I'd take Gemmy, Halley, and Sky, the easy ones, then come home and cook a special dinner for Crane.

One of the blessings of summer were huge blocks of time to fill as I pleased. I planned to make the most of my freedom.

~ * ~

Brent's timing was off. He'd arrived after Crane's and my romantic dinner. But I had strawberry pie to serve and fresh coffee. We ate in the living room under the watchful eyes of the collies. For once, Misty had all four paws on the floor.

Brent was incensed about the destruction of Miss Eidt's garden statue.

"First Lucy, now Miss Eidt. Who's targeting the women of Foxglove Corners?"

"I suspect the culprit might be the self-righteous letter writer who calls herself Angela White. She's on a mission to eradicate the evil in the land, no matter what form it takes."

"I've read her letters to the editor," Brent said. "She's a nut cake. And what's so evil about my statue?"

"She's topless."

"Miss Eidt didn't find her offensive. She has a whole shelf of books on pagan gods and goddesses. That's a depiction of the huntress Diana."

I couldn't suppress a smile. "But those pictures are hidden between covers."

"I don't get it. The public has no business snooping around in Miss Eidt's garden."

"Well, someone saw it and objected to it."

"But that's a crime, to destroy somebody else's property."

"Miss Eidt notified the police," Crane said. "Not much we can do after the fact."

"Plan to meet us at the library next Saturday. A writer named Lily May Hill is giving a talk on romance novels."

Brent scoffed. "That's not my kind of reading."

"Well, she's my second suspect. I think she's copying Lucy.

"How so?"

I had made another discovery about the romance writer, but I'd been waiting to announce it at the right time.

"I don't know if you're aware of it, but Lucy has a website decorated with dark pink foxgloves. So does Lily May Hill. Of all the flowers in the world, why would she choose foxgloves?"

"We *do* live in Foxglove Corners," Crane reminded me.

As always he was logical and fair. Admirable qualities, but I was convinced Lily May Hill had stolen something from Lucy. Not only the spotlight, but Lucy's rather unique website motif.

What else?

Thirty-three

Brent finished the last piece of strawberry pie on his plate and sprang up from his chair. I didn't think my dessert inspired the smirk on his face.

"No self-righteous do-gooder is going to have the last laugh," he announced. "I'm fighting back."

"You're talking about the library vandal?" I asked.

He nodded. "I have a plan."

"To find her."

"Not exactly. I aim to show her she can't mess with me."

"Don't do anything illegal," Crane warned.

"Don't worry, Sheriff. It'll be perfectly legal. In fact, it'll be perfect."

"Can you give us a hint?" I asked.

"Just one. When we go to the library to hear that romance writer talk, keep your eyes open."

He wouldn't elaborate further, and he cut his visit short. We'd have to wait and see. I'll admit that smirk intrigued me.

Candy and Misty followed me into the kitchen where I wrapped the leftovers in foil and stored them in the refrigerator. With the kitchen neatened for the next morning, I joined Crane in the living room, moving the candlesticks from the table to the mantel. He and

Gemmy were playing tug-of-war while Halley and Sky looked on with interest, neither one bestirring themselves to interrupt the game.

"Shall we resume our romantic evening?" I asked.

"With a long moonlit walk?"

"The moon isn't out yet."

"It will be," he said. "We'll take the dogs. Who hasn't gone for a walk yet? Candy? Who else?"

They all gathered around him as he spoke the magic word.

I blew out the candles. "We'll take Misty and Sky."

While Crane attached leashes to collars, I opened the side door. A piece of white paper fluttered to the floor.

"What's that?" Crane asked.

I picked it up. "A note."

Scrolled in dark blue ink, addressed to Crane.

I read:

To: Deputy Sheriff Crane Ferguson,

If you have any control over your wife, please prevent her from snooping into my business. She's done this on more than one occasion, and I find it annoying. She's violating my rights. If she doesn't stop her meddling, she'll have to suffer the consequences.

"It's signed Z. Drummond."

"Let me see that," Crane said.

Stunned, I let the words, the threat, sink in as I handed the note to Crane.

It wasn't so much the vague threat or the accusation of snooping that angered me but the suggestion that Crane was expected to have control over me. That was outrageous. Unforgivable.

"How juvenile," I said, "How cowardly to go running around putting notes on doors. Does the man think he's still in high school?"

"What does he mean?" Crane asked, while Candy pulled on the leash, anxious to be on her way and Raven dashed out of her dog house, wanting to a part of the last walk of the day.

"I have no idea," I said. "Well, in the interest of full disclosure, Leonora and I did stop at River Rose today. He was about to turn in the driveway as we were leaving. He must have recognized the car. You know I've been checking on the blue house, but he hasn't been there in days."

"Why were you girls at River Rose?"

All these questions. I took Sky's leash from him, and Crane closed the door with a little more force than necessary.

"As far as I know, River Rose isn't Drummond's property," I said. 'It's lucky we stopped by. He has another collie locked in the kennel building. She looks like Honey."

I realized I hadn't answered his question. I couldn't remember why we'd decided to drive over to River Rose. It had been Leonora's idea, but I'd gone along with it.

We walked out to the lane, Raven leading the way. The lights were on in the yellow Victorian, but both cars were gone. We had the lane to ourselves, which was good because romance had pretty much dissipated with Drummond's note.

"Didn't you say it looked like River Rose had a new owner?" Crane asked.

"Someone's been making improvements."

I didn't think that someone was Drummond. He'd kept two collie puppies, then a third one at the blue house. I saw a pattern: search for properties with no visible owner; stash collies there prior to opening his back yard breeding operation.

But I'd been wrong before.

"If the man is bothered enough to leave a note on our door, he may be dangerous. I don't want you to meddle…"

"Meddle?" I echoed. My voice carried in the deepening silence.

"Okay. Snoop."

I didn't care for that word either. "I didn't know River Rose was off limits to me."

As we neared the abandoned construction, Candy attempted to lead us into the ever-enticing wonderland of fallen timber, glass, and vegetation determined to win back its territory. Crane yanked her back with a sharp "No." She grumbled but obeyed him.

If I'd been holding her leash, we'd both be several yards into the crumbling ruins.

As we walked on, Crane fell quiet, but I didn't think he'd forgotten the matter.

"I'll have a talk with Drummond," he said. "I don't like cowards sneaking around the house either. Why didn't the dogs bark?"

"They did while I was setting the table. I thought they were barking at deer."

I remembered the commotion. Why hadn't I investigated? Usually I would have.

"I'll try to stay away from Drummond unless I find out he's abusing collies," I said. "But one way or the other, I'll be discreet. He'll never know I'm near."

That was, of course, for Crane's benefit. I didn't want him to worry about me. As for myself, I didn't intend to forget that condescending, accusatory note or the jerk who had written it. I wouldn't have been quite so incensed if he'd addressed his complaints to me. But to appeal to my husband to rein me in?

Inexcusable.

Zachary Drummond would be sorry he'd insulted me.

~ * ~

"That statue-smashing lunatic will be sorry she crossed me."

Brent's voice boomed out in the library. A few people calmly perusing books before the talk turned to stare at him.

Good grief! Last night I had sounded like Brent.

"Shhh," Leonora said.

Brent had insisted on driving us to the library. We had arrived early to preview his surprise.

Miss Eidt waved to us from her station behind the desk. She'd forsaken her signature pastel suits for a plain black dress with a large, sparkly brooch. She looked elegant but different. The library looked different as well, arranged as it had been for Lucy, to welcome Lily May Hill.

"Follow me," Brent said, in a loud voice that wasn't quite a boom.

He led us outside to the garden and to the fountain and a new lawn ornament, a mermaid reclining on a rocky island. Long strands of hair didn't quite cover her ample bosom.

Leonora leaned down to touch the elaborate comb in her hair. "It's appropriate. You know... Fountain... Water... Mermaid."

"It's a coup, Brent," I said. "Is Miss Eidt happy with it?"

"She loves it. We named her Lenore."

A faint hint of color landed in Leonora's face. "After?"

"That poem by Poe."

"How long do you think she'll last?" I asked.

"As long as the library stands, I hope. If not, I have my eye on a pretty Amazon. Statue, that is."

"I didn't know there were so many topless lawn ornaments in Foxglove Corners," I said.

"I had to go all the way up to Maple Falls for this one. I hope the person who killed Diana is here today," he added. "Hope she sees it and has a fit."

"And on that note, we'd better go back inside," I said. "It's one o'clock. Time for Lily May Hill's talk."

Thirty-four

Miss Eidt placed a vase of red roses on Lily May Hill's table and glided back to her chair in front. Red for romance?

My love is like a red, red rose...

The author, a diminutive lady in pink who wore pearls in every place imaginable, presided over tall stacks of paperback books. She appeared older than I'd imagined and slightly frail. Every now and then she lifted a glass of water, took a small sip, then replaced the glass next to an ornate carafe. She seemed nervous, almost as if she were unused to speaking in front of a group.

I couldn't see her destroying somebody else's property.

Don't judge people by appearances, I told myself.

Then a stray thought drifted into my mind. Weren't romance writers all about love in all its forms? Would a bare bosom on a concrete figure drive them into a frenzy?

Keep looking for your culprit. She may be here.

We chose seats in the last row, which suited me as I wanted to observe the audience. Before I sat down, I saw one of my suspects. She had donned a low-cut orange sundress for the occasion and a matching ribbon that blended in with her brassy hair so well one would hardly know it was there. She took her notebook and pen out of a straw handbag, apparently ready to take notes.

What was her name again? Well, I'd keep referring to her as Brassy Hair.

Not counting Brent, Leonora, and I, twenty-two people had braved the heat to hear Lily May speak about romance. Brent was the only male, and several were young girls.

Lucy had attracted more than twice that number.

"Hi, Jennet. These seats taken?"

Jennifer and Molly, clad in summery dresses and wearing makeup, dropped into the last empty seats in the row, bringing the audience number to twenty-four.

"I didn't know you girls were romance readers," I said.

Molly smiled. "We're not. We like Lucy's books and dog stories, but Miss Eidt asked our reading club members to show up today. She wanted to be sure Ms. Hill had an audience."

Jennifer leaned across Molly. "Who's he?" she whispered, nodding her head toward Brent.

"Another non-fan. He's here for balance."

"What's that?" Brent asked.

Jennifer looked quickly away. "He's cute."

"Yes, he is."

From the front of the room, Miss Eidt said, "I think we're ready to begin. Ms. Hill, would you like to tell us what inspired you to write romance novels?"

Lily May favored the audience with a rosy smile. "Thank you, Miss Eidt. Call me Lily May. Well, it's simple. I believe in love. There's a mate for every single person on this earth. Finding that soulmate is a true adventure. My stories are a celebration of that journey from discovery to happily ever after."

Brent turned his choke into a cough.

"Do all of my stories have happy endings? Of course. Remember, there's a pot of gold at the end of every rainbow. There may be snowstorms in winter, but there are always cherry blossoms in spring."

"Not always," Brent said in what, for him, was a whisper. "You have to plant cherry trees first."

"Shhh," Leonora said.

Lily May directed her gaze to Brent. "Do you have a question, sir?"

"Me? Yeah, maybe, but I'll wait till you're done."

Lily May glanced at her notes and twisted the triple strand pearl bracelet on her wrist. She looked flustered, and I felt uneasy. It was as if I were the one sitting at her table, dealing with a heckler, forgetting what I was going to say next.

Brent could thoroughly unnerve a person. Why was I surprised? He believed in speaking his piece. Once I'd attended a play with him when his running commentary had incensed our near neighbors.

He wasn't the sort of person who would enjoy a talk about romance writing. But then, he hadn't come here for the lecture.

Apparently sensing an awkward lull, Miss Eidt asked, "When did you write your first book, Lily May?"

She brightened considerably, although her smile was tremulous.

"When I was fifteen. Using an old portable typewriter, I wrote an entire book, *Love in the Cherry Orchard*. I thought it was wonderful and sent it out to about twenty-five publishers. It always came back. Eventually I realized I had to learn the craft. So I took a course in creative writing at night school and joined a writers' club."

"And wrote happily ever after."

To Brent's credit, his comment was scarcely audible to me, and we were sitting close together.

I *did* wonder about Lily May's obsession with cherry trees. Could I phrase a question about that in a polite way?

Lily May droned on, telling the story behind each of her fifteen books. The heroine and her hero had different names and descriptions. They lived in a variety of colorful places and times, but basically the plots never varied.

Girl meets boy. There's a problem, but not one of earthshaking proportions. Occasionally a rival appeared on the scene, but in the end true love triumphed. The story always ended with an engagement or wedding or perhaps with a chaste kiss.

"I write clean romances," Lily May said.

"Boring," Brent said under his breath.

Beside me, Leonora hid a yawn. Jennifer searched through her purse for something. Brassy Hair had stopped taking notes but appeared to be listening intently. Every now and then she glanced out the window.

I consulted my watch. One-thirty. I found myself wondering what kind of luncheon waited for us at Clovers.

~ * ~

Lily May's question-and-answer session was thankfully short. Miss Eidt asked when her next book, *Cherry Blossom Gold*, would be out. One of the girls asked her to define 'clean,' another wanted to know if she could self-publish the short story for which she'd taken second place in a contest. I decided I didn't really care about her cherry blossom obsession.

Two people bought copies of *Cherry Blossom Wedding*. One of them was Miss Eidt, who certainly didn't need another edition for the library.

Gradually the session limped to a close. Lily May gathered her unsold inventory and dropped the books into a box.

Miss Eidt said, "Lily May invites you to join her at Clovers for lunch. I have maps if anyone needs them."

"Are you ladies going?" I asked Jennifer.

"No, we did what we promised. We're taking Ginger to the lake for her swimming lesson."

"We really wanted to get another Lucy Hazen book," Jennifer added.

"Doesn't Miss Eidt have copies behind her desk?"

"They're all checked out."

"Why does she keep them hidden?" Molly wanted to know. "To make room for clean romances?"

"Somebody has been seeing to it that Lucy Hazen's books are out of circulation," I said and immediately wished I hadn't spoken. I'd definitely captured the girls' interest.

"But why?" Moly demanded. "Who would want to do that?"

"All we can figure out is that this person thinks Lucy's books are bad."

"You mean not clean, like Lily May was talking about?"

"Not exactly."

Did I want to launch into speech about people who thought they had a right to regulate morality for the reading masses?

"You're saying you have another mystery, Jennet?"

Brent rose, towering over us. "Let's go. If they're serving watercress sandwiches and tea at this luncheon, I'm ordering a Reuben."

"What's that?" Jennifer asked.

Ah! Thank heavens for a diversion. "A corned beef and cheese sandwich, I think."

"Yuk."

"You guys don't know what you're missing," Brent said.

A girl in a long dress carrying an armful of books stopped to smile at us. At second glance, she was older than I'd first thought. It was that long straight hair that made her appear younger. I recalled seeing her before at the library.

"Wasn't Lily May wonderful?" she said. "I just love her books."

"They're inspiring." I felt that was a safe comment to make.

"I'm Maryclaire Hastings," she said. "That's Maryclaire, one word. I teach history at the middle school in Spearmint Lake."

"It's nice to meet you. I'm Jennet—Jennet Ferguson."

"Everybody ready to go outside and bake?" Leonora asked.

"Just a second," I said. "I want to see if Lenore is still there."

She was, sitting dreamily beside the fountain, whole and lovely. Sunlight danced off her scales and her fair hair, and her unclothed breasts.

For now, all was well at the library, although I was a little disappointed not to have found the statue basher in the audience.

Oh, well, another day, another search. I hurried past Blackberry and joined the others who were waiting for me at the entrance.

Thirty-five

The tablecloth was pink gingham checks, the roses in the centerpiece were red, and the luncheon consisted of chicken salad with warm cloverleaf rolls and a choice of lemonade or iced tea. Annica wasn't working today. Otherwise Clovers was my familiar haunt, almost a second home. I felt comfortable and very hungry.

Brent ordered his Reuben sandwich with steak fries. He looked out of place. Brent loved the company of women, but on this occasion he reminded me of a bull in a china shop or, more apt, a hunter in a red plaid shirt at a bridal shower. At least he blended in with the table's pink and red décor.

Lily May kept the conversation focused on romance. True Love. Clean books with gold-splashed endings. Miss Eidt made a valiant attempt to see that everyone, especially Brent, felt included.

Brassy Hair had joined us along with three girls from the reading club and Maryclaire, the history teacher, making us eight at a grouping of tables prepared for twenty-five. The small gathering should have been cozy, but somehow the atmosphere was strained.

Having finished his sandwich while the rest of us dawdled over the main course, Brent helped himself to a roll and asked my question.

"Why do you write about cherry blossoms all the time, Ms. Hill?"

His query took her aback. She had been willing to continuing answering questions during lunch but apparently hadn't been prepared for this one.

"I don't, not really," she said. "The cherry blossom is a motif. You know, a pattern. A recurring pattern."

That didn't satisfy him.

"So there's no reason?"

She set her spoon down and slipped into lecture mode. "Cherry blossoms are lovely and delicate and rare. They don't last long. One day they're fresh and dewy on the tree, the next day they're gone."

"You're right there, but tell me. How does that relate to love? Are you saying now that love is rare and doesn't last long? Doesn't that contradict what you said in your speech?"

One of the girls, Amy, giggled, and quickly covered her mouth. Miss Eidt fixed her with a stern look.

Once again Lily May looked ill at ease. We all knew that wasn't what she meant. The opposite, in fact. In fairness to Brent, he didn't realize he was being rude. He was just himself, asking questions in a loud voice that attracted attention from the other diners.

Quickly Leonora stepped in. "True love can be rare. I speak from experience."

We all looked at her. I knew she was thinking about Deputy Sheriff Jake Brown, her sometime love interest who, at the moment, was missing in action.

"Men are single-minded oafs," she added.

"Hey!" Brent said.

"I think cherry blossoms are like bridal veils," I said. "Beautiful pale pink bridal veils. Or floral tiaras. Or fine lace."

Lily May cast me a grateful look. "That's it, Jennet. They're lovely but easily broken. They need to be cared for and cherished. Just like the cherry blossom."

They still faded and fell from the tree, but no one mentioned that.

Thankfully, that brought the discussion to an end. I scooped the last bit of chicken salad from my plate and took a long drink of lemonade.

Throughout the luncheon, Brassy Hair had been silent. Sitting at the table's end with a teenaged girl on either side of her, she obviously concentrated on her chicken salad, not giving anything about herself away. Being mysterious.

My mind drifted from the conversation which, incredibly, Brent had turned to fox hunting.

Could this woman possibly be Lucy's nemesis, destroyer of books and one garden statue?

I couldn't decide. Earlier I had addressed a few innocuous remarks to her. She'd answered in monosyllables and continued her onslaught on the chicken salad. Currently she was cutting the lettuce leaf on which the salad rested into little pieces. She wielded the instrument with precision.

Well, if she was with us here with us at Clovers, the new statue was safe.

"What's for dessert?" Brent asked.

"You'll love it," Miss Eidt said. "Angel food cake with cherry fluff frosting and black cherry ice cream."

Naturally.

~ * ~

"Lenore is gone."

Miss Eidt's voice on the phone held a shrill, panicked note.

For an instant I thought she meant that Leonora had disappeared, which wouldn't have been unusual in Foxglove Corners. Then I realized she meant the garden mermaid.

"Do you mean another statue is broken?" I asked.

"I don't know, Jennet. It may be. It isn't here. Someone took it away."

Someone. While Lily May and Brassy Hair were at the luncheon. The statue had been there at the end of the event, beside the fountain, shining in the sun. We'd all left for the restaurant at the same time. Neither Lily May nor Brassy Hair could have moved it.

"Did Debbie see anything suspicious?" I asked.

"Nothing. She checked the garden before locking the library. Everything was all right."

Our thief had waited until the coast was clear then, possibly until nightfall. Worst of all, the guilty party was somebody other than my initial suspects. What now?

"Call the police," I said.

"I did, and I called Brent. He's furious."

"I'll stop by as soon as I can," I said.

"I appreciate that, Jennet, but what can you do?"

I didn't know how to answer her. My idea of interviewing Debbie might net a clue, but not if the perpetrator had never entered the library.

The library garden wasn't secure. Even if Miss Eidt bought a lock for the gate, a determined thief could simply heave himself over the fence. The white pickets were mainly decorative. Miss Eidt once said she counted on the barking of the shelter dogs next door for protection.

"I'll try to think of something," I said. "Maybe Crane will have a suggestion."

And Brent? I wondered if he'd replace the mermaid with an Amazon? This substitution game could get costly. But that wasn't the point.

Only a lunatic would go to such extremes to rid the library garden of a topless statue. After all, a mermaid's breasts had to be uncovered. She would look silly wearing a blouse.

That was what we were dealing with—a lunatic—which made the mystery of the lawn decorations more than a little dangerous.

~ * ~

"It sounds like a prank," Crane said that evening as we sat on the porch watching the sunset with our collies lying around us.

"We're a long way from Halloween," I said.

A rosy glow engulfed the yellow Victorian, and the long shadows of trees lay across the lane. Only innocuous night sounds intruded on the all-encompassing peace of Foxglove Corners. It seemed impossible that anything would dare shatter that peace.

I was so fortunate to live in this magical place, so blessed to have my husband. So ready to drown in an avalanche of sentimentality. But it was true.

"I was so sure the culprit was a disgruntled romance writer or a certain woman with brassy hair and a surly disposition," I said.

"Could it be a kid?" Crane asked.

"Vandalizing the statues? I suppose so." I thought of a few of the troublemakers I'd had in my classes last year. "But not defacing Lucy's books. That seems to be the work of an adult with a perverted sense of morality. And I feel certain it's someone who's familiar with the library and not very bright. After all, I'm sure Lucy isn't the only writer who deals with devilish matters. How about Bram Stoker? Poe? Stephen King?"

"You have a point."

A casual patron wouldn't be aware that the first garden statue had been quickly replaced by one equally provocative. I'd have to take my investigation back to the library.

"This person is fighting a losing battle," I said. "There'll always be another book to object to. It'll never end."

"Sure it will," Crane said. "As soon as the crazed fanatic is apprehended."

So spoke the law.

Thirty-six

Mornings were magical as well.

Last night's discussion with Crane had turned into a romantic evening—and night. I woke from a dream of cherry blossoms and lace floating on a spring breeze to the chiming of my phone. I reached through a drift of pink petals to answer it.

Four o'clock. Who would call at such an ungodly hour? Something must have happened.

Crane stirred and turned off the alarm clock before it had a chance to ring. I picked up the phone to find that no one had breached the sanctity of our pre-dawn morning.

It was an Amber alert.

Jennifer Marrington, aged thirteen, was missing. She was last seen in Lakeville where she had accompanied her mother yesterday afternoon on a shopping trip.

That was our Jennifer from Sagramore Lake Road! Ginger's owner!

"Oh no!" I passed the phone to Crane. "Jennifer's missing. I just saw her yesterday at the library."

As if that fact were relevant.

"I'll find out more details," Crane said.

"And I'll start breakfast." I swung my legs over the bed and reached for my robe. "Are pancakes okay?"

But he was gone—in the hall, headed to the shower.

Halley leaped to her feet, always leery of being stepped on, although that hadn't happened since she was a puppy. I followed a wagging tail downstairs, started the coffee, and gathered ingredients for pancakes.

An inner voice whispered, *Hurry. Time's running out.*

The peace of Foxglove Corners could never be counted on to last long. It was easily shattered.

~ * ~

By noon there was no word on Jennifer. I walked Halley, Sky, and Misty to Sagramore Lake Road and knocked on Molly's door. No one answered, and I continued on to the lake. With every step, my fear for Jennifer grew. People often disappeared in Foxglove Corners and in other places as well. Sometimes they were found alive. Other times...

I couldn't bear to think about the alternative.

The girls had been going to teach Ginger to swim. Where was Ginger now?

A lone figure stood on the beach apart from the sunbathers. Swimmers and boaters had already thronged the lake, seeking a respite from the morning heat. A sudden breeze aimed a spray of water at my face. It felt wonderful.

God bless the lake.

The figure waved to me, starting walking toward me, and I recognized Molly, her long hair in a single braid that seemed to be coming apart.

"Oh, Jennet..." She had been crying. Her eyes were red, her face flushed.

I gave her a brief hug. "I heard. Do you know what happened?"

"Nobody does. I think she's been kidnapped."

"Let's not jump to conclusions," I said.

"Her mom went into a store, but Jennifer had an ice cream cone. She wanted to stay outside. When Mrs. Marrington came out again, she was gone. No one saw her."

"Someone must have," I said.

"They're not talking then. Mrs. Marrington went in all the stores on the street and waited. Then she called the police. Everybody's been looking for Jennifer."

"I will, too," I said. "I'll take one of the dogs."

Candy would be the best choice, but Crane didn't want me to walk her alone, and I didn't trust myself to handle Candy in an exuberant mood. Sky was too timid, Misty too young and silly... Raven, I decided.

"But where should we look?"

"They're looking in the woods," Molly said and started crying again.

Looking for a body, she implied.

No, I wouldn't let myself think about a body in the woods.

Tears ran freely down Molly's tanned face. "She's my best friend. We were going to the library yesterday. Miss Eidt finally had a copy of Lucy's very first book for us."

"Try to stay positive, Molly. With everybody searching, someone is bound to find her."

"Not if she's been kidnapped."

Molly fixed her gaze on the lake, as if the water held the answer. Instead of continuing our walk, I turned the collies around and headed home again.

I had no idea where to begin looking. Neither did the police, according to the news. They were asking anyone who had seen Jennifer to call them. So far, no one had responded.

That wasn't good.

When I didn't know which way to turn, I usually paid a visit to Lucy at Dark Gables. Lucy couldn't help herself, but perhaps she could help another.

~ * ~

"It's happening again," Lucy said before I had a chance to mention Jennifer's disappearance.

'It' could be anything, and chances were it wasn't anything good.

"What?" I asked.

"I heard about young Jennifer Marrington on the news this morning. Madeline is missing, too."

It took me a moment to divine her meaning. Madeline was one of her teenaged heroines in *The Stone Collie*. I was under the impression that Lucy had abandoned that particular writing project. Apparently not.

"The Voltarians took Madeline," Lucy said. "People are looking for her, but they'll never find her. The aliens have her in their ship. I haven't decided what's going to happen next. I guess I'd better have someone rescue her."

Or in real life Jennifer would be lost forever?

I rejected that notion, but Lucy appeared to believe that once again her fiction set real events into motion. I decided to humor her for the moment.

"Write that scene quickly then," I said. "I'll be on my way. I promised Molly I'd join in the search for Jennifer. Madeline aside, do you have any idea where Jennifer is? Any foreboding or inside information?"

She nodded. "When I heard the news this morning, an image of woods formed in my mind. Dark, dense woods. A vehicle moving against the wind. Darkness."

I shivered at the picture she created. That wasn't encouraging. Foxglove Corners had more woods than houses.

"And fear," Lucy added. "I never met Jennifer, but for a moment, I felt what she was feeling, and she was afraid."

Sky nudged Lucy's hand and uttered a little whimper.

"We have to find Jennifer," I said. "It's so terribly hot out. What if she doesn't have access to water?"

She'll die.

"Have a cup of tea first," Lucy said. "Maybe the leaves will point the way."

I agreed, having known Lucy would offer to read my tea leaves. Not that I was superstitious, but any kind of help would be welcome.

In the kitchen adjacent to the sunroom, Lucy made the tea and for the first time neglected to arrange a plate of her store bought cookies. It didn't matter. My appetite had vanished. It always did when I had pancakes for breakfast or when I came face to face with a life-or-death situation.

I drank my tea, prepared the leaves for reading, and handed the cup to Lucy. She didn't have to peruse the patterns, didn't have to think.

"My goodness," she said. "Jennet, you're in grave danger. You have an enemy who'll stop at nothing to annihilate you. He's close to your home and getting closer all the time."

She looked up. "Be careful."

~ * ~

"Beware," said the witch.

The phrase played over and over in my mind.

Lucy's no witch, and I'm always careful.

I knew I had an enemy. His name was Zachary Drummond, and the threat he'd made in his note was still fresh in my mind.

But annihilate me?

I'd been thinking more in terms of a complaint of harassment to the police or a lawsuit.

Such threats were fairly common to Rescue League members. To help our precious collies, we often had to make ourselves unpopular with their owners.

I might have still another enemy, one I shared with Lucy. I didn't know the person's identity. Neither did he or she know of my involvement in the outrageous effort to purify the literature and art of Foxglove Corners.

So concentrate on Drummond. Better still, push him back to second place on the agenda. Finding Jennifer has to take precedence.

The search had centered on wooded areas near Lakeville. Further details had emerged in a television interview. The street on which Jennifer had waited for her mother was known as Antique Row. Mrs. Marrington had been shopping in my favorite store, the Green House of Antiques. Jennifer might have strolled up or down the street, eating her ice cream cone, never dreaming that her next step would lead to... What?

My speculation ended. If Molly were right and Jennifer had been abducted, she could be miles away. Even in another state.

An image of my own formed in my mind: a collie waiting anxiously at home for the voice and touch of her young mistress.

Let Jennifer come home, I thought.

Thirty-seven

The following day Sue Appleton and I searched the woods on either side of Jonquil Lane. We had dressed in jeans and long-sleeved shirts to protect ourselves from insects and prickly vines. We'd enlisted the aid of my Raven and Sue's blue merle collie, Icy, who had lived in the wild before his rescue.

"It's not likely that Jennifer would be in our neck of the woods when she disappeared in Lakeville," Sue said.

"No, but she *could* be. I don't think anyone looked around here."

In the interest of fairness, I didn't say what I was thinking. For a time Zachary Drummond had stayed in the blue house on the lane with Pepsi and Cola. If he had been Jennifer's abductor, he might have brought her to our woods or even to the house.

Crane was a strict believer in the concept of 'innocent until proven guilty,' Being a civilian, I could follow my instincts, and they told me Drummond was a villain.

"We should check out River Rose, too," I said.

Crane wouldn't be pleased. After reading Drummond's note, he'd practically ordered me to stay away from the place, but this was important. Neighbors and friends of the Marringtons, along with volunteers, had joined the police in the search. It grieved me that people were looking for a body.

Jennifer had been missing over twenty-four hours. Her parents still hoped to receive a ransom note, as a demand for ransom would imply Jennifer was still alive. So far they'd had no word at all.

'Try to stay positive,' I'd told Molly. It was time to take my own advice.

Nonetheless, images of Jennifer tormented me. Jennifer with Molly at their lemonade stand in the summer... Jennifer with her new collie puppy, Ginger... The girls looking grown up at Lily May Hill's library event...

Jennifer had to be all right.

The woods adjacent to the yellow Victorian yielded swarms of mosquitoes and bugs, scurrying wildlife, and twittering birds, but fortunately no bodies.

We came out on Jonquil Lane, hot and dusty. Beyond the dark of the woods, the sun blazed down on the gravel. My clothing was suffocating me. I longed to peel it off, take a shower, and slip into a sleeveless cotton dress. And pull off these uncomfortable hiking boots.

Sue called the dogs and emptied a large bottle of spring water into the collapsible bowl she'd carried.

I looked northward. "The abandoned construction," I said. "Our next stop."

Sue nodded. "And we can look there because we haven't gathered enough petitions to matter. I'd hoped the site would be razed by now."

"It should have been," I said as we trudged up the lane.

The stone collie in Lucy's woods, the bizarre coincidences that mirrored scenes in her work, the ravaged books, Miss Eidt's garden statues... It seemed ages since our last attempt at gathering signatures for our petition, weeks since a disembodied voice had warned me away from the Stone House.

A memory stirred. I had promised Miss Eidt I would read the book she'd found for me, the true account of the murder of Barbara Gorham. When we were finished for the day, perhaps I'd unwind on the porch with another unsolved mystery.

We passed my house and the yellow Victorian, heading north, past barking dogs in both houses who were annoyed they hadn't been invited to join the excursion.

The abandoned construction loomed ahead, dark and uninviting, a place of unrelenting gloom. I couldn't even imagine what the development of French chateau style mansions might have looked like had it been completed. All that remained were ruins: rotting wood, broken glass, and scattered bits and pieces of building materials, everything slowly being reclaimed by nature. An occasional wall still stood, casting grotesque shadows on the debris.

The dogs had a different view of the place. Barking merrily, tails wagging, they entered the site, Icy in the lead. We followed less eagerly, watching for death traps under our feet in the form of vines and rocks.

"We really have to get that petition moving," Sue said as she stepped around a broken windowpane.

"As soon as we find Jennifer."

But canvassing the nearby neighborhoods might be a good idea if Jennifer was still in the area.

I had a sinking suspicion she wasn't.

~ * ~

The ever-disintegrating construction was a place of secrets, but as far as we could tell, Jennifer's location wasn't one of them.

"What now?" Sue asked.

"There's another place we can look," I said. "The blue house where we found Pepsi. If it's still unoccupied, I can't think of a better place to keep a prisoner."

Back down the lane, past houses, around curves, pushing our way through heavy heat. In spite of its newness, the blue house was beginning to look like the construction we'd just left. To be sure, its fresh paint still glowed in the sunlight, but the silence and the atmosphere communicated desolation.

Still, I knocked on the front door. Sue peered in windows, and we both called Jennifer's name.

"Let's check around the back," I said.

A chain lay discarded at the base of the willow tree. Trapped in a clump of blowsy white Queen Anne's Lace I noticed a blue rubber ball. The items awoke memories of Pepsi and Cola— and Honey. Pepsi and Cola had become Mac's dogs as Drummond had never claimed them. The collie in the River Rose kennel might be Honey. Apparently Drummond had stopped using the blue house for his nefarious purposes.

"Do you have time to drive out to River Rose?" I asked.

"Not today. I have a lesson in a few hours."

"Tomorrow then?"

"Yes, but not till the afternoon."

"It won't take long. I hope we don't run into Drummond."

After his note to Crane, it would be more than awkward to encounter him again. If he had kidnapped Jennifer, it might be deadly.

~ * ~

At home I took my longed-for shower and made a beef stew for dinner. While it was cooking I retrieved *The Stone House Murder: An Unsolved Crime in Rural Michigan* from my desk. Feeling comfortable again, I settled out on the porch to read, holding the door open for the collies who didn't want to be separated from me.

I turned to the end. One hundred and nine pages, which was short. On the other hand, it was rather long for a crime that had never been solved.

How much could one write? The victim was murdered. There was no apparent motive. No clues. No suspects. For decades the crime had been considered a cold case.

I took a sip of iced tea. Misty tossed her toy goat at my feet. I threw it for her. She left it on the floor and lay down beside Candy who was looking at something I couldn't see in the woods beyond the lane.

I opened the book and realized the text was even shorter than I'd thought. Illustrations made up roughly twenty pages of the volume.

Here was the Stone House looking fine and imposing with neat landscaping. I glanced at pictures of the land that surrounded the Stone House, decades before the development of the Diadem Estates. A picture of two young women who resembled each other in party dresses. The murdered girl smiling at the collie who sat at her side.

Collie? Wherever I went, whatever I did, I ran into collies.

Turning back to the first chapter, I started reading.

~ * ~

I marveled that the author had written so many pages on a crime about which so little was known. Barbara Gorham, the victim, had been slain at her own engagement party which had been the highlight of her young life. She'd been stabbed in the back with a kitchen knife while her guests, including her groom-to-be, enjoyed a barbecue outside in the extensive gardens of the Stone House.

At some point, Rosemary, Barbara's cousin, noticed Barbara was missing. Not long after, Rosemary made a gruesome discovery. Barbara lay face down on the kitchen floor alongside a table laden with cakes and other desserts.

There was no sign of a struggle.

Approximately fifty guests had attended the party, many of them friends of the young couple. From that number of possible assailants, not a single one was a viable suspect. The doors were open, giving rise to the theory that someone, perhaps a trespasser, had entered, committed the crime, and made his getaway, unobserved in the crowd.

But why? No one could suggest a motive. Barbara was almost too good to be true. Pretty and popular, a girl who truly cared about helping people. She wanted to be a nurse. In another year, she would have realized her dream.

The other sixteen chapters dealt with detailed sketches of the party guests. In the last chapter, I came across an interesting fact. To honor her love for her collie, Kep, Barbara's family had placed a stone collie statue on her grave instead of a conventional angel or lamb.

How sweet. That was what I wanted on my grave. I'd have to tell Crane.

Closing the book, I visualized the crime scene. Guests celebrating a new commitment in the garden on a sunny day. Flowers and laughter and perhaps music, not too intrusive but sufficient to cover any untoward sound. A shadowy figure creeping up to the house. The guest of honor bleeding to death in a cluttered kitchen surrounded by party food. All joy drained out of the day with Rosemary's scream.

How could a case with fifty possible suspects have remained unsolved through the years? Where was the dog, the collie, Kep?

A soft woof brought me out of my speculation. Misty had gotten up and was staring at me. Unnoticed, her toy goat lay on its side at my feet. I picked it up but didn't throw it.

The author hadn't mentioned Kep—where he was at the time of the murder, why he didn't react, what happened to him. Why?

Still holding Misty's toy, I wondered why Kep hadn't known what was happening, why he hadn't tried to protect his mistress?

It was very uncollielike.

Thirty-eight

"We won't have to go to River Rose after all," Sue Appleton said.

I'd been about to slip my phone into my purse when its chime notes rippled out. Five more minutes and I would have been out the door.

"Sure we will," I said. "It may be another dead end, but I want to see if Honey is still there. If the sable is Honey, that is."

"Jennifer's home," Sue announced. "I heard it on the noon news."

Thank God. Thank you, God.

The Amber alert cancelled. Searches called off. Visions of a young girl's body lying in the woods returned to the realm of nightmares.

"Is she all right?" I asked.

"Apparently. She called her mom from Ohio. Her dad drove down to get her. She's exhausted and hungry but safe at home."

Ohio?

"So she was kidnapped?"

"Not exactly. That is, sort of. They didn't say much. Just something about her trying to free a dog from a locked car."

That sounded like Jennifer or any one of us in the Rescue League. Help a dog in distress, no matter the cost. Even if you ended up in another state. There was a story here. In time I'd hear it from Jennifer, but probably not today.

"What's that saying you like, Jennet? 'All's well that ends well'?"

"That's one of them."

Jennifer wouldn't end up as the subject of an unsolved crime in rural Michigan. Suddenly the day which had been overcast looked a brighter.

~ * ~

Lucy said, "I wrote my scene right after you left the other day, Jennet. The Voltarians decide to do something else to make the people of earth sit up and take notice. It isn't my best work, but it brought Jennifer home."

Oh, no. She really believed that.

We sat in the sun room over tea and Oreo cookies with Sky as usual eyeing the cookie plate.

"I'm dying to know Jennifer's story," I said. "I'll wait a few days, then pay her a visit. In the meantime, has anything else happened? With your books, I mean?"

"It's been peaceful so far. Miss Eidt ordered more copies of *Devilwish*. There's a huge waiting list, but the kids are returning the books they borrow. That's good. Do you think it could finally be over?"

"I hope so," I said.

But we didn't know who was behind the vandalism of Lucy's books. Until we did... Well, we could hope. Perhaps Lucy's enemy had run out of books to trash.

"I thought you were going to attend Lily May Hill's library event," I said.

"I thought about it, but I simply don't have an interest in romance writing. Besides, I knew you were going."

"It was quite nice," I said. "Especially the lunch. All hearts and flowers. Brent was—Brent. None of us think she's the vandal," I added. "So it's back to Square One."

"We spend a lot of time there," Lucy said.

She seemed happier. I supposed she credited herself with saving Jennifer, which would make anyone happy. I only hoped there wouldn't be another instance of an event in Lucy's book being echoed in real life.

I didn't allow myself to be too happy, though. When Lucy read my tea leaves she still saw imminent danger. My enemy was advancing on my home. He hadn't quite reached it.

"Don't let your guard down," Lucy cautioned. "He means to destroy you."

My enemy had to be Zachary Drummond. I wished Sue and I had gone to River Rose. I'd have to go another time without a good excuse.

If Honey or another sable were being kept in a locked kennel on these fine summer days, I'd ask Mac to investigate. He was still interested in bringing charges against Drummond for abusing Pepsi and Cola.

I had another favorite saying. 'Forearmed is forewarned.'

~ * ~

I encountered Jennifer and Molly the next day in front of the library.

The young are resilient. Jennifer looked none the worse for her ordeal, although the side of her face was bruised.

"When I fell in the car. Does it look too bad?"

"Not at all," I said.

She was a little self-conscious. She didn't like being the center of attention for what had turned out to be an accident. At least in her view.

"Everybody will be talking about me," she said. "They'll say I brought it on myself. I'm glad we're not in school."

"Nobody's saying that," Molly countered. "I think you were brave."

Ah, loyal friends! How could we exist without them?

We sat on the new lawn bench Miss Eidt had bought for the front yard. Blackberry stared down at us from a wicker chair on the porch. I asked Jennifer what happened.

"Well, I was just walking up and down the street, eating my cone and waiting for Mom when I saw a dog in a car. He was the prettiest Irish setter. All the windows were closed, and he looked so miserable, like he was really suffering. You know what happens when you leave dog in a car in the heat?"

"He bakes to death," Molly offered.

"I know only too well," I said. "And people keep doing it, in spite of all the warnings."

"So I tried the car door. It was unlocked. But the dog didn't want to come with me. I was trying to coax him when suddenly we started moving. The dog knocked me down to the floor, and I guess I lost consciousness."

"And the driver never noticed you?" I asked.

"I guess not. When I came to, I started yelling. He noticed then."

"What kind of car was it?" I asked.

"A big white one. When he let me out I saw the logo. It was a Yukon. Or Huron. Something with an 'on'."

"Didn't he offer to take you back to Lakeville?" I asked.

"He said he couldn't. He was in a hurry. He gave me a ten dollar bill and dropped me off at a diner. By then we were in Ohio."

"I'd have died," Molly said. "He could have been a killer."

Maybe he wasn't a killer, but surely this man should be held accountable for his actions, even though he didn't realize he had an uninvited passenger. He'd left his dog to suffer in a hot car and driven off with a young girl unconscious on the floor. And that bruise on her face. She could have had a concussion.

How could he not have known Jennifer was there? Giving him the benefit of a doubt, who drops a kid off in another state with ten dollars and instructions to call home?

"What did he look like?" I asked.

"He was young with dark hair. He wore a cap with its front backwards and talked with an accent. Southern, I guess it was."

Which would describe any number of men.

"We're just going to let it go," Jennifer said. "Just be thankful I'm home and unhurt."

That was probably best. Jennifer couldn't give the police adequate information about her unintended abductor, and no harm had been done.

"I'd do it again," Jennifer said. "Maybe next time I'll be more careful around a strange dog."

"You meant well," I said, "and you could have saved that dog's life."

And lost your own.

But that hadn't happened. Jennifer was here, the picture of health and youthful exuberance with rosy cheeks and a bit of sunburn.

By the grace of God.

All's well that ends well indeed.

Thirty-nine

It was a slow day at the library. So slow that I wondered if anyone were there other than Miss Eidt, who sat at her desk engrossed in a book and the girls, of course, who were in the fiction section quietly looking for more collie stories by Alfred Payson Terhune.

You could have heard the proverbial pin drop. I *did* hear the sound of falling water out in the garden. On a normal day you couldn't hear the fountain, even with the windows open.

Which made me wonder if Brent had bought another provocative statue to replace Lenore, the mermaid.

"Where is everybody today, Miss Eidt?" I asked.

I'd startled her. She turned to me, a happy smile on her face. "Jennet! I didn't hear you come in." She closed her book. "Debbie's gone to the Hometown Bakery for doughnuts. I have a craving for chocolate iced fried cakes. I'm holding down the fort."

"Molly and Jennifer are here, too. Did you hear Jennifer is home?"

"I heard. Thank heavens for that. Those girls are so sweet."

She glanced toward the back where the thud of a book dropping broke the silence. "Someone was here earlier. That teacher from Spearmint Lake."

I remembered her from Lily May's event. Petite with long blonde hair, she taught middle school history and except for her quaint dresses, looked more like one of her students. Her name was Maryclaire—Something. Spelled with one word.

"She didn't stay long," Miss Eidt said. "Just came and went. Didn't find anything she liked, I guess."

"In the entire library? How is that possible?

"Everyone's not like us," Miss Eidt said primly. "Before I forget, I have four more Gothics for you."

The books were Popular Library paperbacks that had seen better days. Their covers were tattered but enticing. *Scarecrow House* especially looked good, and I loved the cover on *The Third Wife*. It had the requisite heroine in a deep blue gown with a castle in the background—and three sinister monk-like figures.

"By the way, did you read about the Gorham murder yet?" Miss Eidt asked.

"Yes, and now I'd like to see the Stone House again. When I was there before, someone yelled at me to go away. I wonder if one of the Gorhams still lives there?"

"It's possible. The murder isn't that old. But if they're not friendly, why would you want to go back?"

That was a good question with only one answer.

"Curiosity."

"It killed the cat, you'll remember."

"And also solved a few crimes. It's hard to believe someone could commit a murder in a house with fifty people milling around outside."

"I think it was one of the guests," she said.

"The police didn't come up with a motive," I reminded her.

"No, but there was one. They just didn't find it. I always thought Barbara Gorham was too good to be true."

"You sound like you knew her."

"I remember reading the newspaper accounts when it happened. Her friends couldn't say enough in her praise, and her poor fiancé was distraught. Then I read the book, just like you did."

"Even perfect people can have a dark side and secrets," I said.

"If you'd lived in Foxglove Corners at that time and knew Barbara, I'll bet you could have found the killer."

"You give me too much credit. Anyway I'm more interested in the mystery in our own library. Did Brent find another statue?"

"He's bringing it over later today. Brent is determined not to let the vandal win. Like it's a contest between the two of them. I wish he weren't spending so much money on lawn ornaments, though."

The Amazon, I thought, another scantily clad sculpture. Brent must be running out of places to shop.

"We'll see how long the new one lasts," I said.

~ * ~

Carrying four fragile Gothic paperbacks from another time, I stepped outside into the glare of the noonday sun. From the porch I still heard the splash of water from Miss Eidt's fountain. If only it could send a refreshing spray my way. I waited for summertime all year, but I was growing tired of this endless hot weather.

I glanced at the Ice Cream Parlor, tempted to stop for a cone or a sundae.

You have ice cream at home, I reminded myself. *And there's ice cream at Clovers.*

I hadn't seen Annica in a long time. I still wanted to visit River Rose, and Annica was always a willing sleuthing companion.

So it's Clovers. A quick visit. Then home.

A few miles in an air-conditioned car, a few steps to the little restaurant on Crispian Road, where the faux clovers on the border created an illusion of green meadows, and I was inside, cool and comfortable again.

Annica was waiting on a customer in a small back booth. I stopped at the dessert carousel to admire the day's pies and cakes and fancy confections.

Like the library, the restaurant was having a slow day. It was still early for the lunch crowd, and I supposed the more adventurous denizens of the county were at the beach.

Annica swept by the carousel, her tiny silver bell earrings tinkling. "The lemon meringue pie is on special today."

"That sounds good. I'll have a piece with iced tea. Extra ice."

I could choose my own booth, the one with the best view of the woods across the road.

"I haven't seen you in ages," Annica said.

As there was no demand for her services, when she brought my pie and tea, she joined me. "How's your summer going?"

"It's going by too fast. I've been busy looking for Jennifer Marrington. Now that she's home, I can concentrate on Lucy."

"Did you forget about Zachary Drummond?" she asked.

"I haven't seen him lately. That's good, but I heard from him."

I told her about the note he'd addressed to Crane. It still angered me when I thought about it.

"What a jerk," she said. "Does this mean you'll back off?"

"Not a chance. Not as long as I suspect he's abusing collies."

"Because I have some information for you. He was in for breakfast yesterday. He's starting a new business. A collie kennel."

That was unpleasant news, but perhaps not unexpected.

"What does he know about collies except neglecting them?" I asked.

"He says he'll have a litter to sell next month. He wanted to leave a card and pictures with us. Mary Jeanne said no. She doesn't allow advertising."

"Where will this kennel be located, I wonder?"

"I know that too. He's buying River Rose."

Oh, no.

On the other hand, why not? There were a first class kennel and runs on the property. There was land for dogs to run free, assuming he let them off their leashes. At least one collie was already on the premises.

"He must have been the one mowing the grass and painting," I said. "Something seems off though. The way he was using the house on Jonquil Lane, I didn't think he had money to buy a house. Darn..."

"What's the matter?"

"If he owns River Rose, we'll be trespassing."

"When?" she asked.

"When we stop by to check it out."

"Great! I love to break the law. Aren't you afraid of getting caught, though? Don't forget the note."

"We'll be careful," I said. "If we see an orange Volkswagen, we just keep driving."

"When do we go?"

"Whenever you're free."

"Tomorrow, before noon. My shift starts then."

Annica sprang up as the bells at the entrance rang. I went back to my pie. It was good. And it was good to break the law occasionally. All to rescue a collie, if she needed rescuing.

Forty

A wind gust sent the new sign into a violent to-and-fro motion. The words were barely readable: Wildwynd Wood Collie Kennels. He had hung the sign in the same place. It was bright and new. It meant the kennel was a reality.

I brought the Taurus to a stop on the shoulder and watched it, mesmerized. The letters appeared to blur.

Annica turned in the passenger's seat. "I don't see an orange Volkswagen. Shall we keep going?"

I nodded. "All the way, as long as the coast is clear."

I turned and drove slowly over a driveway spread with glittering new gravel.

The changes in River Rose were striking. Well maintained grounds, fresh paint, new plantings around the foundation. One of them looked like the shrub Drummond had purchased at Greenspires. Dark woods still rose on the slope behind Rosalyn Everett's yellow ranch house. I couldn't bring myself to think of surly Zachary Drummond as the new owner.

Dogs were barking. As we neared the kennel, I saw that they were in the run. They gathered at the gate, the dog I thought might be Honey and three tricolors. One of the tri's was heavily pregnant. All were wagging their tails and seemed happy.

So they did have access to fresh air and water and exercise. In a corner I spied a well-chewed rawhide bone. One bone for four dogs to share.

I never gave my collies rawhide for fear a piece would break off and lodge in their throats.

"I wonder if Rosalyn will be happy that River Rose is a dog kennel again," Annica said.

"I don't think so. River Rose meant a lot to her until it all went wrong. She wouldn't have liked Zachary Drummond."

My gaze graveled from the kennel to the house, and old memories stirred. I had found my stolen antique sleigh in that house. On another day I'd been locked in the kennel but managed to escape. For a moment I remembered the ghost in white wandering over the snow swept fields. To this day, I believed the spirit was Rosalyn. There was no need for her to walk now.

"Wildwynd Wood," I said. "I would have sworn Drummond didn't have a poetic bone in his body."

"He was serious about the puppies," Annica said, reaching across the fence to offer her palm to the sable, to the dog I called Honey. "I hope he's going to help the tri have her puppies."

"Let's hope he knows what to do."

A prospective collie mother needed good food and vitamins, a whelping box, and supervision. The puppies would need constant care... I was afraid for them.

"You can't really call Drummond a backyard breeder," Annica said. "Not with all these woods."

"I can call him an amateur and unscrupulous, though, based on the way he treated his first collies."

Alas, there was nothing I could do about the situation. Nothing I *should* do. At present, Drummond wasn't doing anything wrong, wasn't breaking any rules.

Where was he, though? Anyone could scale the fence and steal the dogs.

And what about the way he had treated Pepsi and Cola? He'd left them alone, too.

I sighed. Pepsi and Cola were safe with Mac. As for Honey, the expectant mother, and the other collie girls, I only hoped Drummond would give them the care they needed.

"We'd better go," Annica said. "He could come back at any moment."

He could. And Crane would be unhappy with me if he knew I'd driven to River Rose without the excuse of looking for Jennifer. Unhappy was an understatement. Crane didn't understand curiosity when my life might be in danger. Annica's as well as mine.

"I hate to think of these precious new babies," I said. "Their fate is in the hands of a man who sees them as dollar bills."

"He mentioned he's charging nine hundred for them. Doesn't that seem like a lot?"

"It's what the breeders are asking for pet collie puppies these days. Show prospects are much more."

"If he hopes to get that much for them, it's in his interest to make sure they survive."

Again, all I could do was hope.

"We'd better go," Annica said. "And not come back."

We walked back to the car, our eyes on the road, but there was no sign of anyone else in the area. No orange Volkswagen in sight and no sound except for the dogs who were still barking.

Could Zachary Drummond be the enemy who had appeared in my teacup? Who else could it be?

Just take one false step, Drummond, I said to myself. *"And I'll be back."*

~ * ~

I dropped Annica off at Clovers for her shift and drove to Dark Gables.

I had been thinking about Lucy off and on all morning. Last night, I'd had a strange dream. I couldn't remember the details, but Lucy was in it. Although my dreams were always in color, this one was unique in its sepia tones and shadows.

I wondered if the dream was a type of foreboding. Lucy's tormentor appeared to have backed off, but in Foxglove Corners, one could never count on a prolonged period of tranquility. This might be the calm before the storm.

I turned in the densely shaded drive to the house, hoping I wouldn't walk into another trauma.

Lucy looked happy. Her gold chains and bracelets sparkled, and her black dress had a youthful, stylish cut. Even Sky, who was adept at mirroring Lucy's moods, frisked around me like a puppy, tail wagging a mile a minute.

As we settled ourselves in the sunroom, Lucy said, "I've been working on *The Stone Collie*. It's a mishmash. I kept adding scenes I hadn't planned. I think I can salvage it, though. Those pesky Voltarians aren't as smart as they think they are."

"And writing makes you happy. I'm so glad."

"When it's going well it does, and I had the best news this morning. Something totally unexpected happened. My agent told me about an option for *Devilwish*. There's a good chance it may be a movie on the Twilit Channel."

"That's wonderful! When will you know?"

"I'm not sure. My agent will keep on top of it. For now I just want to bask in the glory. Just think. My own creation brought to life on the screen."

She put the water on to boil for tea. "Now if we can just take care of that troublesome enemy who keeps lurking in your cup…"

"So you're all right?"

"Never better." She broke open a package of chocolate wafers and arranged them on a plate.

"I've been worried about you," I said.

"I was worried about me, too," she said. "All it took was that one phone call to put things in perspective. I'm a writer, a professional. Not everyone will like my work."

But not everyone would take the trouble to hunt books down and deface them. *Devilwish* had come a long way. What would Lucy's nemesis do when it was a movie? Write letters to the *Banner* about the evils of producing immoral films?

"I made the mistake of mentioning the option to Miss Eidt," Lucy said. "It's too early, and it may not happen, but she said something about having a celebration in the library. She's going to bring all of my books out again. I'll give Lily May Hill a run for her money."

"That's exciting."

It was also worrisome. Would the vandal see Miss Eidt's party as a challenge? Maybe the reason he or she had backed off was because Lucy's works had virtually disappeared from the library.

And what if Brent had replaced the stolen garden statue?

Well, of course, he had. Another challenge. Maybe it had already been vandalized or stolen. I'd have to stop at the library soon.

Lucy made the tea, and we sipped it in companionable silence, discussing actors we'd like to see portray Lucy's characters. She hoped they'd shoot it in Foxglove Corners, which was picturesque enough for any major production.

When I finished, I prepared the cup for a reading and handed it to Lucy.

"Is he still there?" I asked.

"Oh yes. He's closer."

She pointed to a long light leaf. "He's holding something."

"A gun?"

"I can't tell. It looks like a stick. Like a shepherd's staff?

"Or a spear?"

"Something," she said again. "But I see your wish."

The symbol was three small dots. *Long years of happiness with Crane,* my usual wish.

Wait! If I could look forward to those years with my husband, why should I fear an enemy holding a staff-like object? Tell me that, Teacup.

You don't really believe this, I told myself. *It's like a parlor game.*

But I did. Lucy had strange powers over which she didn't have control. Her glimpses into the future came and went, never troubling to explain themselves. Tea leaf reading was part of her talent, even if her pronouncements were sometimes contradictory.

The undisputable fact was that I had an enemy. At least one, possibly two. I didn't need supernatural powers to tell me that.

Forty-one

"Any man can breed his dog and have a litter," Sue Appleton said. "We have to let it go, Jennet, until Drummond crosses the line. Even then…"

She trailed off. I refilled her glass from the pitcher of iced tea I'd brought out to the porch.

The 'even then' bothered me.

"We wait until he loses half the litter or sells his pups to people just like him?"

"We wait till one of those adults or pups need rescuing," she said.

I knew that. I just didn't want to accept it.

"I guess you're right."

"Otherwise, he can claim you're harassing him, and he'd be within his rights."

"What about Pepsi and Cola?" I asked.

"We let Lieutenant Dalby handle that. Remember Drummond's note," she added. "He'll be waiting for you to make one false move. Then he'll pounce."

"Just like I'm waiting for him."

Misty, ever on the lookout for a human playmate, stood in front of Sue, holding her toy goat in her mouth, tail wagging, eyes pleading.

"That pitiful collie look," Sue said. "It's irresistible."

She took the toy and tossed it into the yard. Candy and Misty bounded down the steps after it. It was Candy who brought it back—to me. My dogs had their own rules, among them 'the fastest one wins.'

"In the meantime, all our foundlings are in foster homes," Sue said, giving Misty a pat on the head. "We have two enthusiastic new members. The coffers are full, and no one has reported a case of abuse lately. Life is good."

"Finally."

For the Lakeville Collie Rescue League and maybe for Lucy.

"So we should think about getting our petition going again."

"Yes," I said, "before I have to go back to school. I'll never have time then."

"Let's go the day after tomorrow if you're free. Are you ready for a new territory?"

"Almost. I have about four more houses in the Diadem Estates where nobody was home, and I'd like to see the Stone House again."

I had told Sue what I'd learned about the murder of Barbara Gorham, adding that she'd had a collie named Kep.

"Didn't the owner tell you to go away?" Sue asked.

"She did. Maybe this time she'll come to the door."

Something had been nagging at me, a vague feeling that I'd overlooked an important clue. Not one connected to the murder mystery. Something else.

I couldn't give it a name. It was elusive, like the dream I'd had about Lucy. But it was also significant.

I finished my tea and gave the ice cubes a swirl with the long-handled silver spoon I rarely used.

Remember, I ordered myself.

Nothing. Oh, well, it would come to me when I wasn't trying to remember.

"Don't take any chances," Sue was saying. "Most of the people I've met have been civil, but you never know when you'll meet up with a lunatic. The fact that she was rude is a red flag."

"There are two collie statues on the front porch," I said. "I'll take one of the dogs with me. They're wonderful ice breakers. And who knows? Maybe I'll find that the owner is a kindred spirit.

~ * ~

After walking three dogs who were less than energetic in the heat, I took a quick trip to the library. In the pleasant lull between crises, I'd managed to read all four of my Zebra Gothics.

Brent stood at the carousel holding a box while Miss Eidt filled the shelves with Lucy's books. The romances had been demoted to the bottom tier.

Miss Eidt's smile was brighter than usual. "Did you hear Lucy's news, Jennet?"

"She told me. I'm so happy for her."

"It's high time our Lucy received the recognition she deserves. This movie is going to put Foxglove Corners on the map."

"We're already there," Brent said.

"We'll be a tourist attraction like Mackinac Island on those *Somewhere in Time* days."

I couldn't hope for that. In my opinion, Foxglove Corners was perfect. I didn't want it to change.

"I'm planning a party to celebrate the movie option," Miss Eidt added. "You can help me if you'd like, Jennet. I was thinking light refreshments, flowers, mood music… Maybe I can talk Lucy into giving another speech."

"Should you wait until it's official?" I asked.

"Why? Even if they don't make the movie, it's still an honor for Lucy—after the way she's been treated."

"Any excuse for a party," Brent said, putting down an empty box. "Hey, Jennet. I was just going to call you. Come and see the new statue."

Miss Eidt added the last three copies of *Devilwish* to the top shelf. "You'll be amazed, Jennet."

We went through the side door and followed the sound of water into the garden. The statue was imposing. Poised for action beside the fountain, she resembled Lenore, but she had legs instead of a tail, graceful arms and an ample bosom, left unclothed, of course.

The major difference was her size. She was gigantic as befits an Amazon.

"See if you can lift her," Brent said.

"I wouldn't even try."

"She weighs a good sixty-five pounds. Let's see someone try to sneak her out of the garden."

"That's as much as one of my collies," I said.

"Miss Eidt named her Ammie—with two 'm's'."

"For Amazon," I said.

"No, for one of her favorite books."

Ammie Come Home by Barbara Michaels. It was of my favorites too.

"Long may she live," I said.

A sudden breeze blew a spray of water in my face. I had an irrational desire to step into the fountain and be cool for the first time all day.

"I wondered if we could have one in our garden," I said. "I'll ask Crane tonight."

"I don't see why not."

Back inside, we walked into a minor confrontation that was loud enough to draw stares from the people sitting at the tables.

Maryclaire Something-Or-Other, in another one of her old time dresses, stood at the paperback carousel. She seemed agitated.

Beside her, Miss Eidt appeared unruffled, but I suspected she was upset. Miss Eidt tried to avoid or defuse confrontation.

"What are you doing?" Maryclaire demanded. "Where are Lily May Hill's books?"

"Right here." Miss Eidt pointed to the lowest shelf.

"Where are the rest of them?"

"Mmm, probably checked out."

"But why did you move them?"

"For variety. People don't always want to see books in the same places."

That was fast thinking, a quality I hadn't known Miss Eidt possessed. Except to showcase new arrivals, the same place was exactly where the library's patrons expected to find their books.

Her explanation didn't impress Maryclaire.

"With this arrangement, people will only see those creepy vampire books," she said.

"If they know the author's name, they can look in the fiction section. Books are shelved in alphabetical order."

"It isn't the same," Maryclaire said.

Miss Eidt took her stand. "I believe newness attracts readers. The Foxglove Corners Public Library may be old, but we're forward thinking."

Apparently aware that she had an audience, Maryclaire brought the argument to an end.

"Okay. It's your library."

She walked away—stalked would be a better word choice. Past the new desk, almost colliding with Blackberry who was lying in her path, and out the door.

"That wasn't one of Lucy's fans," Brent said. "Which book has a vampire in it?"

"Bram Stoker's *Dracula*," Miss Eidt answered. "Oh, you mean, which one of Lucy's books. I don't recall. That woman is usually so quiet. What set her off?"

"You moved the romance books," I said. "Now they're harder to reach."

"Well I can't please everyone." She walked back to her desk. "What did you think of the Amazon, Jennet?"

"She's unique," I said. "Very weighty."

And when the vandal saw her, he would know he'd met his match.

Forty-two

With three more signatures on the petition and all prospects contacted, I drove the Taurus closer to the Stone House and parked in the shade of an ancient oak tree whose branches hung over the road. I gave Halley a drink in her collapsible bowl and drank the rest of my ginger ale. Then I led Halley up Diadem Lane.

The sun was hot, too hot to stay outside for long, but then I didn't intend to. A quick visit to the Stone House, then home to air-conditioned bliss. I'd had the foresight to wear a long-sleeved blouse, not wanting to risk another sunburn. Unfortunately the sun seemed to find its way through the cotton material.

My destination swam in a light haze. The stones seemed to shimmer and, away from the Diadem Estates, the silence was thick and heavy. The two collie statues at either side of the entrance had a glow. Nothing supernatural. They'd been painted an odd shade of pale green.

The Green Collies, I thought. What a good title for one of Lucy's books.

At the gate, Halley put on her brakes. She stared at the house or perhaps at the statues. Then she lay down on the walkway.

"Come, Halley," I said. "It's all right."

No, it isn't.

She wouldn't budge. This was the kind of behavior I expected from my rebel Candy, not from Halley, my first dog, my heart dog, who had once accompanied me to a safe place as a tornado bore down on us.

I took a jerky treat out of my pocket and offered it to her. It was turkey, her favorite.

She didn't even look at it, didn't lick her chops. She tried to back up to the road, taking me with her.

Just like Candy would. But this was Halley.

Well, Halley *did* behave off-leash. Maybe I could go closer, knock on the door...

A loud voice shouted into the stillness, each word like a separate rifle shot. It originated from inside the house.

"Go away! If you value your life, don't come any closer, and don't come back."

The unseen homeowner hadn't had a change of heart. Her new message was similar to the old one.

Holding a tremulous collie, I stood, scanning the façade, looking for some sign of movement. A curtain pulled back. The glimpse of a face. Any sign of habitation. Who could resist a visitor with a collie on a leash?

Suddenly the voice spoke again:

"Go away! If you value your life, don't come any closer, and don't come back."

And I understood. The inhospitable message was a recording, somehow rigged to activate when a visitor approached a certain spot, well away from the door.

To test my theory, I took a few steps forward. The voice repeated its warning. The same words. The same tone.

There might not be anyone inside, the stone collies keeping their vigil at an empty house. As a further test, I walked around to the back, wading through weeds and plants growing out of control in what had once undoubtedly been a rose garden. Another statue, a stone collie, slightly smaller than the ones at the entrance, lay in a tangle of purple coneflowers. I saw still another one, a standing collie, about three yards from the house.

Apparently all had been placed there in honor of the slain Barbara Gorham. They'd been painted that odd light green color that created the effect of a weird, otherworldly glow.

"All right, Halley," I said. "You win."

We'd leave the mystery of the Stone House and its multiple canine statues for another day.

~ * ~

On the way home, I decided to stop at Dark Gables, which wasn't too far out of my way. As I turned on Spruce Road, I noticed a truly alarming sight, a streak of yellow in the leaves ahead, heralding the imminent approach of fall. Were 'Back to School' sales far behind?

No, it wasn't time. I wasn't ready.

I drove on, thankful the rest of the leaves were still green.

At Dark Gables, while Halley and Sky chased each other around the yard, I gazed toward Lucy's woods, visible beyond the gable tops. These trees showed subtle signs of fall, too. A touch of scarlet, a crunch of fallen leaves underfoot, something in the air. A scent, a feeling. Little things.

Tiring of their game, the dogs bounded up to the porch and lay down, panting heavily.

"Everybody inside," Lucy said. "I'm surprised to have two visits from you so close together, Jennet. Surprised, but delighted."

"I was just in the neighborhood…"

I froze.

In the neighborhood.

That was it! The elusive something that had been lurking at the edge of my subconscious waiting for me to recognize it.

"In the neighborhood," I repeated.

"Are you all right?" Lucy asked.

"Never better," I said.

My thoughts tumbled over one another as they vied for my concentration.

Spruce Road, a mere ten-minute drive from the Diadem Estates. The collies that guarded the Stone House. The stone collie statue in Lucy's woods.

All of them soft green. All glowing, even the one in the dark of the woods.

Lucy stood at the sink, frozen herself in the art of filling the teakettle. "I'm not following you."

"How long ago was Dark Gables built?" I asked.

"Let's see. About five years before I bought it, and I've lived here for twenty years."

"I have a theory about the statue in your woods. Is there a chance your property was part of the Stone House estate?"

"I've never thought about it," Lucy said. "Possibly."

"According to an account in a book I read, Barbara Gorham's family set a collie statue on her grave and didn't stop there. I counted four similar statues at the house, which is empty, by the way. There's a recorded message activated to send visitors away."

"It sounds like a good setting for a story," Lucy said. "My kind of story, that is."

"Do you remember when we hiked out into the woods to see the collie statue?" I asked. "You thought it had a glow."

"Sort of."

"What if the Gorham family erected a statue in the woods, which would have been their property at the time, in honor of Barbara, and forgot about it over time? Maybe that particular spot had some meaning for them."

"That would explain the statue," she said slowly.

"You never explored your own woods, so you wouldn't have seen it."

"You may be onto something!" she said. "The idea that the Voltarians left it came to me out of the blue. It was a coincidence. And everything else?"

"I can't be certain, but I think we're dealing with a mixture. The girls in the library who looked like your heroines and the plane crash were coincidences."

"Really weird coincidences, since I wrote about them in my book first. I don't know, though, Jennet. It's a stretch. What about the copies of *Devilwish* left on my porch?"

"That," I said, "is a separate issue. Let's deal with one at a time. I'm going to check with Miss Eidt. I'm sure there are maps of Foxglove Corners in the library."

Maybe I'd better take another look at the photographs in the book Miss Eidt had found for me.

"I have a picture of your statue on my phone," I said. Let's take a walk into the woods. I want to see it again."

But I was sure I was right.

"Now?" Lucy asked.

"Today, yes."

"But you're dressed up."

"I was collecting signatures for the petition. It doesn't matter. I don't think we should wait."

"Slow down," she said. "Let's have our tea. If you're right, that'll be a tremendous load off my shoulders."

~ * ~

Fortified by tea and chocolate wafers, we entered the woods with two excited dogs at our heels. Not wanting to spend an hour brushing burrs out of Halley's coat, I kept her on her leash, close to me, and I kept my skirt away from grasping branches.

"It's still here," Lucy said when we reached the clearing. "It hasn't moved, and it *does* glow."

"That's paint," I said. "The statue is similar to the ones at the Stone House. I'll bet they were bought in the same place."

"You don't think there's a body buried here then," Lucy said.

"Under different circumstances, I might, but I saw a picture of Barbara's grave in that book I mentioned. She's buried in a proper cemetery. This might have been her favorite place. Somewhere she went to read or just be alone with her thoughts. And she took Kep with her. I'm sure I'm right," I added.

"Now everything's perfect," Lucy said. "I knew you could figure it out."

Forty-three

I was right. I took one last look at the map of Foxglove Corners, circa 1970, and replaced it in the folder.

Decades before Diadem Estates had been developed, the property that now belonged to Lucy had been part of the Stone House's seventy acres.

Add this new knowledge to the presence of stone collie statues at Barbara Gorham's family residence, and I had the solution to one of Lucy's mysteries.

I crossed 'the statue in the woods' off my mental list. So much for the Voltarians.

Miss Eidt peered over my shoulder. "It's obvious, isn't it?"

"A week ago I wouldn't have dreamed of the connection."

"You had to read the book first," she said. "I'm glad you did."

I was, too. I could have solved this particular mystery days ago if I hadn't procrastinated.

"Now we can concentrate on the party," Miss Eidt said. "What do you think about sandwiches to go with cake and cookies?"

"Yes, a variety, and I have an idea for the cake. We can decorate it to resemble Lucy's *Devilwish* cover. I'll order it from the Hometown Bakery."

"It should be devil's food to go with the darkness theme," Miss Eidt added. "We can order the sandwiches from them, too."

"What else?" I asked.

"Coffee and tea, of course. Lemonade. It's bound to be hot. An assortment of soft drinks."

"Excuse me... Ladies? Is this a library or a catering service?"

The question, wreathed in sarcasm, came from none other than Brassy Hair. I could never remember her name.

She looked as if she had just rolled out of bed, as if she were still wearing her pajama bottoms. Even a touch of mascara would be an improvement. Perhaps she just needed a cup of coffee.

Miss Eidt would never invite her into her office for refreshments. She would, however, return Brassy Hair's rude query with civility.

"It's a library, of course, Miss Holland. What can I help you find?"

"Are all your Stephen King books checked out?"

"I don't think so. Let's see."

"I'm looking for *Pet Sematary*."

"I'm sure we have a copy," Miss Eidt said. To me she said, "Don't leave without picking up the new Gothics I set aside for you."

Brassy Hair gave me a look I couldn't interpret. While Miss Eidt escorted her to the fiction section, I let myself out the side door into the garden. The sound of water drew me to the fountain. Ammie, the Amazon statue, stood in the sunlight, proud and ready for battle and so far unmolested. Was it possible the library vandal didn't know she was there?

I moved as close to the fountain as I could, enjoying the caress of water carried on a soft breeze and the splash as it hit the basin. We could have Lucy's party in the garden, bring out chairs and one of the long tables for refreshments.

The door opened and Debbie appeared. She took a step back, and a flush spread over her face.

"Oh, Jennet... I didn't know anyone was out here."

Could that be a look of fear or was she just surprised?

"I came out to check on the statue," I said. "It's so pleasant, I thought I'd stay for a few minutes."

"So did I," she said quickly. "I come outside every hour or look out the window. We're afraid that someone may try to damage this statue or steal it."

"It would be nice to have it in one piece for the party," I said.

Debbie picked up a paper bag that had blown into the yard. "I read that real Amazons used to cut off one of their breasts so they could hold their bows better."

"Good grief," I said. "How gory. But weren't Amazons mythological beings?"

"I guess. Mr. Fowler really likes racy statues, doesn't he?"

"I'm sure he does, but he's trying to make a point."

"Which is?"

"There's nothing immoral about a work of art, even though some misguided individuals think so."

"Well, I'd better get back to back to work," Debbie said.

"Me too."

Back to work? What did I have to do today? Bake a pie for dessert? Buy one at Clovers? It was too hot to turn the oven on. Oh, for the life of a teacher in the summer.

I followed Debbie back inside, picked up two very old copies of Phyllis A. Whitney's *Thunder Heights* and *The Trembling Hills,* thanked Miss Eidt, and went back outside into the heat.

As I crossed the parking lot, a strange thought occurred to me. Could Debbie possibly be the vandal? She had a key to the library and often locked up for Miss Eidt. Who would have more opportunity?

But Debbie had a vested interest in the library. Along with assisting Miss Eidt—as she had for years—she was taking college courses in library science. But there was that remark about racy statues.

No. Miss Eidt trusted Debbie.

But she trusted most people.

No, it couldn't be Debbie. Emphatically no.

By the time I drove out of the Corners, the idea had evaporated, allowing me to concentrate on what kind of pie I was going to buy at Clovers.

~ * ~

Blueberry? Chocolate meringue? Strawberry with a sugar-dusted crust? I stood at the dessert carousel trying to decide. Impossible. Maybe I should buy a half dozen tarts.

I heard the tinkle of tiny bells. Earring bells.

"Chocolate meringue," Annica said, coming up behind me. "It's super good."

"I'm sold," I said. "I'll have a piece for here with iced tea."

"Did you see the *Banner* today?" Annica asked.

"No, why?"

"There's another letter about inappropriate statues in public places and something else I thought you'd be interested in. I saved it for you."

When she served my pie, she handed me a page torn from the Want Ads. One of the ads had been circled.

Champion-sired collie pups for sale. Sables. Males and females. Reasonable prices. Wildwynd Wood Collie Kennels.

"I called," she said. "That's Zachary Drummond's number. Something's wrong. The collie we saw couldn't have had her puppies already, could she?"

"It's possible, but if she did, the puppies wouldn't be ready to go to new homes for eight weeks or so."

"So what's going on?"

"Drummond must have another female collie in his kennel, one we didn't see on our last visit? We have to go back to River Rose," I said. "Wildwynd Wood, I mean."

"But we can't," Annica said. "Crane won't let you."

"We'll be very careful, and I'll tell him after the fact."

"Won't he be mad?"

"Probably."

He wouldn't have forgotten Drummond's note. I remembered it, too. Well, Drummond had placed an ad in a newspaper. He had puppies to sell. That was an open invitation to buyers. He couldn't accuse a prospective buyer of meddling.

I stopped to think. We had to be more than careful if we returned to Wildwynd Wood. The obvious way to proceed was to pretend to be in the market for a collie puppy, but Drummond would never believe that. He knew me, and he knew Annica, too.

But who was to say Annica didn't want to buy a collie puppy? Why else would she be reading want ads?

Our next step called for a plan and Annica's cooperation. I'd be able to formulate a plan with a little thought, but it could wait until I finished my pie.

Forty-four

I decided to accompany Annica openly on our return to the Wildwynd Wood Collie Kennels. Drummond might suspect me of having ulterior motives, but he would hardly turn away a prospective paying customer, which Annica was supposed to be. We agreed not to call first, believing the element of surprise would work in our favor.

"So," Annica said as we neared the kennel. "The story is I had a collie when I was a kid. I want another one."

"You had a sable collie, like Lassie," I added.

"When I saw the ad in the *Banner*, I remembered what he told me about having collie puppies for sale. Do I look like I have nine hundred dollars to spend on a dog, though?"

"It's birthday money from your mom," I said.

"That's a generous present."

"You're not actually going to buy a puppy," I reminded her. "We're there to check out his operation, to see how he takes care of his dogs and what he knows about dogs in general and puppies in particular."

"I'll have to ask questions," she said.

"I can ask some of them for you."

"And you are?"

"Your best friend."

She leaned back in her seat, a smug smile on her face. "What kinds of questions should I ask?"

"You ask to see the mother and the sire, if possible. He may say the puppies' sire is in another state, but he should have a picture of him to show you. Ask if they've had their first vaccinations and eye checks done. Ask to see the pedigree. Have the pups been socialized? Can you buy one outright or will he insist on limited registration?"

"What does that mean?"

"You have to agree to have the puppy spayed or neutered. He holds onto the registration papers until you do."

We heard the Wildwynd dogs before we saw them. Before there had been four. Now there were eight, all barking.

I parked the car and glanced at the run. All of the dogs had congregated at the fence, vying for prime position. Some tails wagged, some of the barking sounded ferocious.

"He added to his family," Annica said.

"I see the pregnant collie is still here."

It must have been like this when Rosalyn Everett's kennel was in its heyday. I hadn't known her then.

"I'm nervous," Annica said.

"How unlike you. We're here on legitimate business. It's perfectly safe."

We walked up to the house briskly, purposefully, and knocked on the door. It opened immediately. Drummond must have seen us through a window. He sent us a scowl dark enough to frightened less determined visitors away.

"Yes?" he said.

"Hi." Annica gave him her brightest smile, most flirtatious smile. "Remember me? From Clovers?"

Keeping his scowl in place, he nodded. "Anne? Annie?"

"Annica. I saw your ad in the *Banner*. I remember you were talking about having puppies for sale," she added.

"So?"

"I want to buy one."

"Really?" He gaze shifted to me and back to Annica.

"I want a little girl dog. Lassie's color. So, could we see them?"

He didn't answer at once but looked at me again.

This wasn't going well. I should intervene. Say something. What? Maybe not. This was Annica's show.

"You want to buy a collie?" he asked. "Seriously?"

"Yeah," Annica said. "I had a collie when I was a kid. I want another one. It's my birthday present from my mom."

"Is this another one of your tricks, Mrs. Ferguson?" he asked me.

I met his look. "Not at all. Annica is my friend. She asked me to come with her to look at puppies."

"I just adore collie puppies," Annica added.

Sending her a silent message not to overdo it, I said, "Are they in the house?"

"In the kennel," Drummond said brusquely. "Come on, then. You can see what I've got."

As we approached the run, he glanced at the barking dogs. "Shut the hell up! Can't hear yourself think with all this racket."

What a way to talk to your collies! But they were a commodity to him, not flesh and fur and loving hearts. Drummond might be attractive but his personality didn't match his rugged features and blond hair.

He pulled open the door to the kennel building and turned on the light. For a moment I remembered the time I'd been locked inside, left, as I thought, to die. Well, that hadn't happened. No need to relive past trauma.

"Over here," he said, leading us to an ex-pen where five roly-poly puppies fell over one another to greet the newcomers.

"Oh, my God," Annica said. "They're so beautiful."

Three tricolors and two sables.

"Jennet—look at the one with all the white in her coat," she said. "Are they boys or girls?"

"The tan ones are female. They're nine weeks old."

Annica appeared to have forgotten her role. She knelt on the cement floor, trying to entice the little sable girls to come to her. One wobbled over on pudgy little paws. She was the puppy with the most white in her coat. I supposed Annica had forgotten her questions.

"Do you own the puppies' mother?" I asked.

"Yes, but she's staying with my friend now."

"And the sire?"

"He's in Indiana. Show quality but they haven't showed him lately."

"Could we see their pictures?"

His smile was infuriating. "Later. When I see some money. I want five hundred dollars to hold a pup. Cash."

Annica tore herself away from the pup who was nibbling on her finger. "How much are they again?"

"Nine hundred dollars."

"Can Annica buy them outright?" I asked. "She isn't interested in limited registration."

"Then I ain't interested in selling."

"Oh, no…"

"For nine hundred dollars, the puppy should be completely mine," Annica said. "I want her papers when I take her home. If I want to breed her, the decision will be mine."

"That's not the way it's going to work," Drummond said.

"Not everybody has almost a thousand dollars to spend on a puppy these days," I pointed out. "What if you can't sell them and they get older? They're at that adorable stage now. Lots of people don't want a pup who looks lanky and awkward."

"That's my problem," he said, "and that's my offer. Now if you girls are through here, I've got business."

"Thanks for letting us see them," I said stiffly.

"Look," Annica said. "Let me think about it. Okay?" She ran her hand down the puppy's pretty white blaze. "Maybe I can work something out."

Drummond parted with his first smile of the encounter. It looked fake to me—about as phony as anything he had said.

Annica had proved herself to be an accomplished actress. Only... I hoped she was still acting. She didn't seem to be pretending. Could she possibly be thinking of buying one of Drummond's puppies? She lived in a small apartment, went to college, and worked at Clovers. It was unfeasible. Moreover, it was unlike her.

He strode toward the door. "Coming?" he asked.

We had no choice. In truth, I didn't mind leaving. Old memories were closing in on me. I took a deep breath, telling myself that soon I would be out in the fresh air. Where the puppies should be.

I wondered if they'd been outside yet. At nine weeks, they must have been.

"Thank you again," I said.

"Yes, thank you," Annica echoed. "We may be back."

Uh oh. I was afraid of that.

~ * ~

"I'd have to move in with my mother again," Annica said. "She won't mind. She didn't want me to leave in the first place."

"You're not serious. When would you have time to raise a puppy?"

"My mom will help. She loves dogs."

I steered out to the road, wondering how to dissuade her. It wouldn't be easy. A person who truly wanted a collie would make it happen. In this case, there were other considerations.

"We didn't ask Drummond whether he'd had the puppies vaccinated or had their eye checks. Conveniently we couldn't see the parents. You know his track record. You might be buying a puppy who has serious health issues."

"I can have any testing done myself," she said.

"Yes, but you're basing the decision on emotion."

"But isn't that how you acquired every one of your dogs?" she asked. "From Halley all the way to Misty? Emotion?"

That was true, but all of my collies except for Halley had been rescues.

"It was love at first sight for that little girl," I said. "People fall in love with puppies. They do. You never talked about wanting a dog before."

"I didn't think I could have one," she said. "Now I do."

"Just like that?

"She was so sweet. She wanted me to choose her. What if someone else buys her? Someone who won't treat her right?"

"Owning a dog is a life-time commitment," I reminded her.

"I know that."

"And that story about your having nine hundred dollars birthday money to spend... Can you afford to buy her?"

"I have some savings, and I'm working. I have a scholarship at the university."

"Well, as you told Drummond, think about it," I said.

The city limits of Maple Creek lay ahead. "In the meantime, how about stopping for lunch? I'm starving."

"Yeah, me, too."

I wouldn't say anything more about the puppy, and perhaps Annica would change her mind.

How had this happened? This was a complication I had never anticipated, not in a million years, and the life and well-being of an innocent collie puppy at stake.

What have you done, Jennet? I asked myself.

There was no answer.

Forty-five

"Annica wants to buy a collie puppy," I told Crane that evening after dinner.

"Isn't she too busy to raise a puppy?" he asked

"You'd think so." I paused and plunged on with my pseudo-confession. "The real problem is she wants a specific puppy, one of Zachary Drummond's new litter."

Crane looked up from the *Banner*. "He has a litter?"

"And eight adult collies."

"How do you know?"

"I went with her to see them."

He fixed me with that frosty gray eyed stare I seldom saw anymore. "Weren't you going to stay away from River Rose?"

"I did." I assayed a lame smile. "It's Wildwynd Wood now."

"Tell me the rest," he said with a sigh.

"Drummond has set himself as a breeder, but I can't imagine a worst one. The pups look healthy and happy, not neglected like poor Pepsi and Cola, but he wasn't forthcoming with information, the kind every buyer should know. He couldn't show us pictures of the sire and dam. Heaven only knows if he's had the pups tested. To top it off, he's as surly as ever. Maybe that was only with me, but a leopard doesn't change his spots."

"Now Mac knows where to find him," he said.

"He will—when I tell him."

"Make sure you do."

"I will."

"There are a lot of unanswered questions in this story," Crane said. "The blue house down the lane is still vacant. We don't know why he was keeping dogs there."

"Maybe we never will."

"Back to Annica. If you think there might be a problem with this litter, you'll have to talk her into buying from a reputable breeder or maybe wait for a young rescue."

"She wants *this* puppy," I said.

At the restaurant, she had even come up with a name for her. Angel.

"Where did she get the idea in the first place?" Crane asked.

I thought I could dodge the issue of full disclosure. Apparently not.

"I'm afraid I gave it to her. I was curious and saw a chance to check up on Drummond."

"After that note he left at our door?"

"I'm sorry," I said.

"No you're not."

He knew me.

"Okay, you're right. But how do I talk Annica out of buying the puppy? Because I think she'd be making a mistake."

Crane picked up the *Banner* again. "She probably won't listen to you, although she's the last person I'd picture with a puppy. All you can do is try."

"It might work out," I said. "I guess I should step back and let fate make the decision."

"That's my girl," he said.

Sometimes Crane was right. Sometimes I was willing to admit it.

~ * ~

Lucy didn't want to attend her own party. She'd had a premonition.

"You have to," I said. "You're the guest of honor."

Her gold bracelets clanged as she set her teacup on the wicker coffee table. "It's all in my teacup. Encroaching darkness. Danger. Doom."

I would have smiled had the situation not be so serious. Trust Lucy to fall back on alliterative key words.

The cakes were ordered, twin devil's food cakes both decorated to resemble the *Devilwish* cover. Miss Eidt had prepared flyers and taken an informal count of those who planned to attend. She had ordered fifty copies of *Devilwish* and been wondering if she should order fifty more.

"I don't want to disappoint Miss Eidt," Lucy said, "but I feel strongly that I shouldn't go. If I do, something terrible will happen."

"I think this once you should ignore your premonition," I said. "As for your teacup, I thought you didn't read your own tea leaves."

"I don't usually."

I'd finished drinking my tea but lost interest in hearing my fortune. I could live without darkness, danger, and doom. I supposed my enemy still lurked in my teacup. He could stay there.

"Besides it's supposed to rain tomorrow," Lucy said. "They're predicting thunderstorms."

So much for having the party in the library garden. Well, we were flexible.

"What's a little rain?" I asked. "You won't melt."

"Will you be there?" she asked.

"Sure, with Annica and Brent. Leonora can't make it, but Crane's coming, and he has his gun."

"My premonitions never fail me," Lucy said.

"This one will be the exception," I said. "We'll laugh in its face."

Whoa! Did that sound like a challenge?

"We'll take every possible precaution," I amended. "Please say you'll reconsider."

"I guess I should show up. Otherwise, I'd be letting my fans down."

"That's the spirit," I said and drained my cup.

At least there wouldn't be spirits in the library tomorrow.

~ * ~

Miss Eidt was the next one to balk at the prospect of giving the party—and it had been her idea. Her previous enthusiasm evaporated when more of Lucy's books disappeared from the carousel.

"Just when I let my guard down," she wailed. "The whole first tier was empty this morning when I unlocked the library. They were there last night. It has to be an inside job."

"Or someone has a key."

"That's impossible. There are only three keys in existence. I have one, Debbie has one, and I keep the third key at home."

"Anyone can make a copy of a key," I said. "They do it at Zollers' General Store. How careful are you and Debbie?"

"Speaking for myself, very careful. I keep them in my purse."

"You never left your keys lying on the desk?

"Never! Well, I don't think so. I might have a few times."

"What about Debbie?" I asked.

"She called in sick today."

"You have to talk to her."

I'd briefly suspected Debbie of vandalizing the garden statues, then dismissed the idea. It still seemed outrageous to me. More likely, Miss Eidt had forgotten to put her keyring back in her purse one day and the vandal had seized his opportunity.

"All the new copies of *Devilwish* are gone," she said. "How can we have the party?"

How could we *not* have it? Lucy's enemy was determined to continue his or her nefarious activities. Perhaps the idea of a celebration in Lucy's honor, combined with the news that *Devilwish* might be a movie, had inspired the vandal to try to ruin it.

"Is the Amazon statue still all right?" I asked.

"Last time I looked."

"Well, then…" I surveyed the carousel with its empty tier. "Here's what we'll do. You can leave more space between the books you have left. You'll have to leave those romances where they are. In the meantime, I'll drive out to the mall and see if I can find copies of *Devilwish* in the bookstore."

"I'll give you some money," she said, moving toward her office.

"Wait till I see if I can buy any. In the meantime, keep an eye on the statue just in case we have two vandals rather than one."

"Two?"

She sank into one of the armchairs set out for readers who wanted to feel as if they were reading in their own homes. Blackberry leaped into her lap. From where? This was the first I'd seen her.

"For what it's worth, I think we're dealing with one misguided person who wants to make as much trouble for you and Lucy as possible."

"I'm glad Brent is going to be at the party," she said. "I feel safer when he's near."

"We'll all be there," I said.

Forty-six

I stopped at Clovers the next morning for a Danish and coffee. With her golden-red hair, Annica looked like the embodiment of sunshine in bright yellow and antique topaz earrings.

The restaurant was crowded, but I found an empty booth and placed my order.

"Are you still thinking about buying the puppy?" I asked when she brought my second breakfast.

"I can't wait to bring her home, but that won't be until I move to my mom's. My apartment doesn't allow dogs. Brent is going to help me move," she added.

Brent and a new collie puppy. No wonder Annica was glowing.

"That means you're going to pay Drummond his five hundred dollar deposit," I said.

She nodded. "And I'm going to buy my puppy a leash and collar and some toys." She glanced around and slipped into the booth. "I know you don't approve, Jennet, but could you come shopping with me? If you have time?"

"It's not my place to approve or disapprove, Annica," I said. "I'm sorry I gave you that impression. It's just that it's all happening so fast, and I don't trust Zachary Drummond. You're my friend. I don't want you to get hurt. And, oh, sure I'll go with you. Let me know when."

"Isn't there always a risk when you buy a puppy?" she asked. "You can do everything right and still have problems down the line."

"That's true."

"I only know I want her," she said.

Of course that was enough. That was how I'd felt when I had first seen Halley.

"Sooner or later, all of my friends end up with a collie," I said. "I wonder why?"

"Miss? I'd like more coffee please." The voice was sharp, tinged with impatience.

Annica gave me a sunny smile. "Gotta go. See you later."

~ * ~

My errand to the mall proved frustrating. I walked into an abundance of fall merchandise. Dresses in dark plaids, camel purses, cashmere scarves, and costume jewelry with faux stones of blue and red and green. Autumn was right around the corner. And school. Long hours spent away from Foxglove Corners.

Soon now. Begin counting days. In Michigan, summer is the shortest season.

Setting those grim thoughts aside, I stopped at The Written Word. Not a single one of Lucy's books was there. Undaunted, I asked at the service desk. Perhaps they were in a special place.

"We should have them," the young clerk said. "Let's see."

She led the way to the Young Adult section. "Hadley... Heatherby... I guess we're sold out. Her books are so popular and not just with kids. I can order a copy for you."

"Thank you," I said, "but I need it now."

"I'm sorry. You might try Barlow's."

The store at the other end of the mall was also sold out of Lucy's books.

Discouraged, I left the mall and headed for Antique Row on Lakeville where a new bookstore had opened up last month. They specialized in vintage books, but they might showcase the books of a local author.

At one time, Lucy's books had filled entire shelves in bookstores. When *Devilwish* was released, The Written Word had displayed multiple copies of the book near the cash register. If *Devilwish* were made into a movie, the booksellers would have to scramble.

Were Lucy's books so popular that bookstores couldn't keep them in stock? Or—frightening thought—had the person who wished to rid the world of Lucy's influence—swept up all her works? He'd have to spend a lot of money at a store, whereas, if he were stealthy, he could just spirit them out of the library.

Even though Miss Eidt and Debbie were vigilant or so they claimed? I couldn't understand how so many books could simply disappear. They couldn't both be distracted at the time the thief chose to strike.

I couldn't cast off the feeling that some power was hard at work to undermine Lucy's party.

Well, you won't get away with it, I vowed. *If I have to borrow a copy of Devilwish from everyone I know. Lucy's book is going to have a presence at the celebration in her honor.*

~ * ~

Thunder rumbled through my dream.

Rain, rain go away...

I was in the library, at a strange party where the revelers moved like sinister gray-clad figures, their features wreathed in shadows.

It wasn't supposed to be like this.

Instead of the classical selections Miss Eidt had chosen as background music, there were creepy sounds, like those one listens to at Halloween parties. Winds wailing. Floorboards creeping. Skitterings. A scream...

I looked for a familiar face in the crowd, for Annica and strong, reliable Brent. Even the ones I didn't particular want to see— Maryclaire and Brassy Hair.

And where was Miss Eidt?

I couldn't see her.

Lucy was missing, too? Had she decided not to come?

I didn't know these people, didn't feel comfortable with them. They were invading my space, making it difficult for me to breathe.

At last I came to the buffet table laden with sandwiches, fancy iced cookies, decorated cupcakes and the twin devil's food cakes decorated to resemble the Devilwish cover.

Something was wrong.

I looked again. The two cakes were smashed, chunks scattered in every direction and on the floor. Spatters of chocolate fudge icing marred Miss Eidt's white tablecloth, melting in the heat of the candles. The clever designs were obliterated.

No!

In spite of all the precautions we'd taken, the vandal had been here.

He'd won.

~ * ~

I woke in my own bed, safe beside Crane, my heart pounding, as the horrible images faded.

It wasn't going to be like that. Not if I could help it.

262

Forty-seven

A crash of thunder is an inauspicious beginning for a party. I could almost believe that Lucy's premonition was making itself felt. Danger... Doom... Darkness?

Dark. Yes, the storm made it dark, but the lights provided illumination and a promise to ward off evil.

Anticipating a rainy day, Miss Eidt, Debbie, and I had rearranged tables and chairs inside the library to accommodate a sizable crowd. Outside the storm continued to brew. Any minute it would be pouring.

I'd only found seven copies of *Devilwish* in the vintage bookstore in Lakeville, but that was seven more than I'd thought I'd have. Miss Eidt was still unhappy. She'd been hoping the stolen books would somehow reappear, an unrealistic wish considering what had become of the previous copies.

That didn't happen. She'd taken my advice and arranged the seven books on the carousel with ample space between them.

"Let's assume that most people are familiar with Lucy's works," I said. "And look on the bright side. The cakes are gorgeous."

The people at the Hometown Bakery had created two identical masterpieces, using dark chocolate fudge icing with dollops of red and yellow that adorned the actual book cover as symbols of hell fire.

"They look delicious," Miss Eidt said. "Do you think there'll be enough for everyone? Maybe we should have ordered three cakes."

"Stop worrying, Miss Eidt," Debbie said. "Everything looks great. If we run out of cake, we have cookies and cupcakes."

She jumped as thunder crashed directly overhead. "I'm afraid of storms."

"That was close," Miss Eidt said. "I hope Lucy will be okay."

"Brent is bringing her," I said. "They'll be fine."

At that moment, I remembered fragments of my nightmare. The dream thunder. The eerie sounds, the gray-clad figures, and the smashed cakes.

It was only a dream, I told myself. *Dreams have no existence in reality.*

The vandal might be among us, but Brent would be here soon, and Crane would stop by after his shift. An armed deputy sheriff. Nothing could possibly go wrong.

People were starting to arrive, and, of course, a few had been here all along checking out books or reading newspapers. I saw Maryclaire at the carousel and Brassy Hair hovering over the refreshments. They weren't our friends; neither were they our enemies—as far as I knew.

Then I saw three arrivals who were definitely friends, Lila and Letty Woodville from the animal shelter escorted by their neighbor, Henry McCullough. Henry gave me a broad smile while Lila set her wide umbrella in the stand Miss Eidt had brought from home.

"Jennet! It's been ages since we've seen you." She enveloped me in a warm hug. "This is such a good idea. I hear they're going to make a movie of *Devilwish* in Foxglove Corners."

"Maybe. An option isn't a certainty, but we're hoping."

"This is a perfect place for a movie," Letty said, patting the raindrops out of her silver hair. "We have so many beautiful old houses. Ours, for example."

"And mine," Henry added.

The shelter and Henry's house were similar in style, picturesque old white Victorians. In fact the block was filled with charming turn-of-the-century structures. Across the street we had the municipal park bordered by woods. Foxglove Corners could provide matchless scenery for a movie set.

"You don't expect to run into the devil in our town, though," Henry pointed out.

"That's exactly where you'll find him," Letty countered. "In a wholesome little backwater like ours. I wonder if they'll use the middle school."

"They can use any school," Lila said. "What I wonder is who's going to play the teenagers. I don't know the names of any of these young actors."

"Then why wonder?" her sister countered.

"Where's Lucy?" Henry asked.

"She'll be here," I said.

Henry lowered his voice. "I heard somebody wants Lucy's books banned from the library."

"Where did you hear that?" I asked.

"At Zollers' General Store just the other day. I don't remember who was talking about it. Some woman."

I hadn't thought Lucy's problems were general knowledge. Well, her friends would rally around her.

"I remember when that other woman wanted Miss Eidt to remove books from the library," Letty said. "What was her name now? She came to a bad end."

"Marla Holland."

Marla had died in front of the library after tumbling down the steps. But it wasn't the fall that had killed her.

"Retribution," Henry said. "It'll get you in the end."

"No. As I recall, there was a motive unrelated to Marla's vendetta."

"Censorship is still evil, if you want my opinion," Henry said. "No one's going to tell me what not to read."

No one argued with him.

The office door opened and Miss Eidt beckoned to me. Fortunately, she looked slightly less flustered and pretty in her dressy lavender suit. As the hostess, it was her duty to set the tone of the party.

"If you'll excuse me, I have to help Miss Eidt," I said.

With the coffee and tea and the lemonade, which was Debbie's specialty.

"What can I do?" I asked.

Miss Eidt closed the door. "Help us carry in the beverages, if you will. Then, I think we're all set. This carafe goes on the table I set up for Lucy when she gives her talk."

I picked up a tray covered with tall glasses of homemade lemonade while Debbie carried the coffeepot, leaving Miss Eidt to bring the carafe. Once I found a place for them on the table, I could relax and enjoy the party.

Well, I'd enjoy myself, but relax? Never. Not with the thunder and lightning and Lucy's premonition, which I'd advised her to ignore. Had that been wise?

I glanced out the windows as a lightning bolt illuminated the Amazon statue. Ammie. She was still intact, still poised for battle.

Really, Jennet, I told myself. *There won't be a battle.*

After all, a dream was only a dream. Premonitions could arise in the wake of fear, and certainly Lucy had been fearful beginning with the discovery of the stone statue in her woods.

Take a deep breath. Ready?

I walked into the crowd.

~ * ~

I knew Brent had arrived when I heard his booming voice drowning out the more sedate conversations flowing around him.

"Here she is!" That was Lila.

Lucy, striking in a black cocktail dress and gold bracelets, stood close to Brent as if loath to step out of the protective circle he offered. For a moment they surveyed the gathering and the candlelit buffet table where the *Devilwish* cakes were showcased. Lucy whispered something to Brent. He laughed.

Then one person rushed forward to greet her, then two more, and presently a crowd surrounded her. Her friends, fans, and support system.

After a short while, Brent escorted Lucy to the small table set aside for her talk. Miss Eidt had found a *Devilwish* poster and a black pillar candle left over from a past Halloween. Poster and pillar, the simple articles conveyed the essence of Lucy's story.

The stage is set, I thought. *Let the fun begin.*

Brent came out of the crowd to pull me into a hearty embrace. "What a night! It's raining cats and dogs out there. Lucy almost bailed. She's convinced something bad is going to happen tonight."

"Let's make sure it doesn't," I said.

"It won't. I'm here."

Sue and Annica arrived together, drenched in spite of the umbrella they shared. Next came Camille and Gilbert, followed by Nikki Holland, niece of the unfortunate Marla. Like the Woodville sisters and Henry, Nikki had only to walk from her house to the library.

"Doesn't Lucy look pretty?" Annica said.

I smiled. Was there a wistful note in Annica's voice? She admired Lucy and considered her a friend, but because she also had a crush on Brent, she likely considered Lucy competition.

"She always does. I've rarely seen her wear any color except black."

"It suits her," Annica said. "And what better color is there for a mystery writer?"

At that moment Blackberry streaked across the floor and leaped onto the table.

A black cat. The final atmospheric touch.

I could stop watching the entrance. Everyone I expected except for Crane had arrived. I'd feel more at ease when I saw him, even though so far everything was going according to plan.

~ * ~

Lucy mingled with the crowd, appearing to lose her apprehension as she accepted congratulations and responded to questions. When she resumed her seat at the table, silence fell on the library. Against a background of falling rain, she spoke.

"I want to thank everyone for coming out in the storm today to celebrate the success of *Devilwish*. It's a bit early. I don't know if the movie will become a reality, but as they say, it's an honor just to have an option. I owe it all to my loyal readers, especially you young people who keep buying my books."

The candlelight cast a golden glow on her. She was truly lovely. I wondered if she'd be offered a part in the movie. Not one of the main characters, of course, but wasn't there an aunt in the book?

Then she began to talk about her work-in-progress, *The Stone Collie*, which she had finished yesterday. Remembering that she had described it as a mishmash with all the last-minute scenes she'd had to add, I was amazed to discover she'd made it work.

"In my new book, my teenaged heroines move into in a new town. It's a small town like Foxglove Corners where nothing ever happens. At first they're bored and unhappy. Then they find a stone collie statue in their woods and soon learn that aliens from Voltar have arrived on our planet, planning to annihilate mankind and establish a new colony..."

Will the girls defeat the Voltarians or is life on earth as we know over? Stay tuned."

She held the audience's attention as only a professional writer could. Gone was any trace of nervousness or fear. She had given us enough details to arouse interest in the new book but didn't give anything crucial away. Especially not the ending.

I'd definitely buy *The Stone Collie* when it was released. Of course I had all of Lucy's books, but I was certain she'd garnered new readers for herself. Maybe people like Maryclaire would venture beyond the romance genre.

Brent made his way to our side. "See, everything went well. I told Lucy it would. Now let's hit the buffet."

A bolt of lightning punctuated his words.

"Not so fast," I said. "The party isn't over yet."

Neither was the storm.

Forty-eight

Debbie had appointed herself guardian of the buffet table, making sure it stayed neat and the beverages were kept warm or cold, depending on their requirements. Her homemade lemonade had proved to be in particular demand. She'd already made a second batch.

I helped myself to a piece of the *Devilwish* cake and joined Brent and Annica at a small table close to the main desk. My slice had a red flame in a corner—in another words, a dab of strawberry frosting masquerading as hellfire. Curiously it tasted warm.

The baker had given me a tiny sample when I'd picked up the cake. The finished product tasted even better. "It's delicious," I said.

"As long as it's raining, people will stay and chow down on sandwiches and cake," Brent said. "Suits me."

Annica nodded. "Me, too."

A few of the party goers, among them the Woodville sisters and Henry McCullough, had left during a lull in the rain. But the library was still fairly crowded.

I looked for Lucy in the crush. She was surrounded by a group of young girls, her favorite audience. I recognized a few of them from her library event. In all likelihood they were members of Miss Eidt's summer book club.

Everyone wanted to know more about the *Devilwish* movie. Several people had asked me what I knew about it. I, of course, had no answers. One young woman wanted to know if they planned to hire locals as extras.

"Maybe. We'll have to wait and see."

I frowned. I wanted Lucy to have every success possible. At the same time, I didn't want Foxglove Corners to change. I couldn't imagine our beloved haven of woods and waters overrun by Hollywood types.

Uh oh. I'd said that aloud.

"It'll take more than a movie to change us," Brent said.

Annica tossed her head. Predictably her gold earrings jangled. "I wish I were a little younger. I'd like to play the part of Olivia."

Olivia was one of Lucy's devil-bargaining teenagers.

"You could do it, Annica," Brent said. "You look young enough."

She blushed. That wasn't what she wanted to her from her secret crush.

Miss Eidt walked over to talk to us. "It's going well, isn't it? Did everyone have enough to eat and drink? There's plenty more in my office."

"I'm good," I said.

"I could have another piece of cake." Brent looked down at his empty plate. "The one I had was pretty small."

"Help yourself," she said. "If there are leftovers, you can take them home."

I glanced at my watch. Crane's shift was over. He should be walking through the door any time. Since the party had been so blessedly free of trauma, he could eat his fill in peace.

He'd have to. I hadn't made any dinner for us.

Brent sauntered over to the buffet table, plate in hand. Annica was chatting with Nikki Holland with whom she'd had a class at the university. I finished my cake and decided to congratulate Lucy on finishing *The Stone Collie* in spite of the myriad of obstacles in her path. At one point I'd thought she would abandon it.

Lucy?

She'd been talking to the girls by the window, but I didn't see her now. Or the girls either, come to think of it.

Quickly I scanned the room. She was probably talking to more of her fans. They were legion, and they rarely had an opportunity to visit with her as she seldom left Dark Gables.

She hadn't wanted to leave today.

A ripple of unease insinuated itself into my conscious mind. Just a ripple. Everything was all right. Miss Eidt had thrown a successful party. Lucy was the undisputed star of the show. The seven copies of *Devilwish* were still in the carousel, and people were convinced Lucy's book was going to be a movie.

Lucy was probably in the office with Miss Eidt or maybe in the restroom.

I waited for a few minutes, still gazing into the crowd. The ripple grew stronger.

The library had been transformed for the party, but the stacks remained, almost ceiling high and swimming in shadows. Lucy could be in one of the aisles with another group of admirers, seeking a quiet place to converse away from the heart of the party.

I strolled casually down each aisle. No one was there.

Miss Eidt's office, then?

It was empty.

The restroom?

A girl stood in front of the mirror applying gloss over ruby red lipstick. Another brushed her hair.

Outside then. She had stepped outside for a breath of fresh air.

The rain had tapered off, the sky brightening imperceptibly. Unnoticed I opened the side door. The fountain water continued its never-ending descent to the basin. The Amazon statue, washed clean, had a subtle shine. Rather like the stone collies.

Don't think of that.

No one had wandered into the garden. Why should they? The action and the food were inside.

It wasn't time to panic. I'd managed to miss Lucy. She was somewhere in the room happily discussing *Devilwish* and the possible movie. People didn't disappear in Foxglove Corners.

What was I saying? I should know better.

All right, but they didn't disappeared at parties.

From somewhere deep inside I heard mocking laughter.

Sometimes they do. Remember the case of Barbara Gorham? Missing from her engagement party. Stabbed to death in the kitchen of her own home, her murder unsolved to this day.

That was a rare occurrence, an isolated incident.

I returned to the buffet, spied a lone glass of lemonade, and reached for it.

"Nice turnout, isn't it?"

Maryclaire held a cupcake wrapped in a napkin. She bit into the orange icing. A flame from hell.

"Wonderful!" I said. "It's great to see so many of Lucy's fans out to celebrate with her."

"Did you ever read *Devilwish*?" she asked.

"When it first came out."

"I prefer lighter fiction myself," Maryclaire said. "I never thought a book could scare me. That one had me looking over my shoulder for weeks."

"That's what movie goers like these days. Oh, excuse me. I see my friend over there."

I hadn't seen anyone I knew but didn't want to engage in idle chatter until I found Lucy. Until I assured myself that she was all right.

Of course she is. You just didn't see her yet.

Unwanted images danced in my head. A multitude of sinister figures in gray against a background of dream thunder and wailing wind. Maybe it was time to take forewarnings seriously.

That inner voice, the one I counted on to be the voice of reason, was growing fainter.

If Lucy's here, you would have seen her by now.

Sipping my drink, I crossed the room, trying not to break through socializing groups. So many people milling around… Just like in last night's dream.

Undaunted, I looked for a sleek black dress. Glossy black hair with a blue cast in the light. A splash of gold jewelry.

There were only so many places Lucy could be. Had I missed an obvious nook or cranny?

More to the point, wasn't it time I alerted Brent to the possibility of trouble?

~ * ~

The party had become alarmingly like my nightmare. Throngs of revelers, over a hundred people. No familiar faces in sight.

Annica, Nikki, Miss Eidt, Debbie, Brent of the booming voice— I couldn't see any of them. Crane should be here by now. I didn't see him either.

The lights flickered, came on again, died. If we had a power outage, at least the party was winding down. None of the food required heating, and the candles were already lit. Also it was brighter outside.

Was it? I glanced out the window. The sky was growing dark again.

I needed to find Brent. He should be easy to spot with his dark red hair.

I heard another thunderclap. The storm, which had retreated, was making a comeback.

Another sound caught my attention, a loud crash. Incredibly no one else appeared to have heard it.

It could only be…

The statue!

I rushed to the window in time to see a decapitated stone head lying in the mud.

The vandal!

Without giving sufficient to thought to what I was about to do, I rushed to the door.

Forty-nine

I sensed that I was alone in the garden—alone with the decapitated stone head and what remained of the statue. Whoever had struck the death blow had effectively ruined the Amazon statue. It might serve as a macabre Halloween decoration in the future. The Headless Amazon of Foxglove Corners. Certainly that wasn't its original purpose.

Along with her head, she'd lost another part of her anatomy. Her right breast had been caved in. Pieces of concrete lay at her feet.

I'd guess the vandal had been waiting somewhere, in a car perhaps, for the rain to stop to enter the garden and smash the statue. Or perhaps he hadn't minded committing his crime in the rain. He'd then jumped over the fence. Not the high one that separated the animal shelter from the library, but the ornamental picket fence. Yes, there was the gate was partially open. Miss Eidt always kept it closed.

Once again acting without considering the consequences, I dashed through the gate and out to the street. The Corners was steeped in an unearthly mid-afternoon stillness, the air muggy after the rain. Across the street the park was deserted, the swings and slides too wet to use. I didn't see a single person on Park Street, which wasn't unusual.

Next door, in the yard of the animal shelter, a dog howled. Once, twice, a third time. I shivered. Was it a forewarning? Or a different form of alarm bells?

Perhaps five minutes had passed since I'd heard the crash. Where could the vandal have gone?

Into one of the houses or a yard? To a car? Before I'd even left the library, he could have driven out of the Corners.

To come so close only to have the culprit get away was unbearable. Out of town, out of reach, identity still unknown. Once again we were back in Square One.

Where we spent a lot of time. I recalled Lucy saying that.

Lucy… She was still missing.

The vandal was gone. There was no point in lamenting a failed chase.

Inside the library, I saw Brent talking to Miss Eidt and eating another piece of cake. Or was it still his second? How long had I been outside chasing a virtual shadow?

Brent would be furious about the damage done to the statue, but Lucy's whereabouts took precedence.

"Have either of you see Lucy?" I asked.

Miss Eidt looked out into the crowd. "Not for a while. She wouldn't leave without saying goodbye to me."

"She wouldn't leave without me," Brent said. "I'm her ride."

She wouldn't. Alarm bells started ringing again.

"We'd better look for her," I said.

Apparently catching the note of anxiety in my voice, Miss Eidt said, "What's so important about finding Lucy right this minute? She's probably mingling with the guests."

"I don't think so," I said. "Do you see her?"

Miss Eidt scanned the crowd. "Oh, my!" Holding her hand to her chest, she searched for a chair. Brent found one for her.

"No, I don't, but…"

"Lucy has to be around somewhere," Brent said. "Come on, Jennet. Let's find her."

He started off into the crowd, colliding first with one person, then another, leaving me to trail behind him.

Where was Crane when we needed him? Always in some other place.

If Lucy was still missing after this last search, I'd call the police.

Once again, Brent's voice boomed out to all corners of the room, effectively silencing every other speaker.

"Lucy Hazen, report to the front desk immediately!"

People broke off their conversations and looked around the room. Whispers began. Somebody laughed. I half expected Lucy to emerge from some unknown part of the library, indignant that Brent had shone a figurative spotlight on her.

Gradually the whispers faded. Blackberry streaked across the floor and disappeared behind the desk. A few people moved surreptitiously toward the entrance.

Lucy didn't appear.

In Miss Eidt's office, I pulled my phone out of my shoulder bag and dialed nine-one-one. Then I caught up with Brent who was already going through the side door.

~ * ~

We found her in the garden, in the one place not immediately visible to the casual observer—behind the branches of a wide Scotch pine. Her long black hair was spread over her face like strands of a darkening cloud. She lay on the ground as still as the beheaded statue. As still as death.

"Lucy!"

Brent was the first to reach her. He knelt beside her, felt her wrist. He touched her face and stared at the blood on his hand.

"She's been hurt!" he shouted. "She's alive. Back, everyone. Get back inside."

Slowly, reluctantly, the party goers melted back into the library goaded by Miss Eidt who had found an inner source of strength. The order didn't apply to me. Miss Eidt and I stayed outside with Lucy and the few people who hadn't been intimidated by Brent's order. Brent held Lucy's wrist again.

Maryclaire detached herself from the dispersing crowd and slipped out of the library. "Will she be all right?"

No one answered.

"How could this happen? I was just talking to her. I asked her what her aliens looked like."

"When were you talking to her?" I asked.

"A little while ago. Fifteen minutes, maybe."

"Go inside with the others," Brent said.

For some reason I noticed Maryclaire's shoes, sparkly flats to match the rhinestone sequins on her dark blue top. The shoes looked as if she'd stepped in deep mud. They weren't meant to be worn in rainy weather.

"I hope she'll live," Maryclaire said. "Do you think she hit her head when she fell?"

"On what?" I asked. "The ground?"

"Those rocks."

I'd never noticed them. Miss Eidt or Debbie had lined the flowerbeds with the beautiful colored rocks that were so plenty in Foxglove Corners if one expended the energy to unearth them. Pink-veined rocks holding back pink and yellow snapdragons, the variety known as Rockets. Beautiful to behold, but lethal if you chanced to come in contact with one in the dark.

"I'll bet she tripped," Maryclaire said.

"She'll tell us what happened when she comes to," I said. "I meant when she wakes up."

I believed that would happen. Lucy was going to wake up and tell us what had prompted her to leave the security of the party for the isolated garden. And how she came to be lying unconscious on the wet ground.

In the distance I heard the sirens.

~ * ~

Brent insisted on accompanying Lucy in the ambulance. She still hadn't regained consciousness.

I couldn't stop thinking about her premonition. I'd advised her to ignore it. I had encouraged her to come to the party. I should have had more respect for her talents.

"I brought Ms. Hazen here," Brent said in his booming voice. "I'm responsible for her. So step aside."

The paramedics did as they were told.

"Let me know," I said. "As soon you know something."

He promised to do so, and a subdued Miss Eidt and I returned to the library. The crowd had thinned, the festive air dissipated.

"I need a cup of hot tea and privacy," Miss Eidt said. "Won't you join me, Jennet?"

"I will. I'm going to wait for Crane."

Annica rushed up to us, breathless and pale. "What happened?"

I told her. As I did, I remembered the decapitated Amazon statue. Poor Ammie. I'd forgotten her plight, but she was made of stone. Lucy was alive.

For now. She had just hit her head on a rock.

Or did someone hit her?

Could she have surprised the vandal in the act of destroying the statue?

Thank heavens he hadn't dumped Lucy into the fountain.

Annica said, "Brent went with her to the hospital? He is so loyal."

"He'll call us with an update. She'll be all right," I added. "They'll know what to do for her in Emergency."

"I'm going to make a fresh pot of tea," Miss Eidt said. "Please join us, Annica."

"That sounds good. I will."

I looked around. Out of over a hundred people, only twenty or so remained. Someone had blown out the candles and removed the refreshments from the buffet table. The library was dim and shadowy. I'd forgotten about the power. It must still be out.

"What a way for a party to end," Annica said. "It's like the *Devilwish* movie is cursed."

"It's only an option," I reminded her.

"Then *Devilwish* is cursed."

At that moment we passed the carousel. The top tier was empty. All seven of the *Devilwish* copies I'd bought at the vintage bookstore in Lakeville were gone. Our vandal had been busy, smashing a statue in the garden and stealing books inside the library.

"Maybe it is," I said.

Fifty

The missing copies of *Devilwish* hadn't gone far. Miss Eidt discovered them in the wastebasket saturated with coffee. There'd been no attempt to conceal them under the rest of the trash.

"It's like they wanted us to see them," Annica said.

She made an attempt to dry a book with napkins.

"Don't bother, Annica." Miss Eidt's voice faltered. "They're all ruined. I can't take any more of this."

"I'm glad Lucy didn't see them," I said.

For the first time since she'd learned about Lucy's disappearance from the party, Miss Eidt smiled. It was a pitiful attempt at a smile but better than tears. "Unknown to everybody, I have a secret *Devilwish* stash in the office. Some of my friends found copies for me. I'm going to fill the carousel before I leave tonight."

The only good news of the day was that Lucy was going to be all right. Brent had called from the hospital to tell us she'd suffered a mild concussion. Over her strongly voiced objections, she was being admitted to the hospital for observation. It could have been so much worse.

"Was she able to tell you what happened?" I asked.

"A little. She didn't see who attacked her. She was standing at the window when she saw someone in the garden and went out to investigate. Someone hit her with a rock or some sharp object, they think. These writers always have to be investigating something."

I remembered being thankful that Lucy's assailant hadn't thrown her unconscious body into the fountain. If he had... I didn't need to think about that now. Lying on the wet ground was bad enough.

"Whoever wrecked my statue tried to do Lucy in," Brent said. "That's going way too far."

"He must have been afraid he'd identify him."

"*She*, Jennet. It was a woman."

I reviewed my list of suspects. A frequent visitor to the library. A self-righteous crusader who regarded Lucy's books, especially *Devilwish*, as immoral. A woman with no respect for anyone else's property or, for that matter, life. Unscrupulous, stealthy... Getting reckless.

It took a bold woman to carry out her demented plan with more than a hundred people on the premises.

About those discarded books, though... It would have been easy to sweep them off the carousel while practically everyone was focused on Lucy.

Which of the suspects fit the pattern? I realized they were all female.

Now that she'd caused physical harm to Lucy, she could be charged with attempted murder along with destruction of property.

When we found her.

~ * ~

Crane strode into the library, almost stepping on Blackberry who was sleeping in the entrance. He looked slightly rumpled, hardly resembling the crisp, dapper deputy sheriff who'd left for his shift this morning.

"Is the party over?" he asked.

"You missed the action, Crane," Miss Eidt said. "Let me get you some sandwiches and coffee."

"Could we take them home?" I asked.

Home was the only place I wanted to be. I imagined Crane would agree.

"Sure thing," Miss Eidt said.

Annica jumped up. "I'll get them."

Crane gave me a quick kiss. "Sorry, honey. I was held up. What happened?"

"The library vandal struck again and got away." I told him about Lucy's close call. "We know it's a woman."

"Only you could find danger in a library," he said.

"I was never in any danger."

But if I had seen a mysterious figure in the garden where no one should be, I might have gone outside to investigate as Lucy had done. I might be the one with the concussion. There was no need to point that out to Crane.

To Miss Eidt I said, "We'll help you move the furniture back so it'll be business as usual in the morning."

"It can wait till tomorrow. I'm thinking of opening the library at noon." She frowned, tapping her finger on her desk. "Debbie has a headache. She's taking tomorrow off, and I'd like to sleep in. Trauma is so tiring."

"My energy level is highest in the morning," I said.

"Tell you what. I'll give you the key. Come any time you like. I'll be here around ten with the doughnuts," she added.

"That'll work."

Annica came back with Crane's food in a white bag. "I'd like to help, but I have an early class tomorrow."

"That's okay. I can manage."

"Lucy's books will be back in the carousel," Miss Eidt said. "I'll shelve them now. You can't keep a good library down."

~ * ~

The Corners felt like the loneliest place on earth the next morning—silent, eerily silent and already sweltering. It was too early for the ice cream parlor and the general store to open, and the park was deserted. Even the shelter dogs were quiet.

I'd never been here at this hour. I parked in the lot, the only car in sight, and walked up to the porch. Blackberry wasn't lying on her favorite wicker chair, but that wasn't unusual. She went home with Miss Eidt at night.

Eerie indeed. I felt like a nineteenth century lady entering a forbidding white mansion. In a way, it was exciting. But this was no time for fancies. I had work to do. It shouldn't take long; then I'd be home walking with the dogs before the temperature started to climb.

Quickly I opened the door and stepped into a silence so deep I could slice through it with the proverbial knife. And it was cool, not a pleasant cool but the kind associated with isolated places like the kennel at River Rose before Zachary Drummond bought the house and property. Or the mausoleum that Gothic heroines are forever getting locked in. Not that I'd ever been in a mausoleum.

I walked past the main desk and surveyed the buffet table. All of the plates and utensils remained—as well as the candles, all blown out. The crumbs on the cake platters reminded me of my dream from two nights ago. The smashed devil's food tribute to Lucy's book.

Well, that hadn't happened. We'd eaten every morsel.

The feeling dropped down on me like a piece of the ceiling. Something was wrong.

I looked around and saw immediately what it was. The top tier of the paperback carousel was once again empty. I had watched Miss Eidt fill it last night with the *Devilwish* copies donated by her friends.

How was that possible?

In a moment, the library became a frightening place holding itself apart from the bright morning sunshine. A place of shadows and silence and danger. It was positively ghostly.

There were no spirits in the library. I recalled saying that or thinking it. Suddenly I realized it was untrue. Once a ghost had haunted the library's secret room. Even before that there'd been stories about a woman who had gone into the stacks in search of a particular book one day and vanished into thin air.

Well, not actually. Something else had happened to her. I couldn't recall what it was.

Get a grip!

I was letting a vacant house and old memories spook me.

And new ones as well. The beheaded Amazon statue and Lucy's misadventure in the garden.

I'd have to let Miss Eidt know that still another batch of Lucy's books had disappeared. But why call her? She'd be arriving in about an hour, doughnut box in hand, presumably rested and, I hoped, ready to take on still another aspect of the ongoing mystery in the library.

From the carousel I had a clear view of the table at which Lucy had sat with the poster of *Devilwish* and the black pillar candle.

Get rid of the books but leave the poster? Who could know how the vandal's mind worked?

A sound pierced the heavy stillness that hung in the air. A sneeze.

I froze, my feet melded to the floor. An allergic ghost?

Not likely. A human had sneezed, which meant I wasn't alone in the library as I'd thought. The vandal was still here, concealed by the tall stacks. I didn't think he knew he wasn't alone. I hadn't made a sound, but my breathing sounded unnatural loud.

I looked for a weapon, saw Miss Eidt's stapler on her desk and about a million books. Nothing useful. Still, I grabbed the stapler.

"Who's there?" I demanded.

My voice threw an echo back at me. Footsteps filled the silence. Another sneeze. More echoes.

From the back of the library, Maryclaire appeared. She looked as startled as I was.

"I'm just..."

I didn't let her finish. "What are you doing here? The library's closed. How did you get in?"

"Oh... The door was open. Why would the library be closed? It's always open at this time."

True, and Miss Eidt's 'Open at Noon' sign had been posted on the door.

I had my vandal, and she had a book in her hand. She took a few steps forward and set it on a table. Her hand trembled. She shoved it into the pocket of her long brown dress. I noticed it had a pattern of small daisies. Old time charm.

"I know what you're doing," I said. "It's called breaking and entering. I'm calling the police."

"You can't do that." Her voice rose. "This is a public place. I have as much right to be here as you do."

She spoke boldly, brazenly, but I sensed she was unsure of herself—trapped and obviously guilty. She twisted a strand of long, pale hair around her finger.

"Not when it's closed."

I opened my purse.

"No, wait," Maryclaire said. "This isn't what you think."

"What is it then?"

She hesitated. "I need a book. A book on gardening. I'm planting one of those fairy gardens, and I don't know what kinds of plants to buy."

I closed the space between us. Maryclaire was a little shorter than I was and thinner. Was she strong or as fragile as she appeared?

"Did you attack Lucy?" I asked.

"No. No, of course I didn't. I wouldn't. I was just there. We all were. At the party."

At that moment I remembered noticing mud on her shoes yesterday. One doesn't come to a party wearing muddy shoes. Shoes don't get muddy if the wearer stays out of the mud.

"You're the one who's been stealing Lucy's books and destroying them," I said. "I happen to know Miss Eidt added several copies of *Devilwish* to the carousel yesterday. They're not there now."

"I don't know anything about that."

"May I see your fairy garden book?" I asked.

She didn't need to give it to me. I saw the title. *The Exorcist.*

"All right," she said with a toss of her head that didn't indicate surrender. "They're gone, but they're diabolical. Lucy Hazen has contaminated a whole generation of impressionable kids with her vile books. Now there isn't a single Hazen book in the library or the book stores either. It's going to stay that way. The woman has to be stopped. We're going to stop her."

"We?"

"My friends and I. People who think like I do." She shook her head and went on. "I always knew you were our enemy, but I didn't think you'd figure it out. Now that you have…"

I still had many questions, but it wasn't important that they be answered at this point. I'd make my call. Let Mac find the answers and the names of the other people who were involved. As for Maryclaire, she was deluded but not especially dangerous.

"I won't let anyone stop my work," she said. "You have to die. I didn't want it to come to this, but I don't have a choice. I hope you can understand." She pulled a gun out of her pocket. It was small. It looked like a toy, but I wasn't going to make assumptions.

"I'm sorry. Really, truly sorry."

I'd underestimated Maryclaire Hastings, history teacher from Lakeville, if that's who she was.

Fifty-one

I had been in life-and-death situations before, had faced down killers in the past, some of them delusional. But how had I escaped unscathed? What had I done?

My mind was a blank.

I had to think quickly. I couldn't expect help, couldn't dial nine-one-one with Maryclaire holding a gun on me and couldn't count on intervention of any kind.

No one seeing the 'Open at Noon' sign would attempt to enter the library earlier. Miss Eidt? She was coming at ten, carrying doughnuts, not suspecting treachery. I didn't want her to walk into danger.

Think! What can you do?

Not much. Except to stall Maryclaire. Stall for time and keep her talking. Use her own hesitancy against her. Anyone could tell she had a fragile hold on reality.

"The devil you fear so much... He must be proud of you," I said.

She stared at me. "What do you mean?"

"You're doing his work. Making people aware of him. I'll bet he doubled over in laughter when you attacked Lucy. I'll also bet that most people never think of him."

"That's crazy," she said. "Everybody knows he's real. I saw him. One evening in the park. It was twilight..."

"Stop to think about what you're doing. Sure, there are no more Hazen books in our library and bookstores, but what about other towns in Michigan or in the country, for that matter? You can't burn them all. The written word will always live on."

"We have to start somewhere," she said, which didn't address the question. "The world will be a better place when all this filthy rubbish is gone."

"Like nude statues?" I asked. "Are you going to take this crusade of yours to the museums of Europe?"

She touched *The Exorcist*.

"I'll bet your other name is Angela White," I said.

She didn't deny it.

"I just want to live in a clean, wholesome town. I want that for everybody. Books about the devil don't belong in a Christian library." She took a few steps forward. "That's enough talk. Please forgive me. I don't want to do this."

She raised the hand that held the gun.

With all the force I could muster I threw the stapler at her. It landed in the center of her chest and bounced under a table. Still standing, she screamed and pulled the trigger.

Nothing happened.

Her gun wasn't real. There were no bullets. The weapon was part of her delusion.

"You're still alive!" she cried. "You're one of them. You're a devil."

"I've been called worse."

Now that I didn't have to worry about dying, this was fun. Well, almost.

"You've guessed my secret," I said. "What gave me away?"

She twisted a strand of pale yellow hair around her finger. She didn't answer but dropped into a chair.

"You have to know that resistance is futile," I added, borrowing my favorite line from *Star Trek Voyager*.

I pulled my phone out of my purse. Maryclaire didn't object. She didn't even look at me. In her long floral-patterned dress, she looked like a waif lost in time.

All's well that ends well, I thought. *Sometimes.*

~ * ~

The police arrived before Miss Eidt.

Maryclaire still sat in the chair, acting as if she hadn't heard the sirens. She'd let *The Exorcist* fall to the floor.

"What do we have here?" Mac asked.

"The library vandal," I said. "Lucy Hazen's attacker. She was going to kill me. Fortunately the gun isn't real."

"You lucked out this time, Jennet."

"Yes, well, she made it easy."

They took her away, along with her makeshift weapon. She didn't resist. In a way I felt sorry for her. Almost.

Then I remembered Lucy's books, charred and defaced. Lucy in the hospital. Sky alone and wondering where she was—although Brent had taken care of her. The damaged statues, for I had no doubt that Maryclaire had taken a hammer or axe to them. Probably the same object she'd used to disable Lucy.

Thank heavens it was over.

It was nine-thirty. I had time to return the library to its normal pristine state and make coffee to go with the doughnuts Miss Eidt was going to bring. Time to worry about what might have happened if the gun had been real. Time to wonder whether Maryclaire was really a teacher. She was so obviously psychotic. How could she function in classes with typical middle school kids? And where had she come from? Mine had been the only car in the parking lot.

When I finished vacuuming, I found the copies of *Devilwish* tossed into the basket that had been emptied of previous trash.

Fortunately they were salvageable, and Miss Eidt could order additional copies without worrying about them disappearing.

We had won this battle.

~ * ~

Later that week, Brent and Lucy continued the interrupted celebration over dinner at our house. I'd baked a devil's food cake but hadn't decorated it. After dinner Crane carried generous slices on a tray into the living room. I followed with coffee for him and Brent. Lucy and I were having tea.

"Was that strange young woman responsible for everything that happened to me?" Lucy asked.

"I'm sure a lot of it was coincidence. The thunderstorm and the airplane crash, for example. Oh, and Jennifer's almost kidnapping. We can lay the burned books at Maryclaire's door. She as much as admitted it. And we know where the collie statue in the woods came from."

"It's funny," Lucy said. "I was lying in the hospital thinking about everything, and I remembered. I *did* see that collie statue when I first moved to Dark Gables. I'd completely forgotten about it. I thought when you had a concussion you were supposed to forget things, not remember them."

I couldn't resist commenting. "I knew it. That was one of my early theories."

"There were too many coincidences in this affair," she said. "What's going to happen to Maryclaire?"

"She'll have to undergo psychiatric testing. Not that there's any doubt of her instability, especially if she talks about seeing the devil in the park."

I had the answers to some of my questions. First, Maryclaire's teaching position was a fabrication. She'd rented a suite of rooms in one of the renovated Victorians on Park Street, which enabled her to visit the library virtually unnoticed. She hadn't yet revealed the names of her confederates.

I suspected that Brassy Hair might be one of them, but I could be wrong. Appearances are deceiving. Only once had I observed Maryclaire in a temper—when she discovered that Lily May Hill's romance novels had been moved. That should have been a clue, but at the time I didn't have any reason to suspect her.

Brent dove into his cake with relish. "My favorite," he said.

Lucy sighed. "I never had a piece of those wonderful cakes from the Hometown Bakery."

"Jennet's cake is better," Brent announced. "I was thinking I'll have to replace the Amazon statue."

"Maybe you can find one fully clothed like a little girl holding a watering can or an animal."

"Might as well. "There's no need to make a point."

"We still don't know who shares Maryclaire's twisted ideas," I said. "Don't tempt fate."

Brent agreed to look for an innocuous garden statue. Perhaps a dinosaur, a larger version of the one I'd bought at Greenspires.

"I thought my enemy was Zachary Drummond," I said. "I wanted it to be him, but he would have been a formidable opponent, not like Maryclaire. Then the story might have had a different ending."

"Don't count Drummond out," Crane said. "By the way, I saw a moving van at the blue house this morning. I'll introduce myself tomorrow and ask if Brooks even knows Zachary Drummond."

"I won't, especially since Annica is buying one of his puppies. Believe me, I'm going to keep an eye on him."

"From far away," Crane said. "I guess I can't convince you to stay out of the library."

Gothic novels, private tea parties in Miss Eidt's private office, the lure of those million books that hadn't lifted a hand in my defense?

"Not a chance," I said.

Candy padded in from the kitchen with Misty who had her toy goat in her mouth.

"Another country heard from," Crane said.

"Who wants to play?" Brent asked.

Five collies began barking.

Brent and Crane took all the collies outside, leaving Lucy and me alone with our tea.

"I was right about the premonition," Lucy said, "but wrong about your enemy. I thought for sure it was Drummond, too."

I glanced into my cup. "Tea leaves are sexless."

"Drink your tea," Lucy said. "Let's see if Maryclaire has gone for good."

I did and, following the proscribed ritual, made my wish. I handed the cup to Lucy.

"She's gone," Lucy announced. "From your life anyway. And I don't see any more trouble. There is something though…"

I knew three dots meant a wish to be granted. An overflowing basket meant unending happiness. I'd have to consult a tea leaf reading book for more meanings.

"Do I want to hear this?" I asked.

"I don't see why not. I see a key." She pointed to a small light blob.

All right. A key. It looked harmless enough.

"You're opening a new door," Lucy said. "Starting a new adventure."

In the waning days of summer I planned to concentrate on my 'Raze the Construction' petition and help Annica with her new puppy, interspersed with peaceful visits to the library for Gothic novels. I didn't think any farther into the future than that.

But a new door and a new adventure sounded exciting.

"I'm ready," I said.

Meet Dorothy Bodoin

Dorothy Bodoin lives in Royal Oak, Michigan, not far from the town that serves as the setting of her Foxglove Corners cozy mysteries. A graduate of Oakland University with Bachelor's and Master's degrees in English, Dorothy taught secondary English until leaving education to write full time and stay at home with her collies. *The Stone Collie* is #20 in the Foxglove Corners series. Dorothy is also the author of a Gothic romance and six novels of romantic suspense.

VISIT OUR WEBSITE
FOR THE FULL INVENTORY
OF QUALITY BOOKS:

http://www.wings-press.com

Quality trade paperbacks and downloads
in multiple formats,
in genres ranging from light romantic comedy to
general fiction and horror. Wings has something
for every reader's taste.
Visit the website, then bookmark it.
We add new titles each month!

95702620R00169

Made in the USA
Lexington, KY
11 August 2018